BEACON STREET GIRLS

This book belongs to:

VERITAS AMICITIA GAUDIUM
truth friendship fun!

D0736144

BEACON STREET GIRLS

Be sure to read all of our books:

BSG Special Adventure Books:

Sweet Thirteen

BY
ANNIE BRYANT

ALADDIN M!X

NEW YORK   LONDON   TORONTO   SYDNEY

Special thanks to Rabbi Stacia Deutsch
and Rhody Cohon for their expertise and sensitivity
in handling the story of Maeve's Bat Mitzvah.

ALADDIN M!X

Simon & Schuster Children's Publishing Division

1230 Avenue of the Americas, New York, NY 10020

First Aladdin M!X edition October 2009

Copyright © 2009 by B*tween Productions, Inc.,

Home of the Beacon Street Girls.

Beacon Street Girls, KGirl, B*tween Productions, B*Street, and the characters Maeve, Avery,

Charlotte, Isabel, Katani, Marty, Nick, Anna, Joline, and Happy Lucky Thingy are

registered trademarks of B*tween Productions, Inc.

All rights reserved, including the right of reproduction in whole or in part in any form.

ALADDIN is a trademark of Simon & Schuster, Inc., and related logo is a registered

trademark of Simon & Schuster, Inc.

ALADDIN M!X and related logo are registered trademarks of Simon & Schuster, Inc.

For information about special discounts for bulk purchases, please contact

Simon & Schuster Special Sales at 1-866-506-1949 or business@simonandschuster.com.

The Simon & Schuster Speakers Bureau can bring authors to your live event. For more information

or to book an event contact the Simon & Schuster Speakers Bureau at 1-866-248-3049 or visit our

website at www.simonspeakers.com.

Designed by Dina Barsky

The text of this book was set in Palatino Linotype.

Manufactured in the United States of America

2 4 6 8 10 9 7 5 3 1

Library of Congress Control Number 2009921936

ISBN 978-1-4169-6438-4

ISBN 978-1-4169-9685-9 (eBook)

Who's Who

BSG

Katani Summers
a.k.a. Kgirl . . . Katani has a strong fashion sense and business savvy. She is stylish, loyal & cool.

Avery Madden
Avery is passionate about all sports and animal rights. She is energetic, optimistic & outspoken.

Charlotte Ramsey
A self-acknowledged "klutz" and an aspiring writer, Charlotte is all too familiar with being the new kid in town. She is intelligent, worldly & curious.

Isabel Martinez
Her ambition is to be an artist. She was the last to join the Beacon Street Girls. She is artistic, sensitive & kind.

Maeve Kaplan-Taylor
Maeve wants to be a movie star. Bubbly and upbeat, she wears her heart on her sleeve. She is entertaining, friendly & fun.

Ms. Razzberry Pink
The stylishly pink proprietor of the Think Pink boutique is chic, gracious & charming.

Marty
The adopted best dog friend of the Beacon Street Girls is feisty, cuddly & suave.

Happy Lucky Thingy and alter ego Mad Nasty Thingy
Marty's favorite chew toy, it is known to reveal its alter ego when shaken too roughly. He is most often happy.

more on beaconstreetgirls.com

Part One
It's My Party

1

Excuse Me

"W ow!" Katani exclaimed, taking in the scene at the
Museum of Science. Flashing disco lights and blar-
ing music had transformed the museum into party
central.

"Unbelievable!" Isabel said with awe as the girls
stepped under an enormous rainbow made entirely of
black, red, and silver balloons. "Henry totally deserves a
nice party, but this . . ." Isabel ducked as a paper airplane
decorated with streamers went sailing past her head.
Henry Yurt whistled and waved from a crowded video
arcade room. A goofy crown on his head read "BAR
MITZVAH BOY."

"OMG!" Maeve yelped as she dodged the airplane,
and, of course, Avery caught it.

"Yurtmeister!" Avery was about to throw the airplane
back at him, but Katani grabbed her arm.

"Wait, it says 'look inside' on the wings!"

Unfolding it, they discovered a map with all the night's

activities. There were directions to the lightning show, the Omni Theater, the butterfly garden, and the monkey habitat—and those were just the museum's regular activities. Then there was the gaming arcade, the photo booth, and more.

"Everything fits into a science theme—even the food!" Avery pointed to the dinner menu at the bottom of the paper: astroburgers and space fries with galaxy smoothies or stardust sodas to drink.

"Hey, Maeve, there's dancing later!" Isabel nudged her friend, who was being unusually quiet for such an exciting occasion. The DJ was mixing in another room, but everyone could hear the hottest dance tunes echoing through the lobby.

"Who knew science could be so romantic?" Maeve gushed absently as she fingered one of the floral bouquets lining the entryway. Her own Bat Mitzvah and thirteenth birthday were only two weeks away, on May 9. Maeve pinched her pink glossed lips together and tried to ignore the fact that she was wearing the world's worst dress, an early birthday gift from her great-grandmother. *I'll have roses, all in pink. Or maybe white and yellow, too. Those are perfect spring colors. . . .*

"Where's Charlotte?" Isabel asked. "Anyone heard from her?"

The Beacon Street Girls had planned to arrive at the party together, but Charlotte called at the last second to say something had come up, and she'd be there ASAP.

"I'm sure she'll be here soon," Katani assured her

friends as she led the pack toward what normally would have been the museum's information desk. A man in a black tuxedo and a red bow tie was standing behind the desk, handing out little cards to a line of Henry's friends and family.

"The best part about this is there won't be a test on the exhibits tomorrow," Avery said with a small laugh.

"Ahem." A deep voice sounded from behind the girls. "Name three reasons Pluto is no longer considered a planet."

Avery flipped around to find Mr. Moore, their science teacher, standing directly behind them in line.

"Wait! I know this one!" Katani crossed her arms and tapped her foot, stalling for time.

Mr. Moore began to laugh. "I'm just fooling with you." He grinned widely. "No school tonight." The science teacher was a short man with wild brown hair. Tonight he was wearing a black-and-white cow-spotted tie with a Star Wars pin. He was strange and nutty and a whole lot of fun.

"What do you mean, 'no school'?" Ms. O'Reilly turned around from farther up in the line. "I'm taking notes for a quiz on teen party trends first thing Monday. Looks like goofy crowns and paper airplanes are *in*." The social studies teacher winked.

"Did Henry invite *all* the teachers?" Avery whispered. The Yurtmeister often acted more like a class clown than a class president. . . . But he had obviously taken his duties as chief executive seriously and invited the entire school!

Ms. O'Reilly got her card and gave the girls a last wave. "You all look wonderful! I hope you have a good time."

"I do *not* look wonderful." Maeve rolled her eyes. "I still can't believe Mom talked me into wearing this."

"You should have called me ahead of time," Katani chided. "I could have done something about those bows. And maybe hemmed it a little."

"No offense, Katani," Maeve mumbled, "but I don't think even your design genius could ever make this thing fashionable."

The lavender tank dress was a shocker to everyone who knew Maeve. It was covered with boring, pale purple flowers and oddly placed white bows, with not even a hint of glitter or pink, her signature shade. *Pink is the only color I will ever wear when I'm a famous movie star, setting trends and making my own rules!* Maeve decided.

Maeve had spilled the entire dress saga to her best friends when they'd met up outside the party. It was either wear great-grandma's surprise birthday gift tonight or wear it for her own Bat Mitzvah. They all agreed, wearing it tonight was definitely the lesser of two evils!

Isabel squeezed Maeve's hand as the line moved forward. "It's okay, Maeve. You look *maravilloso* in everything!"

"And Great-grandma Gigi will be overjoyed when I show her this picture!" Maeve whipped a digital camera out of her purse and held it up to snap a picture of herself in the horrid dress. Giggling, the friends checked out the preview screen. "I'll get a *new* dress for my own mega Bat

Mitzvah bash!" Maeve announced suddenly. "One worthy of a future movie star!"

Katani looked at Maeve sideways. "I thought you were just having a small—owww!" Katani yelped as Maeve's strappy white sandal landed firmly on top of her gold slip-on. Maeve's dress might have been terrible, but at least her shoes were stunning.

"Oh, I am so sorry." Maeve placed one hand delicately over her mouth, checking to be sure Katani was all right.

"I'm okay." Katani stared inquisitively at Maeve, who obviously didn't want to talk about her family's plans for a small luncheon after her Bat Mitzvah.

"Of *course* I'm having a big party," Maeve said with a flourish of her hand. "A really humongo-gigantic party." She paused for a brief second, then added, "With a movie star theme."

"Next," called the tuxedoed man at the information counter, before Katani could ask, "How?"

Avery rushed up to the desk. "Hi. I'm Avery Madden." The man looked through his stack of cards and handed her one.

"Table twelve," Avery announced. The other girls got their cards and were thrilled to discover they were all sitting together.

"Let's get Charlotte's table card, too," Isabel suggested.

"Thanks, but I can get it myself!" Charlotte said, rushing up to join her friends. She took her card from the attendant. "Awesome, table twelve. And you guys'll never guess—"

"Party tiiiiiiime!" A whole slew of seventh graders barged through the big glass doors, pushed one another under the balloon rainbow, and piled into the back of the line.

"Dudes, what up?!" Dillon popped Avery a casual knuckle butt.

Charlotte stood there with her mouth hanging open, waiting for an opening to finish her sentence, but she didn't get a chance.

"Hi," Betsy and Danny greeted the BSG.

"Do you think the natural history exhibit is open?" Betsy asked nobody in particular.

"I hear you can categorize specimens there," Danny continued as the two class brainiacs got in the back of the card line.

"Where have you been?" Katani asked Charlotte.

"Well, I—," Charlotte began.

"Isn't this *fab*?" Maeve trilled. "I can't *wait* for my own party!"

"Your what?" Charlotte looked from Maeve's sparkling eyes to her less-than-sparkling dress. *Obviously, I've missed a lot being just a few minutes late!* Charlotte smiled. But before she figured out what was going on with Maeve, she had something really, really important to share! "Guys, I was late because—"

"Isabel! There you are." Chelsea Briggs walked in from the exhibit halls, carrying her camera. "Take a look at this shot I got of the dance scene!" Before Charlotte could say another word, Isabel scooted away. Charlotte wanted the

BSG to be *together* when she shared her wonderful news. *Something this BIG has to be shared with all my BFFs, all at once!*

The crowd carried them past the information desk and into what were normally exhibit halls. There, black, red, and silver balloons and streamers adorned a row of booths, each of which were crowded full of people. Isabel bounced over, clapping her hands with excitement.

"There's a place to decorate T-shirts! Come on, we can make matching ones!"

"Guys, can we go over there for just a sec?" Charlotte pointed to a relatively empty corner.

"Whatever *for*?" Maeve stared quizzically at the empty spot.

"Because, there's something important I wanted to—"

"Wait up!" Dillon called out as he came running over, trailed by Riley and Nick.

"'Sup?" Riley asked the girls, blushing when Maeve sidled over to stand next to him. Everyone at school knew he had a huge crush on her. Riley was incredibly brave and outgoing when he was onstage playing his guitar, but in person he was very shy. Riley's face turned totally red when he said, "Hi, Maeve."

Maeve flashed her famous movie star smile and curtsied. Her awful dress didn't seem to bother Riley one little bit! "Pleasant evening, isn't it, gentlemen?"

"You're sooo weird." Dillon grinned crookedly at Maeve.

Charlotte had hoped to tell her friends alone, but it

looked like she wasn't going to get a chance. "So what I wanted to say was—," she started.

Just then, Nick Montoya gave Charlotte's hand a squeeze. He let go after a second, but Charlotte felt her hand still tingling. She and Nick had had this weird thing going ever since a magical kiss after the Valentine's Day dance. He wasn't her boyfriend, but he was . . . special.

"What did you want to say?" Katani asked.

"Ummm . . ." Charlotte's mind had gone completely blank! All she could think about was how warm Nick's hand had been.

By the time she caught a hold of her thoughts, Dillon was going on and on about how they all had to check out the arcade room. "I got the all-time high score on Acid Blast, and Riley wiped the floor with Nick at Astro-Pong."

"Yeah, but I crushed you at foosball," Nick boasted.

"So now we're off to the Theater of Electricity to check out the DJ," Riley added.

"Wanna come?" Dillon asked.

"I need—," Charlotte began, but once more she was interrupted.

"Hey, dudes," Billy and Josh Trentini cheered as they came over and joined the group, waving their seating cards. "Table twelve all around!"

Charlotte didn't want to be rude, but her secret was burning up inside her. She glanced at Nick, Riley, the Trentini twins, and Dillon, motioned with her hand, and said, "You guys go on ahead. We'll meet you in the theater in a few."

"What's up, Char?" Isabel asked, sensing that something was going on with her friend.

"Yeah," said Dillon. "You're acting almost as weirdo-wacko as Maeve."

Maeve tried to step on his foot, but he pulled it out of the way just in time.

"Izzy really wanted to go over to *that* booth," Charlotte said, struggling to act as normal as possible. "There's a graffiti artist over there helping decorate T-shirts." There was no one else by the T-shirt girl at the moment. It was the perfect place for telling secrets.

"See ya on the dance floor, then," Dillon told them.

"I'll go with the boys," Maeve announced. *Riley's so adorable in that tie! But he'll have to wear white to my party,* Maeve thought. *White or light blue.*

"Come on, Maeve," Isabel took her arm and tugged gently. "We'll catch up with them in a few."

Reluctantly Maeve sighed and turned back to her friends. "Save a dance for me," she called after Riley.

While the boys followed Dillon toward the music, Charlotte led the girls past a trivia game room filled with prizes and toward the T-shirt booth.

Once they were out of everyone else's earshot, Charlotte began fresh. "Okay, so I didn't really want a shirt." She paused. "I wanted to get you guys alone because I have something to tell you! You aren't going to believe it, but—"

"Nice dress, Maeve," Anna McMasters interrupted in a snooty voice.

"Did your mommy pick it out?" Joline Kaminsky asked, sidling up beside her partner in meanness. Together, the BSG called them the Queens of Mean, or QOM.

"Look at little Maeve-y wavy; her mommy still dresses her!" Anna mocked.

Katani's eyes flashed with anger as Maeve's face burned bright red. "Need help?" she asked softly, but Maeve shrugged her away.

"I can handle this," she whispered. *If I'm going to be a big star, I'll have to deal with the critics.* Maeve puffed out her chest and put her hands on her hips, "Classic styles never go out of fashion."

Katani, known throughout school as a fashion expert, turned to Maeve and asked pointedly, "Didn't I see Lola Lindstrom wearing those *exact* same shoes to her red carpet premiere last week?"

"Why, I think you did!" Avery added, getting in on the fun of watching the QOM's triumphant expressions fade a little. Isabel wrapped her arm around Maeve's shoulder, and Charlotte stepped in right beside Maeve, giving her best stare-down glare.

Maeve grinned. She had the greatest friends. Really. The best ever.

With a loud grunt, Anna raised her nose and turned to walk away. "Come on, Joline, let's go find people worth talking to," she said, and the two of them disappeared in a swirl of matching black taffeta.

"Who made *them* the fashion police?" Maeve sputtered after the QOM were out of earshot. "I mean, who wears black to a Bar Mitzvah?" Maeve waved one hand in the air. "At *my* party, there will be a rule: pastel only!"

The BSG laughed, all except for Charlotte, who had missed most of the party talk. "I didn't know you were having a big party. I thought your parents said no."

"They'll come around," Maeve said assuredly. "My party *has* to be supermarvtastic! And I need you all to help me. We'll have decorations and flowers and activities and"—she waved her hands around the redecorated museum—"it will be *just* like this party . . . only pink!"

Charlotte was happy for Maeve and wanted to help plan the party too, but still hadn't gotten to share her own news. *Yay for Maeve,* she thought, *but if I don't get this out soon, my brain's gonna explode!*

"Anyway—," Charlotte began.

"Oooh! I love this song!" Maeve dashed off toward the Theater of Electricity, where the DJ had just put on the latest hip-hop sensation.

"It's almost time for dinner!" Katani realized, checking her watch.

I guess it's just going to have to wait. Charlotte sighed and followed her friends.

The Big News

"These astroburgers are huge!" Avery exclaimed when they got to table twelve. "Yum."

"I want something fancier to eat at my Bat Mitzvah party," Maeve remarked. "Maybe something fitting into the movie star theme?"

"Marilyn Monroe Muffins?" Katani suggested with a grin.

"Guys, I—" Charlotte struggled to get a word in to change the subject, but Nick spoke faster.

"Terminator Tacos?" Nick chimed in from the boys' side of the table.

"Batman Burritos?" the Trentini twins suggested at the exact same time.

Charlotte couldn't wait anymore. Planning Maeve's menu might go on forever, and she couldn't stand keeping her news a secret for even one more second. *I'm never going to get a chance to tell the BSG alone,* she realized. *I'll have to just blurt it out.* But did she have the courage to do it? Right here? Right now?

"Sophie—," she started.

"Okay, let's go with that," Dillon said to his buddies. "How about Sophie Sandwiches?"

"Sophie's not a—" Charlotte tried to stop the boys and explain who Sophie was, but they kept going. Like a runaway train.

"Sophie Spaghetti!" Billy Trentini snorted.

"No, no . . . Sophie Sundaes!" his twin suggested.

Suddenly a great tune came on from the DJ's station, and Maeve jumped up. "We'll work on my theme later. We need to dance. Now!"

Isabel jumped up from her chair too, as Avery started to pull out some of her funky, crazy moves right by the table. "I love this song!"

Everyone was getting up and moving off to the dance

floor! It was noisy and chaotic, and Charlotte felt tears of frustration burning against her eyes. *If I'm ever going tell the BSG my news, I'll have to act fast!*

Charlotte jumped up on her chair and waved her arms over her head to get her friends' attention. Once they were looking up at her, she shouted out at the top of her voice, "Sophie Morel is coming to Boston!"

2

Rock the Party

This wasn't how Charlotte imagined giving her news. Not at all. As she looked around, Charlotte felt her heart racing. Sure, the Beacon Street Girls had all heard her, but so had most of the people in the room. It was Maeve who liked being the center of attention, not Charlotte. And yet there she was, standing on a chair in the middle of the party, acting like a complete spaz.

Charlotte carefully stepped off the chair, taking her time so she wouldn't make a double fool of herself by falling flat on the floor. There were a lot of strangers looking at her oddly—most of them Henry Yurt's family and friends. Then there were the people she knew—Mr. Moore, Ms. O'Reilly and a whole table full of teachers, Chelsea and the rest of the school newspaper staff, Betsy and Danny at the nearest table—all were watching Charlotte with curious expressions, clearly wondering why she was making such a scene. Even the Yurtmeister himself had stopped dancing and was now gazing at Charlotte.

Charlotte could hear whispers around the room. People were asking, "Who's Sophie?" and "Why is Sophie coming?"

The Queens of Mean even moved in closer to listen. They loved juicy gossip. If Charlotte knew them at all, they probably wanted to be the ones to tell everyone *exactly* who Sophie was and why she was coming to town.

The first one to recover, Katani squealed, "I can't believe this! Mega-awesomicity!"

"You've been trying to tell us about Sophie since you arrived tonight, haven't you?" Isabel realized. "Sorry we haven't been listening."

"Yeah, we can't wait to meet her!" Avery added.

"Tell us more!" Maeve gushed. "We need details."

"Okay." Charlotte told her friends . . . and the whole crowd of random people gathered around! "I got a call from Sophie in Paris right before I was about to leave tonight. This trip was a surprise for her thirteenth birthday, so I guess my dad and her dad have been planning this for months, and we didn't find out until now. But it's definitely happening. Sophie is flying in Monday night! That's in, like, two days! Isn't that amazing?"

"Who's Sophie?" Dillon asked, confused.

"Yeah. What's the deal with her? Is she famous?" Henry Yurt looked completely baffled at why this was such big news.

The Beacon Street Girls all knew exactly who Sophie Morel was.

"She was Charlotte's BFF when she lived in Paris," Avery explained.

"Charlotte went to visit Sophie last year to look for her missing cat, Orangina," Isabel added.

"Cool," Henry said. "Can't wait to meet Frenchie!" He smiled enthusiastically, then the Yurtmeister grabbed Dillon and his other buddies and went back to the dance floor.

"I'm glad your friend is coming," Nick whispered to Charlotte before running off with the guys. "I can't wait to meet her."

The Queens of Mean looked truly disappointed. "Who cares that some French snob is coming to town?" Anna remarked.

"Big, fat deal," Joline agreed as the QOM wandered off to find more interesting gossip. The rest of the crowd, also realizing that this news didn't seem to involve them, went back to their dinner, drinks, and dancing.

When the BSG were finally alone, they huddled around Charlotte.

"This is thrilling news!" Maeve exclaimed.

"We simply *must* make a list of everything to show her in Boston," Katani added.

"We should start right here!" Avery suggested. "Even on a regular day, the Museum of Science is pretty cool."

"Oh, how about a visit to the ICA?" Isabel hadn't lived in Boston as long as the other girls, but she'd already found her favorite place: the Institute of Contemporary Art, Boston's modern art museum.

"Or the New England Aquarium!" Avery loved watching the penguins.

"Another day we could go horseback riding," Katani said. "How long will Sophie be here?" There were so many places to go, like Montoya's Bakery and the Movie House and Irving's Toy and Card Shop.

"I'm not sure yet," Charlotte admitted. "I only just found out this was Sophie's surprise birthday present, like, an hour ago!"

"I hope Sophie'll stay long enough to come to my Bat Mitzvah," Maeve pondered. She was now so excited that she started talking a mile a minute. "She can come with me to Think Pink to shop!" The BSG all knew that the slightly eccentric owner of the store, Ms. Razzberry Pink, used to live in Paris. Maeve chattered on, "Ms. Pink and Sophie could totally bond about French things, like the Eiffel Tower and baguettes and—"

"Slow down, Maeve," Katani interrupted. "You're going so fast, even I can't keep up! Also, I had another idea. She should come by my house. We can design and sew French fashions together!"

"Sophie is going to LOVE the BSG!" Charlotte exclaimed, overwhelmed by her friends' exuberant reactions. "I'll e-mail her when I get home tonight and tell her *all* our ideas."

The DJ's voice interrupted their conversation. "Ladies and gentlemen, I have a special surprise for you tonight! In honor of Henry Yurt's Bar Mitzvah, I want to introduce to you"—a drumroll started building up in the background—"the third runner-up from everyone's favorite reality contest *Rock and Roll Survivor* . . ." The swell of drums from the speakers grew as the crowd hushed. "I give you . . . John Thomas!!!!!"

From behind the DJ a shower of fireworks rained down and gray smoke slithered across the stage. The DJ moved aside just as John Thomas, teen singing sensation, burst through the fireworks curtain. He was wearing a black T-shirt with a neon skull on the front, and tight black leather pants.

JT, as he was known by his fans, shouted out, "Mazel Tov to the Yurtmeister!" and then broke into his number-one hit song. It was a fast and catchy pop tune that he'd recorded the day after he was booted off *Rock and Roll Survivor*, the only reality TV show where contestants had to sing and perform daredevil stunts at the same time.

"You make my heart spin! Yeah, yeah, yeah! You make my fears fly away on wings of light. Without you the day faaaaades to night!" JT sang.

The BSG and everyone else at the party rushed the dance floor. This was huge! A Bar Mitzvah party moment no one would ever forget.

"Check out Dillon." Isabel pointed over Maeve's shoulder. True to form, Dillon was flirting with Henry Yurt's twin girl cousins, in from New York. Even from this far away they could tell he was talking sports. He moved his arms, as if he were hitting a baseball, then flexed his muscles.

"Probably retelling every moment of the last game," Katani said, rolling her eyes. "Hope he doesn't bore them to death with the details."

"Hey—don't knock it! That game was amazing! Dillon's double in the seventh inning won us the game," Avery remarked. She and Dillon had been sports buddies since preschool.

Nick grabbed Charlotte's hand and spun her around the floor. Charlotte had no idea where he'd learned his moves and was just glad she didn't fall. But then when he dipped her, she started to stumble and put her hand on the floor to steady herself. *Great, I can't even keep up with a simple dip without a major klutz moment!* Charlotte thought, mortified. But Nick didn't seem to notice. He just swept her back up and spun her around again.

"You must be psyched that Sophie's coming!" Nick shouted over the music. "We should go hiking sometime while she's here."

"Great!" Charlotte exclaimed as the song came to an end. "I'd love to. Umm, I mean *she'd* love to!" It was a little difficult, actually, to imagine proper city girl Sophie Morel out in the woods, but Charlotte couldn't say no to spending a whole day with her crush. *I'm sure Sophie will understand!* Charlotte thought as JT moved into his next song, "I'm the Apple of My Own Eye," and Nick once again took her hand.

Walk of Fame

As the girls danced and sang along with JT, Maeve was on a mission. She boogied over to Henry Yurt and told him, "You know, I'm having a party too! I hope you can come."

"Sick! Can't wait," the Yurtmeister said.

Riley told her nothing could keep him away. Nick said he'd be there. Danny, Betsy, Chelsea, and the Trentini twins promised to come. Soon, the entire dance floor was buzzing about Maeve's big bash.

"Watch for invitations in the mail," Maeve told them all.

"I was thinking about your party," Isabel said when Maeve returned. "We should have a walk of fame, like in Hollywood," Isabel continued. "I could cut stars out of cardboard and paint our names on them!"

"Oooh! And you should have an arcade and game room, too," Avery suggested. "Just like this party."

"What about mannequins in movie costumes?" Charlotte mused. "Like how Henry has those ice sculptures of famous scientists around the dance floor. Your dad could probably help us get real props from the Movie House!"

Maeve's head was crowded full of ideas. In her mind she saw a limo driving her to the bash. *Slowly I step out of the limo, wearing the dress of my dreams, matching sparkly shoes, the pinkest of pink nail polish, glitter lipstick, and a diamond tiara! Riley is walking next to me, carrying a new, silver guitar as we walk down the red carpet. Inside, there's a towering Hollywood-style cake and little Oscars for the party favors. . . .* It was a Maeve fantasy times ten!

No one noticed the worried look on Katani's face.

"We heard you're having a Bat Mitzvah party," Anna, QOM #1, interrupted Maeve's daydream.

"Why haven't we been invited?" Joline, QOM #2, asked. "I mean, it *is* only two weeks away, isn't it?"

"*Normal* people send invitations at least a month in advance," Anna added. "It's common knowledge that that is proper etiquette."

Maeve just shrugged, still in heavenly bliss from her fantasy. "Everyone's invited, but you don't have to come if you don't want to," she jested.

"Where's this big bash going to be, anyway?" Anna asked, stepping in closer and digging for information. "In your tiny apartment?"

"And what's on the menu?" Joline said, following Anna's lead. "*We* don't eat red meat. Or french fries."

"I—" Maeve shook her head, backing away slightly. She didn't know all the details. Not yet anyway. "It's all a mystery." She brushed their questions off, too excited about her planning to let even these two get her down. "You'll find out soon enough."

The girls snorted and walked away.

Maeve rolled her eyes and stuck out her tongue at their retreating backs. "They are sooo annoying sometimes," she said with a sigh.

"Not just sometimes," Avery remarked. "Those two are annoying *all* the time."

"Hey, look at Dillon," Isabel exclaimed. "Wow!"

"Is he still flirting with the twins?" Katani asked.

"Not anymore!" Isabel pointed over to where Dillon was riding around the dance floor on a bicycle. It was a brand-new bike, the kind that Maeve had seen A-list celebrities posing with in her favorite magazines. In fact, Maeve could tell that it was the exact same model that her favorite

Hollywood director, Ozmond, had given to his crew at the wrap party for his latest film. The same color even.

Dillon rode the bike across the floor and straight up to Henry. "Thanks, Dillon, for your help," Henry's dad announced. "This bicycle is from Grandma and Grandpa Yurt. They are sorry they couldn't be here tonight, but send their best from the deck of their cruise ship in Spain!"

A cruise ship! Maeve's fantasy doubled and tripled as she moved her red carpet party to the deck of a ship in the Boston harbor . . . then a yacht off the coast of France.

Dillon high-fived Henry before turning the bike over to the Yurtmeister, who then took it for a spin around the dance floor, trying out some crazy moves and nearly running over his twin cousins.

"After this last tune," JT announced, putting a temporary halt to the bike fun, "everyone head on over to the Omni Theater for a photomontage presentation about Henry, class president of AAJH and today's Bar Mitzvah boy! Congrats, kid."

After a flurry of applause, JT assured everyone, "Party's not over yet," and launched into a new song he'd written with that exact same name.

Party Planning

While the crowd was distracted by the music, Katani sidled up next to Maeve. "Hey," she whispered in Maeve's ear. "Can we talk for a sec?"

Maeve nodded, and the two of them moved to the side of the dance floor.

Katani sighed, then unloaded. "Although I hate to admit it, I think that the QOM might be right about a few things," she began. "The plans for your Bat Mitzvah party are growing bigger and bigger by the moment, and until tonight I thought you weren't having a party at all."

"Of course I'm having a party!" Maeve replied with a wide-eyed, innocent look on her face. Inside Maeve was forced to admit to herself that Katani had a point. *But with a little planning it'll all be perfect and come together like a dream,* Maeve thought.

"All I know is that for the last month you've been moaning and groaning about how your parents say they can't give you a big party now that they're separated and all. And how you were only having a family luncheon. Even the BSG weren't going to be invited."

"I know," Maeve said with an elegant wave of her hand. "But that's all changed."

"When did it change?" Katani asked pointedly. "I mean, you *are* talking about the kind of party where things need to be done in advance . . . like mailing out printed invitations, choosing a menu, ordering personalized party favors, and even picking a DJ."

"Don't worry so much, Katani," Maeve told her, rocking back on her heels, ready to return to the dance floor. "It will all work out, and I'll have the party of my dreams." She paused, then smiled her award-winning grin. "I'm talking to my mom about it tonight!"

CHAPTER

3

One Perfect Pink Dress

The BSG left the party loaded down with goodies and giveaways. Maeve wore a baseball cap she'd won in a limbo contest. Isabel and Charlotte had hand-painted shirts, Katani looked stylish in a brand-new pair of huge sunglasses and a glowing necklace, and Avery had some hilarious photos the BSG took in one of those booths where you all squish onto one seat. Oh, and then there were the "Henry Yurt Bar Mitzvah" tote bags that all the guests received to fill with their stuff.

"Looks like you five made off with all the loot," Charlotte's dad remarked. He'd volunteered to meet the girls at the museum and ride the subway home with them.

"Oh, Dad! It was amazing," Charlotte gushed. "But I'll tell you later."

"We want all the details about Sophie's visit!" Katani added.

No one seemed to notice that Maeve just sat there,

preoccupied with her own thoughts while the others planned Sophie's Boston visit day by day.

When they reached their stop in Brookline, Maeve had a whole speech to her mom worked out in her head. *My dream party has to come true! It just has to!* she told herself.

"Call me tomorrow." Isabel stuck her thumb and pinky out like a phone as she headed for her aunt Lourdes's car.

"I'll be on IM," Avery announced.

Charlotte waved. "And I'll send an e-mail as soon as I hear back from Sophie!"

Katani leaned over and whispered in Maeve's ear, "Good luck with your mom tonight."

Maeve nodded, then she straightened her new Henry Yurt baseball cap and started walking the short distance to her family's home above the Brookline Movie House. *I wonder what kinds of gifts I should hand out at my party. Maybe faux jewelry and movie gift cards and boxes of theater-style candies—*

Suddenly Maeve stopped in her tracks. Her head turned, slowly, until she was gazing over her shoulder into the darkened windows of Think Pink. *Did I just see what I think I saw?* She put it in reverse, stared into her favorite boutique, and gasped.

Ms. Pink must have changed the window display that very afternoon! The party favors were completely forgotten as Maeve stood, jaw dropped, looking up at the most perfect pink dress she'd ever seen. *This is the most amazing, glorious gown in the history of the world!*

The top of the raspberry pink dress swooped slightly

off the mannequin's shoulders. A satin sash with just the right amount of shine adorned the empire waist, and the soft fabric trailed down to the floor in a shimmering cascade. The simple elegance of the gown was totally movie star glam and beyond perfect, but it was the sequins that sold it for Maeve.

Sewn into the fabric, all over the dress, top to bottom, were tiny sparkles. They cast rainbows even in the faint glow of the street lamps, and Maeve could only begin to imagine how the sequins would flash as she entered the brightly lit ballroom of her party. Maeve saw herself parading down the red carpet, her Hollywood gown sparkling as she moved. She'd glow and glimmer, as if she were wearing a thousand stars.

Maeve was breathless. *I have to have that dress. Have to. Have to. Have to.*

The Battleground

Maeve sprinted the short distance remaining to her home and hustled up the stairs at top speed.

"Mom! I'm home," she announced, bursting through the door of their apartment.

"Shhh. You'll wake Sam," Maeve's mom called in a soft voice from the kitchen. "Come have a glass of milk and tell me about the party."

Maeve was too jazzed to drink anything, but if her mom was sitting down, that was a good sign. Carol Kaplan was always easier to talk to when she was relaxed.

"Coming," Maeve called quietly, setting her tote of

favors in the hallway and taking off her shoes. When she passed the hall mirror, she frowned at her boring, lavender dress. Hopefully she'd never have to wear it again. *Because I'll have a gown worthy of a star!*

"Careful of Gettysburg," Carol warned, poking her head out of the kitchen and motioning to the mess on the floor in the living room.

But it was too late. Maeve's bare foot landed solidly on a blue plastic soldier carrying a bayonet. "Owww," she yelped. After confirming that she wasn't bleeding, Maeve stood the soldier up again. *Honestly*, Maeve thought, *It's creepy how much Sam knows about war.* Her brother loved historic battles and was always reenacting them. Messing up the battle right before an incredibly important talk with her mom was not a good idea.

Maeve carefully navigated the rest of the way through Sam's mini military encampment, noting that the Confederates were holding their own. There were a lot of dead Union soldiers piled up in a shoebox cemetery.

In the kitchen her mom sat at the little table, a coffee mug in one hand, book in the other.

"Whatcha reading?" Maeve plopped down in a seat across the table.

Her mom showed the cover: *Management for Managers.*

"Yikes," Maeve blurted out, then corrected herself. "Umm, sounds interesting." Her mom had taken to reading a lot of business books lately—one big, boring one after another. After the separation, her mom had gone back to work as a part-time office manager. Maeve was impressed at how seriously her mom took her new job and how much she wanted to succeed.

Jokingly, Maeve asked, "Can I borrow it when you're done?"

Her mom ignored the comment. "So, sweetie, how was the party?"

"Fabuloso," Maeve gushed. "It took up the whole museum! JT, you know, from *Rock and Roll Survivor*, did this whole dance set. Then there was a butterfly garden and this photomontage all about Henry. He got this awesome bicycle for a present, and we all took turns riding it, and I won a baseball cap in a limbo contest, and . . ." Maeve paused then said, "And I want my party to be just like his. Only better, of course."

Maeve's mom began to say something, but Maeve cut her off. "I've got it all planned out. We are going to have a movie star theme. Isabel will make a walk of fame, and we can have old posters and costumes on mannequins, or maybe even on real models who can wander around! I am going to arrive in a limo and walk down a red carpet—wait till you see the awesomely amazing dress I just found in the window at Think Pink!"

Ms. Kaplan put a hand on Maeve's shoulder to get her daughter's attention. "Maeve," she said firmly. "It's fine to dream about a nice party like that, but you *know* we can't afford all that." Her mom looked hard at her. "We've already discussed this a thousand times. After the ceremony, we're having a small lunch, just for family. No friends. No party. And certainly no limo."

Maeve sighed. In a matter of thirty seconds, her mother had all but crushed her dreams. "Mom, that's so not *fair*. Stacy's having her Bat Mitzvah on a *yacht*!" Maeve pointed to the fridge, where a fancy invite to her cousin's party hung between family photos.

"Maeve. I think you need to really consider the meaning of becoming a Bat Mitzvah," Ms. Kaplan continued, sounding very much like Rabbi Millstein. "Instead of getting all wrapped up in these other kids' fancy parties, think about what a Bat Mitzvah really means. At the age of thirteen, you are becoming a 'daughter of the Commandments.' It's a Jewish child's rite of passage. Being a Bat Mitzvah is about way more than having a party. It's about taking on adult responsibilities in the community."

Maeve nodded. "Right! I wore Great-grandma Gigi's dress tonight, and yesterday I put all the dishes away without you asking, and I got a B minus on that math quiz. . . ."

Her mom sighed. "And I'm very proud of you. But we've already discussed a party, and no means *no*." She paused, then added, "Rabbi Millstein called yesterday to discuss your community service project form."

Maeve sat up a little straighter. *Maybe if I'm really responsible and do a great project, she'll change her mind!* she decided. *I mean, how much could a big party actually cost?*

"Well," Maeve began, "I was thinking that I might go and fix up the park behind Jeri's Place. I could plant flowers and make a new playground for the kids."

"It's lovely that you want to do something for the homeless shelter," her mom said. "But there isn't much time left, honey. You only have two weeks to get a project done."

"If I started tomorrow," Maeve said. "Then I could get—"

"Maeve," Ms. Kaplan interrupted. "You've had a year to do this project. Remember when you wanted to get movies for cancer patients?" Maeve nodded. She'd only made a list of the movies. Never actually collected any of them. "Or when you were going to send books to a needy school?" There was a bag of books in the Movie House's storage closet that Maeve never got around to sorting.

"I know you love the idea of helping others," her mom said compassionately. "And you dream really big. But we are down to the wire here. You need to write up something you've already done and get the form in to the rabbi this week."

"I guess I could write up Project Thread," Maeve said, after considering her mother's words. Maeve had won an award for organizing the project to sew and donate blankets to Jeri's Place at the beginning of the school year.

"That's exactly what I was thinking, too," her mom replied.

"But I sorta wanted to do something new for my Bat Mitzvah project," Maeve continued. "And bigger this time."

"Project Thread is big enough," Maeve's mom told her. "Please get your community service form signed at the shelter ASAP."

"Okay," Maeve said with a sigh. It was late, and she was tired and a bit deflated. *I guess I don't need a huge new project, but maybe there's still a chance for the party if I get my form signed and memorize all my Hebrew perfectly and if I'm really, really nice to Sam . . .*

With this new tactic set in her mind, Maeve hopped up from her chair. "Good night!" She kissed her mom's forehead, and headed back out into the war zone, toward her bedroom. She'd start over, trying to convince her mom about the movie star party, in the morning.

"Hang on, Maeve," her mom called after her.

They met at the Confederate cavalry headquarters, a walled garrison built of gray LEGOs.

"I nearly forgot," Ms. Kaplan continued, "one of Sam's classmate's mom called to see if you could babysit after school. I told her that you might be too busy with Hebrew and hip-hop classes and your friends."

Maeve immediately thought about the dress hanging in the window at Think Pink. "I'll do it!" Maeve said, without hesitation. Babysitting meant money, and money meant she could help pay for the party! *I'll start by buying that dress.*

"Well, only if you're *sure* you can handle the extra responsibility. We'll have to work hard to rearrange your schedule to fit Mrs. Franklin's needs. Make sure you call her in the morning to set it up. I left the number on the kitchen counter." Ms. Kaplan gave Maeve a hug and said, "Good night."

Maeve went to her room, happy and excited again, certain that once she owned the dress, everything else would fall into place.

Writer's Block

On Sunday morning Charlotte rushed to her computer as soon as she woke up. She'd sent a long e-mail the night before with a list of the BSG's ideas for Sophie's visit. Sure enough, there was a response waiting in her in-box.

> To: Charlotte
> From: Sophie
> Subject: Re: See you soon!!!!
>
>
> *Mon amie*, I am so very excited to come
> to Boston and see you! This is the best
> surprise birthday gift ever. . . . Can
> you believe our dads kept it secret for
> so long? I cannot wait to meet your
> *meilleures amies*, the BSG. I have heard
> so much about them, and I only hope they
> will like me!
> My plane arrives 6:45 p.m., Monday, and
> I will stay until 10 May in the early
> morning. I want to see everything you
> tell me about!!! The museum and horseback
> riding sound *très* wonderful. I hope we
> can have tea at Montoya's Bakery. I know
> it is your favorite, and there I can meet
> your *petit ami* Nick! See you soon.
> *Je t'adore*,
> Sophie

Charlotte clapped her hands, having trouble containing her excitement. The sound woke up Marty, who started dancing around under the chair legs, yipping for breakfast.

"Just one minute, Marty!" Charlotte hit reply and began to write:

```
To: Sophie
From: Charlotte
Subject: Re: Re: See you soon!!!!


Dearest Sophie,
Good morning! Guess what??? Your last
night in Boston is the same night as
Maeve's birthday! She's turning thirteen
too. And she's having a huge party!!!
Oh, and don't worry about anything.
Of course the BSG will adore you. . . .
```

Charlotte stopped. She didn't know what else to say. Marty sat down at her feet and whined. Suddenly things inside her felt all churned up. *What if Sophie doesn't get along with the BSG once she meets them? What would I do? What if they don't want to hang out, all of them together? What if—?*

"Charlotte?" It was her dad calling her name from the hallway just outside her bedroom. Deciding to finish her e-mail to Sophie later, Charlotte pressed save and closed the window.

"*Entre,*" she said, practicing her French a little for Sophie's visit.

Her father came right in. "*Bonjour,*" he said, playing along. "*Ça va?*" he asked.

"I'm just fine, *merci*," Charlotte said. "And how are you, Papa?"

"*Ça va bien*," he replied. "I'm fine too." Then he asked, "We talked about Sophie the whole way home. You never told me anything about the party."

"It was wowmazing, as Maeve always says." Charlotte sat back in her desk chair and told him the whole story. " . . . then, I stood up on my chair to tell everyone about Sophie, because no one was listening to me!"

Her dad chuckled and took a seat on the side of Charlotte's bed, scratching Marty's ears. "But your friends were excited to hear about Sophie's visit, weren't they?"

Charlotte pulled a beaded bracelet out of her collection and stared at it. "They had a zillion ideas about what we should do and where to take her. It was great." But she knew she sounded less than totally sure about things.

Her dad had spent years studying people and places as a travel writer, and he knew Charlotte better than anyone. "What's going on, Char?" he asked.

"I'm worried." Charlotte loved that she could be honest with her dad, but sometimes it wasn't easy to share her feelings. She put the bracelet on, then took it off again. "I want to make sure that Sophie feels welcome, but I don't want to seem overeager or overwhelm her or anything."

"Hmmm, I see," he replied. Then after a moment's thought, Mr. Ramsey added, "I think there are a few things we can do to prepare for her visit. One: We'll talk to the principal and make sure everything's all set at school. Two:

We'll make an itinerary with plenty of wiggle room, and three—"

"I know!" Charlotte smiled. "A welcome gift."

"Actually I was going to say, we should go shopping to pick up some groceries for French meals, but that works, too!"

Charlotte leaped up and kissed her father on both cheeks, European style, then rushed back to her desk. "When I was in Paris," she told him, "I promised Sophie I'd write a story about Orangina. When we finally found him and he looked so happy living on the barge, we both wondered what adventures he'd been having." She clicked the mouse to open her word processor. "I'm going to write Orangina's story for Sophie!"

"Good luck!" Mr. Ramsey waved and left the bedroom, with Marty at his heels. "But don't forget to eat. I'm making pancakes." Charlotte nodded, fingers over the keyboard, staring intently at the cursor blinking on the blank page. Then she began to type.

- -

Orangina's Travels
Part 1
A Wet Cat

A wet cat is a miserable cat. Orangina woke and stretched, sending droplets of dew flying off his spiky orange fur. "Wherrre is my boat?" he asked, only it sounded more like, "Ooo est mon bateauuu," which is how cats

35

speak in France. He didn't expect an answer, but he got one. "It floated off, mate, in the night. Say, you're mighty wet, huh? Care to dry off?"

An Australian accent was the last thing Orangina expected to hear on the banks of the river Seine. He looked left, then right.

"Down here, mate!" Orangina blinked, and struck out with his paw, trapping the strange little human-shaped creature, like a mouse.

"Ouch! Hey, that's no way to treat a bloke," the tiny man complained. He was only a little taller than Orangina's paw and wearing the most ridiculous outfit the cat had ever seen: a tan explorer's suit with pockets everywhere, tall brown boots, and a wide-brimmed hat with orange feathers sticking out. "You want the gold, don't you? They always want gold. Well, I've got something even *better* than gold, feline friend!"

The first three paragraphs came easily, but then Charlotte got stuck. What did the tiny man have that was better than gold? The tastiest cat food in the world? A huge sailing ship? Adventure? And what was he doing in France, anyway?

Throughout the day Charlotte returned to the computer again and again, to stare at the story. Sometimes she typed a new sentence, then deleted it. Other times she just stared. At dinner her dad asked, "How's your writing going?"

"Harder than I thought," Charlotte remarked, pushing

her food around. "I have a lot of ideas, but they aren't coming together yet."

Her dad put down his fork and said, "A great story cannot be forced. What you have is a common problem known as writer's block." He winked. "I've suffered from this condition more times than I can count, and the only remedy I know of is to just give it time. Let the story cook in your head."

"But, Dad, she's coming *tomorrow* night! And this is her welcome gift!"

"Try again early tomorrow morning. And here's an important bit of advice I remember reading somewhere when I was a young writer: Every central character has to want something."

What does Orangina want? Charlotte mused as she finished her vegetables. Even though she didn't have an answer yet, she was relieved that her dad, a real writer, also knew what it was like to feel stuck.

While Charlotte was eating dinner, Maeve was perched on her bed, typing on her laptop. But she wasn't writing a story; she was planning a party.

Maeve's Notes to Self

1. *Need shoes to go with dress* ☺ ☺ ☺
    Sandals? Heels? Flats?
2. *Hand out save the dates 2morrow.*
3. *Hairstyle and makeup: ask Katani!!!*
4. *Do I have to invite Sam?*

5. *Party favors: trophies, DVDs, mini Oscars, makeup kits, etc.*

6. *Centerpieces: I can't choose! Candles, flowers, snow globes, mirrors, or all four?*

7. *DJ or band? Hip-hop? Rock and pop? (Ask Riley!)*

8. *Games: Balloon pop, musical chairs, Coke versus Pepsi . . .*

9. *Location! Hotel—must have a ballroom. Cruise ship?*

10. *Oops . . . Forgot to call about the babysitting job today. Call 2morrow.*

CHAPTER
4

A Stupend-Delicious Idea

H ey, what's going on?" Charlotte arrived at the lunch-
room Monday to find a buzzing crowd centered
around Maeve! She twirled toward Charlotte and
handed her a card.

It had bright pink stars drawn around the border of
a light pink postcard. In the middle, Maeve had written
"SAVE THE DATE! MAY 9. MAEVE KAPLAN-TAYLOR'S
BAT MITZVAH BASH." Beneath that, in smaller letters it
said "7–11 P.M."

"Wow!" Charlotte exclaimed. "These are really nice!"

"Thanks." Maeve smiled as she handed cards to Danny
and Betsy. "I printed them on my computer, then drew the
stars myself."

"Did Isabel see them?" Charlotte asked. "She's gonna
LOVE these cards."

"Isabel said they were *muy bonita* and took some for
Katani and Avery," Maeve replied as she handed two more
cards over Charlotte's shoulder to the Trentinis.

"The BSG are saving us seats," Maeve told Charlotte. "I'll be there in a minute." She held up the small stack of cards left in her hands. "I just want to make sure everyone gets one."

Charlotte headed into the caf. Since she'd brought a bag lunch, she bypassed the lunch line and went straight over to where the BSG were sitting.

"Nice, huh?" Charlotte commented, holding up one of Maeve's cards.

Everyone agreed that the cards were deathly cute. Well, everyone except Katani. She was being oddly quiet.

"What's up?" Isabel asked her. "Don't you like Maeve's save-the-date cards?"

"It's not that." Katani sighed. "They're really adorable." But she was conflicted. *Maeve is definitely dreaming too big. With the party less than two weeks away, I just don't see how Maeve is going to get it all worked out.* Katani also wondered if Maeve had cleared the bash with her parents yet. *I'm not getting a clear vibe on the situation,* she thought. *I'll just have to pull Maeve aside and ask her. After all, that's what good friends are for!*

Katani changed the subject by asking Charlotte about the math homework.

It wasn't long before Maeve flounced into the caf. She came out of the lunch line carrying a tray with the day's mystery meat and a banana on it.

"There's so much to do for my party!" Maeve plopped onto the bench next to Avery. "What are you all wearing?"

"Right now? Soccer shorts and a T-shirt," Avery quipped.

But Maeve was distracted by someone across the room.

Riley's looking this way! Maeve felt a warmth inside that made her smile. She often rehearsed her Academy Award acceptance speech, and for the past few weeks she'd added Riley to the picture, standing by her side. She knew exactly what kind of suit he'd wear. What color tie. Even which brand of shoes. *But what's Riley going to wear to my party?*

"I think I'll buy a pink tie for Riley to wear," she announced.

Avery laughed so hard, milk dribbled out of her nose.

"What?" Maeve was unfazed. "We should be color-coordinated at the party."

It wasn't that Riley and Maeve were an actual couple or anything. It was just that everyone knew they liked each other, and if she was going to have a date to her own party, it would certainly be Riley. *So of course,* Maeve thought, *we should plan our outfits together.* "Would a blue or white suit look better with the pink tie?"

The BSG looked to Katani. She was the fashionista after all. Katani just shrugged. "Maeve, I think we need to ta—," Katani began, but the QOM chose that moment to saunter up to the table. Joline and Anna were each holding one of Maeve's save-the-date cards.

"Interesting card," Joline said, turning it over in her hands, like she was scrutinizing an alien object. "Did you make these yourself?"

"I did," Maeve said proudly, trying to ignore the tone in Joline's voice.

"So Maeve, where are you having this par-tay?" Anna snipped.

"Uh . . . well . . . " Maeve stalled, her face starting to flush. "It's a surprise."

"If you are inviting us all to a party," Joline said, "don't you think you should tell us where it's gonna be?"

Anna tossed her hair dramatically over her shoulder and said, "Because we might have better things to do that day."

Joline flipped her hair the exact same way before the QOM left the scene.

"Better things, like picking out matching nail polish?" Maeve muttered. "Maybe I should tell my mom that inviting Anna and Joline is going to be my mitzvah project."

Avery asked, "Isn't the mitzvah project something good that you have to do for the world?"

"Yeah," Charlotte added. "Remember the Yurtmeister collecting cans for the soup kitchen?"

"Uh-huh." Maeve nodded. "Every Bar or Bat Mitzvah has to do something charitable." She used her acting skills to look like she was really thinking about what she said next. "Do you think the rabbi would sign off on my form if I promise to be nice to the Queens of Mean?"

The BSG broke into giggles. "Somehow, I don't think he'll go for it," Isabel said with a chuckle.

Maeve smiled and shrugged. "I guess I have to think of something else, then. Mom wants me to get the project form signed for our work on Project Thread."

"Perfect!" Katani exclaimed. "The BSG did a mitzvah project all together."

"Okay, guys," Charlotte broke in. "I have a different kind of project to ask you about."

"A Sophie project, right?" Avery hopped up and down on her seat, nearly knocking over Maeve's juice.

"Yeah, I wanted to make her a welcome gift."

"Coolio! Like what?" Isabel asked, intrigued.

"Like . . . a story. About Orangina. But it's not done." Charlotte rolled up her lunch bag and swung her legs back and forth under the table.

Maeve shrugged. "You can finish it. No biggie. When's she coming?"

"Tonight!" Katani reminded them.

"Yeah, we're picking her up this evening," Charlotte said.

The table went silent as they all realized Charlotte wouldn't have time to finish her present.

Suddenly Isabel's face broke into a wide smile. "I've got a great idea! Let's meet at my house after school and make cookies! I'm sure it would be okay with my mom."

"Chocolate-chip cookies are an American classic," Avery said, patting her belly.

"And chocolate is the greatest food of all," Charlotte said. "You're a lifesaver, Izzy!"

"Great idea, but I can't come," Katani said apologetically. "On Mondays I take Kelley horseback riding. It's her favorite day of the week. I can't let my sister down."

Maeve took out her day planner to check her schedule. "Bummer. I'm out too. I have to meet my Hebrew tutor today." Maeve was dyslexic, which meant she had trouble deciphering letters. English was hard enough. The Hebrew alphabet was completely different, and the words went backward, right to left. Once a week a tutor came to her house to make sure she was pronouncing things right.

"Charlotte, maybe we could have a party for Sophie in the Tower later tonight?" Katani suggested.

"Fantabulous!" Maeve cheered.

"Perfectomundo!" Isabel agreed, and set the plan. "Avery and Charlotte can come over this afternoon to bake. Then we'll all meet at the Tower later for the big welcome."

After lunch Katani took Maeve aside. "Look, I don't mean to be a party pooper, but I think the QOM have a good point. It's nearly impossible to throw the kind of party you're talking about in less than two weeks."

"I'm on it," Maeve promised, reassuring Katani yet again. "Don't be such a worrywart."

Katani crossed her arms and stared Maeve down. "I'm getting the vibe that nothing has really been arranged."

"Ummm . . . ," Maeve stalled, and Katani knew she was right.

"Can I make a suggestion?" she asked. "As your friend?"

Maeve shrugged. She really *did* have it all under control, but if Katani wanted to stick her two cents in, well, then . . . "Go ahead," she said.

"I think you should show your parents that you're responsible. They might get on board and help you with the party if you can prove that you're really taking this whole becoming-a-Bat-Mitzvah thing very seriously."

Maeve nodded her head thoughtfully. This was sounding like the idea she'd already had: to be really nice to Sam, be helpful around the house, and earn money babysitting.

But Katani wasn't done. "I think you should make a list of places and prices for the party." Katani put her arm around Maeve. "During study hall I'll help you look up some possible locations. Then you can show your parents all your research. I bet they'll be impressed."

"Wow, Katani, you're totally right! I could book a cruise ship *and* a hotel. . . ."

"No, don't make any reservations yet, just a list!" Katani tried to explain, but she wondered if Maeve even heard her. "And remember to keep the cost reasonable," Katani added, half to herself. Maeve had *that* look in her eye, the one she got when her mind was spinning a million miles an hour.

"Stupend-delicious idea, Katani!" Maeve shouted. "Gotta get started!"

Smelly Dog

"We're here," Charlotte called out as she and Marty let themselves in through Isabel's front door.

"In my room with Avery," Isabel called back.

"Come on, Marty," Charlotte said. Normally she wouldn't bring him on a cookie-making expedition, but he needed a walk, and there was no other time today to take him out!

Marty bounded into Isabel's room and dropped his chew toy on the floor by Avery's feet so the happy face was staring at Avery. "Happy Lucky Thingy!" Avery exclaimed.

She snatched up the toy and tossed it for Marty to chase. Only Marty didn't go after his favorite thing. He

trotted to the corner of the room and barked at a covered cage hanging near Isabel's desk.

"Want to meet Franco?" Isabel asked Marty, scratching him behind one ear. He wagged his tail eagerly. Isabel pulled off the cage cover and inside, a gray parrot shuffled on his perch to peer down at his doggie visitor.

"Smelly!" the bird squawked. "Smelly dog!"

"That's not nice!" Isabel scolded Franco, but the bird didn't seem to notice. He just jiggled the latch of his cage, like he wanted to come out.

Marty barked and jumped around, his tongue lolling out.

"He's excited to meet Franco!" Avery said with a giggle.

"Unfortunately Franco doesn't seem overly excited to meet *him*," Charlotte pointed out.

When Isabel opened the cage, Franco flew out and landed solidly on her shoulder. "Franco love Izzy," he said, completely ignoring the dog.

"Want to come cook with us, Franco?" Isabel asked. "I might have some *pineapple* for you!"

"Pineapple!" Franco squawked, flapping his wings while Charlotte and Avery cracked up. When they first discovered Franco on a Hawaiian cruise, his love of pineapple nearly got them all in big trouble!

Isabel carried Franco to the kitchen, with Avery and Charlotte following. Marty snatched up HLT in his teeth and trotted along behind the girls.

"I printed out a recipe I found online," Isabel said, putting Franco on the back of a kitchen chair and handing each girl a piece of paper from the counter. "I made copies for all of us!"

Avery read the list of ingredients that they needed while Isabel got out the mixing bowls. Charlotte's job was to look in the cabinets for the cookie sheets.

But Marty was making her job nearly impossible as he darted between her legs, over to Franco's chair, and then back to Charlotte again, his toenails clicking and clacking on the linoleum floor.

"That dog is going to give himself a heart attack!" Isabel's older sister, Elena Maria, griped as she entered the kitchen. "And what's Franco doing in here?"

"Are they helping us make cookies?" Scott joked. Avery's brother was also Elena Maria's boyfriend.

"Pineapple!" squawked Franco as Marty tried to tug a cookie sheet away from Charlotte.

"Oookay . . . how about this," Elena Maria offered, spreading out her hands and backing away from the hyper animals. "While you make the cookies, Scott and I will make a cake. That way you'll have two desserts for the welcome party!" She picked up the bag of sugar that Isabel had pulled from the pantry and set it down on the kitchen table. "We'll work over here. *Away* from your *loco* cooking zoo."

Pineapple Frenzy

It all started out well enough. Charlotte read the cookie recipe, Avery did the measuring, and Isabel mixed the ingredients. On the other side of the room, Elena Maria and Scott worked on a cake batter. In the middle, Marty and Franco stared at each other.

"Did we add the vanilla yet?" Charlotte asked, keeping

one hand on Marty's back so he couldn't jump up on the chair where Franco was perched.

"No, Scott has it." Avery waved over to her brother. "Vanilla, *por favor*?" She held up her hand to catch the bottle, but Scott was staring into Elena Maria's eyes, completely oblivious to the rest of the world.

"They'll never finish that cake if they don't stop making googly eyes at each other," Isabel whispered to Avery.

"Seriously!" Avery griped. "I am *never* falling in love."

"Oh, really?" Isabel teased, crossing the room to get a stick of butter from the fridge.

At the kitchen table, Elena Maria reached over to open the cocoa powder at the same time as Scott, and their hands touched. Isabel's sister let out a high-pitched giggle as Scott lifted her hand for a quick kiss, pushing the can of cocoa powder to the side—a little *too* close to the edge of the table.

"Blech!" complained Avery.

Isabel opened the fridge, and Franco took off in a flurry of feathers!

"WANT PINEAPPLE!" The parrot was heading straight for Isabel! Marty ran after him, jumping and barking.

"Huh . . . ?" Isabel stood with the fridge door open, holding the butter, and watched as chaos broke loose in the kitchen.

"Ahhh!" Elena Maria screamed at the top of her lungs as Franco's tail feathers brushed against her head. When she reached up to flail at the bird, she bumped into the table, sending the open cocoa container flying!

Isabel leaned forward, thinking maybe, just maybe, she could catch it, but it was already too late.

Crash! The tin slammed onto the floor. Cocoa spilled all over, coating Marty and Isabel with brown powder.

"Pineapple!" Franco said triumphantly, landing inside the still-open refrigerator and grabbing a small plastic container of pineapple chunks.

Avery and Charlotte were laughing so hard, their stomachs hurt. Marty was licking the dropped stick of butter, and Scott had his hand on Elena Maria's back.

"Are you okay?" he asked.

"We still need to add cocoa powder!" she wailed. "And we don't have any more!"

While Isabel tried to brush herself off, Charlotte scooped up the tiny bit of powder remaining in the container. "Is this enough?" she asked Elena Maria.

But Marty must have thought Charlotte had a treat for him, and leaped into her legs with such force that she crashed into the counter, knocking a bag of flour onto the floor.

Poof!

A cloud of white powder exploded in the air as the bag hit the floor with a solid thud.

"Woof, woof, woof!" Marty barked at the fallen bag.

The noise terrified Franco away from his pineapple, and he flew around the room, cawing nervously, "Smelly dog! Smelly dog!"

"These *animals* are ruining everything!" Elena Maria hollered.

"Here, this'll stop the bird!" Scott soothed his girlfriend.

"They go to sleep when it's dark, right?" He reached for the light switch . . . but hit the ceiling fan switch instead! As the blades whirred in a blur, Marty started barking himself into a frenzy, and Franco swooped around under the fan, whooping and cawing as the spilled flour and dry cocoa swirled into a powdered tornado.

"Turn it off!" Elena Maria yelped. "Stop that dog! Get that bird!"

Everyone watched as Avery somehow managed to dodge the swooping bird, hop over the running dog, hurdle the slick flour-cocoa mixture, duck past the flailing Elena Maria, and outflank her unbalanced brother to reach the switch.

"Got it!" Avery announced as she scored the touchdown and stopped the chaos. The fan's breeze died down and the powder began to settle. "Whew."

"Desert" in the Kitchen

When it was all over, there was a fine brownish powder covering most everything in the kitchen, from the toaster to the table. A cocoa-flour mist sifted down and settled on the kitchen floor in gentle sand dunes. Mixed into the desert-like terrain were fallen feathers and wisps of dog hair.

"Well, it's a good thing your mom isn't home," Avery pointed out.

"What are we going to do now?" Isabel wondered, surveying the mess.

"You," Elena Maria directed, "will clean this up!"

"But what about our cookies?" Charlotte asked.

"We've got to finish our cake first," Scott said, holding Elena Maria's hand.

"I can't!" she wailed. "Not with that *bad bird* staring at me!"

"Bad bird, bad bird!" Franco repeated. He was inside the open fridge again, picking at the plastic lid on the container of pineapple.

Isabel shook her head at the parrot. "That's enough, Franco."

"Franco love Izzy!" he announced, as Isabel lifted him out, closing the fridge door and taking him back to her room.

"Marty," Charlotte called to the dog. "Maybe you should wait in the backyard."

When the kitchen was quiet—messy, but quiet—the girls turned back to their mixing bowls. "Where were we?" Charlotte asked.

"I think we were on the eggs," Isabel said.

"Did we already add the vanilla?" Charlotte asked.

"Let's skip ahead and add the chocolate chips," Avery suggested.

Elena Maria leaned against Scott. "It's pointless! Everything's ruined," she said with a moan. Scott gave Avery an apologetic look, and the teenagers left the kitchen, stepping carefully around the drifts of powder.

"Well, then." Isabel stared into the bowl of unfinished cake batter. "Shall we pop this in the oven?"

CHAPTER
5

Sophie Shines

"What took you so long?" Katani demanded when the three hapless bakers finally showed up at the Tower.

"And what . . . in the *world* . . . is that supposed to be?!" Maeve pointed with one hot-pink fingernail to the cake platter Isabel was carrying. Maeve was decked out in a pink beret, a pink leopard-print shirt, and black skinny-leg jeans. Her pink and black tennis shoes completed the look.

"Um," Isabel answered.

"It's a cake!" Avery announced, waving one hand over the lopsided mess. "And *these* are cookies!" She held up a plastic container full of dry, crumbly pieces that only vaguely resembled chocolate-chip cookies.

Upon hearing the word "cookies," Marty started barking wildly, his nose high as he searched around for the treat. He found them and was about to attack Avery's container when Charlotte grabbed him by the collar.

"Dogs can't eat chocolate," Charlotte warned Marty. "It'll make you sick." She tugged Marty away from the temptation.

"Maybe we should give him the cake," Avery suggested as Maeve leaned down and took a whiff of the desserts.

"We sort of missed a few ingredients," Charlotte explained. "All 'cause this little dude couldn't keep his nose out of things!"

"Franco wasn't much help either," Isabel apologized.

Katani stopped taping streamers to come take a look. "The cookies are hopeless," she surmised after a quick taste. "But the cake can still be rescued . . . with a little TLC."

Maeve puckered up like she was going to give the cake a big kiss. "Mmmmm, *je t'aime!*"

"Not *that* kind of TLC, Miss Pink Paris Fashion!" Katani laughed.

"I wanted to dress special for Sophie," Maeve declared, striking a modeling pose, one hand on her hip, the other tucked behind her head.

"Chic!" Avery joked, resisting the impulse to snatch Maeve's beret and toss it to Isabel in a quick game of keep-away.

"I'll need a kitchen knife to save the cake," Katani told Charlotte. "And maybe some more frosting, if you have any."

"Could you also get me some glue?" Isabel requested. "I'm going to add glitter to the welcome sign!" She was spread out on the floor, with a pack of markers and the poster board Katani had brought, hard at work. Right now, she was illuminating a drawing of an eagle with gold shading.

"I'll go get it," Charlotte said. "Any other requests?"

"Charlotte!" Mr. Ramsey called up before she had even left the room.

"Yeah, Dad?" Charlotte shouted back, her voice echoing down the stairwell.

"It's time to go to the airport."

Charlotte's heart began to race. She looked at her watch for the first time all night. "Wow! I guess we really were late!" she exclaimed, her face flushed. "And I never got to finish my story about Orangina!"

"You'll finish the story later this week," Maeve assured her.

"That's right," Isabel insisted, getting up off the floor. "Don't worry about a thing."

"Have fun," Katani said, handing Charlotte a printed chart. "I meant to go over this with you first, but . . . I made a calendar for Sophie's visit. It is a day-by-day schedule, including the subway stops and exhibit hours for everything we talked about doing."

Charlotte looked down at the list. "Thanks, Katani!" She gave her a quick hug, "These are going to be the best two weeks ever!" With that, Charlotte rushed down to the driveway, where her father was already waiting in the car.

"I guess I'll go look for the glue and stuff," Avery said

after a few minutes of watching Katani tape streamers, Maeve blow up balloons, and Isabel block out letters on the sign.

"Mmmm," Katani answered. Isabel was so absorbed in her work, she didn't even seem to hear!

Avery dropped down the ladderlike stairs, two at a time, landing in the second-floor hallway of the old Victorian house. The first-floor apartment belonged to the landlady, Miss Pierce, and she barely ever came out. *Shy and mysterious,* Avery thought as she made her way into the Ramseys' kitchen. A search through the drawers and cupboards revealed not a single bottle of glue, and there didn't seem to be any frosting, either. *At least I found a knife for Katani to fix the cake. . . .* Avery thought, ready to head back up with the bad news.

Then she had an idea. *I'll ask Miss Pierce!*

The reclusive but kind landlady opened her door on the second knock. "Hello?"

"Do you have any glue or cake frosting?" Avery asked bluntly. "We're having a party!"

"Oh yes, I know! Charlotte told me all about it," Miss Pierce declared. "I'm so glad to hear you girls are doing so much to make Charlotte's friend feel right at home." She gestured for Avery to follow her into the kitchen. "Here is the glue, and I only have strawberry frosting. I hope that will be helpful to you."

"Thanks!" Avery turned to leave, but Miss Pierce spoke up again.

"Would you and the girls like it if I brewed up a pot of

my special tea?" Miss Piece winked. "It's my special-ty."

Avery laughed at the silly pun. Charlotte always raved about her landlady's special green tea with honey, so Avery knew exactly what to say. "Fabulosi-ty!"

Avery bounded back up to the Tower. "Delivery!" she announced as she walked in. Then her jaw dropped. "Wow!"

While she'd been downstairs, Katani, Maeve, and Isabel must have gone into overdrive, because the Tower was totally transformed! There were pink and orange streamers wrapped around each of the four windows and dipping across the slanted ceiling. There were multi-colored balloons tied onto streamers and taped together into arches.

"Wowzers!" Avery said again.

"You like it, *mon amay*?" Maeve danced around the room.

"It's *mon amie*," Katani corrected her as she did a quick repair job on the cake, cutting away the flat part and creating a smaller, rounded treat out of the raised half. Then she coated the whole thing with strawberry frosting and decorated the top with chocolate-chip cookie crumbs.

"That looks sooo much better," Isabel remarked. "Now, all we have to do is hang the sign!" Isabel used the glue to accent her artwork with pink glitter. Then the girls hung it up so "Welcome to America!" would be the first thing Sophie saw when she came into the Tower.

"We're ready!" Maeve sighed happily re-adjusting her pink beret. "I wonder how it's going for Charlotte at the airport."

Air France

"Terminal E, arrivals," Charlotte pointed up at a large sign.

Her dad nodded. "We're here."

Charlotte kept her eyes pinned on the glass doors separating customs from the airport lobby. *That's where Sophie and her parents will come out,* she said to herself. Every minute that passed she got more and more antsy. For the thousandth time, she found Sophie's flight number on the computer screen over their heads.

"It says *arrived,*" Charlotte pointed out.

"Yes, but she still has to get her luggage and go through customs," Mr. Ramsey reminded her.

Charlotte bounced on her toes, watching the groups of travelers coming through the glass doors, hauling and dragging huge bags as they arrived in America. All around her other people stood waiting, eyes searching for familiar faces.

"Grandma Sully!" A young woman next to Charlotte practically leaped over the divider to embrace an older woman wheeling a cart full of luggage.

"G'day, lovey!" The grandma engulfed her in a hug, and Charlotte was sent back to the year she and her father spent in Australia. Once, she got to go on a rescue mission with a naturalist to save an injured boomer that got attacked by a dingo! When she told the BSG about it, though, they just gave her weird looks until she explained that a boomer was a kangaroo and a dingo was a wild dog.

Charlotte let her eyes follow the Australian grandma and her granddaughter as they pushed the luggage cart out the terminal doors toward the taxi stand. As they went out, a whole group of women wearing native African clothing came in. Charlotte didn't know what part of Africa they came from, but when they stopped and chattered excitedly a few feet away, Charlotte could tell from their accents that it was probably near Tanzania. *I wonder who they're waiting for,* Charlotte thought. *Someone's son or daughter? A friend? Do they live in Boston, or are they just visiting?*

Then her mind started to wander. She wondered what it would be like if instead of airplanes, people could just travel through tunnels underground from one country to another. Maybe there could be elevator-like chutes that would deliver you instantly wherever you needed to be, without lines or customs or anything. *Remember this for Orangina's story!* she told herself, wishing she'd brought along a journal to jot down some notes.

"Charlotte!" A girl's high-pitched squeal interrupted Charlotte's musings.

"Sophie!" Charlotte cried out, a smile spreading out across her face. *"Bienvenue!"* The two friends rushed to each other, first saying hello Parisian style with a kiss on both cheeks. Then came the American-style hello—they jumped up and down, holding hands and screaming.

"You're here! You're here! You're really here!" Charlotte shrieked, and Sophie's only answer was musical laughter and a tight hug.

When Sophie finally let go, her mother squeezed

Charlotte tightly. *"Bonjour ma chérie!* How I've missed *ma petite* Charlotte!"* She kissed Charlotte on both cheeks.

Mr. Morel was more restrained than his wife, but he still gave Charlotte a small hug. After greeting Mr. Ramsey, he reminded them that he and his wife were only staying a few minutes to see Sophie off, then they had to change terminals for their flight to Florida.

"Adieu!" they called as they set off with their bags.

"Bon anniversaire," Mr. Ramsey greeted Sophie. "Happy birthday."

"I can't believe you and Papa kept this trip a surprise!" Sophie scolded Charlotte's dad. "But it is the best birthday gift ever!" She put down her matching suitcases and shrugged off her caramel-colored jacket.

"Wow!" Charlotte exclaimed, stepping back to take a look at her friend. "You look amazing!" Even though it was the end of April, Sophie was wearing a soft, flowery scarf with a thin black sweater. Caramel-colored leggings under a brown and black plaid skirt finished off the look. Very stylish. Even the shoes she wore were adorable—petite ballet-type flats. She looked like a model. Sophie had always dressed nicely, but there was something different about her this time. Something had changed, but what?

"You too look very nice." Sophie smiled, and Charlotte wished she had taken a few minutes to pick out something nicer than jeans to greet her friend. *Sophie looks so great after traveling seven hours on a plane,* she thought. *And I didn't even change clothes after baking.* She touched something crunchy on the bottom of her T-shirt. *What's that? Cookie batter?* She was embarrassed that she hadn't at least thrown on a clean shirt or combed her hair.

"You're just being nice," Charlotte grimaced. "I look awful. Wait till you hear about the great cookie disaster!"

As they talked Charlotte noticed that it wasn't just the stylish outfit that set Sophie apart. She'd gotten at least two inches taller since Charlotte had visited Paris. *And she's filled out!* Charlotte thought, feeling acutely aware that she *still* didn't really need a bra. *Wow, I can't believe this is the same Sophie who used to toss pebbles into the Seine with me while we made up silly stories about the fish living in the river.* Charlotte walked proudly beside Sophie toward her dad's car, answering all her questions about the people and places she was going to see in the next two weeks. *I'm going to be the one to introduce Sophie to America for the very first time!* Charlotte couldn't wait to get started.

Welcome to America

When Sophie's dark hair emerged at the top of the stairs leading up to the Tower, Katani, Maeve, and Isabel erupted into cheers of "Welcome!" and *"Bienvenue!"* Avery had even found a kazoo, on which she was trying (and failing) to play "The Star Spangled Banner." By the time the noise died down, Charlotte had made her way up behind Sophie. She watched as the BSG welcomed her friend with open arms and a rain of compliments.

"We are sooo happy you're here!" Isabel embraced Sophie first.

"We're going to show you all the coolest places in Boston!" Avery promised.

"Ooh, where can I get shoes *just* like yours?" Maeve asked.

Katani touched Sophie's scarf. "I just looove this. It's so Parisian!"

Sophie just kept nodding and saying thank you in her dainty accent. "You look *magnifique*," Sophie told Maeve, but Maeve wasn't so sure. She wished she had picked something more . . . *mature* . . . something more like what Sophie was wearing!

"*J'adore* the welcome sign! It must be the work of Isabel, the *artiste, non*?" Sophie admired the poster while Isabel beamed happily.

"You also made me a cake?" Sophie wandered across to the table of refreshments. "And . . . cookies? How wonderful!" She reached for a piece of cookie.

"Uhhh, I wouldn't recommend eating those unless you have a steel stomach," Avery warned.

"Steal a stomach?" Sophie asked, confused.

Charlotte was about to explain, but Isabel got there first. "It means, like, a strong stomach. We sort of forgot some of the ingredients."

"Ah!" Sophie leaned down and opened up the one small bag she had hauled up to the Tower. "Well, good thing I have brought you all some special treats from Paris," she pulled out a box that Charlotte recognized immediately.

"La Baguette!" Charlotte exclaimed. It was her favorite French bakery. Not better than Montoya's, of course, but a really close second. "You didn't get the meringue cookies, did you?" Charlotte asked as Sophie lifted the lid.

"But of course!" Sophie exclaimed.

Everyone had a cookie, then kicked back on the cushions scattered on the four window seats. Miss Pierce stepped in with a pot of tea during a rare moment of silence in the conversation.

"Welcome." She nodded to Sophie.

"*Merci.*" Sophie smiled and offered her a meringue. "Have tea with us, *s'il vous plaît.*"

"Gosh, no." Miss Pierce looked nervously back down the stairs. "I should be going."

With a few excuses about how busy she was, Miss Pierce told Charlotte to bring the teapot down later and just leave it; she'd clean up in the morning. "*Au revoir,*" Miss Pierce said, leaving as quietly as she'd come.

"Hey, Sophie," Maeve began out of nowhere. "Did Char tell you about my party?"

Sophie nodded, already sipping on a cup of tea.

"I already have my dress picked out, but maybe you could help me accessorize?" Maeve asked.

"*Bien sûr!* I'd love to," Sophie replied. "Perhaps I could help you with your hair and makeup also?"

"Fabulous!" Maeve jumped up and spun around the Tower, using her meringue like a microphone as she explained her party down to the finest details: the exact shade of red for the carpet, the number of doves to be released, and the thirteen different layers of the cake.

Katani glanced around at the other BSG, wondering if

any of them had questions about how all of this was even remotely possible. *Maybe they're just playing along for fun,* Katani supposed as Avery pretended to release doves out the Tower windows. *And they don't realize Maeve is serious—seriously in trouble of getting in way over her head!*

"Where are you having this *fête,* sorry, this party?" Sophie asked innocently.

"Oh, I haven't decided yet," Maeve replied. "There are so many places to choose from."

"Sophie," Avery interrupted, turning from the Tower window that looked out over downtown Boston. "We have a long list of things in town we'd like to show you."

"I made a chart." Katani proudly pulled it out of her pocket.

"I thought you gave it to me," Charlotte remarked. She'd looked at the list in the car and wondered if it was too ambitious for such a short visit.

Katani handed papers to all the girls. "I made copies for everyone!"

"I love to horseback ride," Sophie commented. "And the art museum sounds wonderful."

"That was my idea," Isabel said.

"Oooh, there is a Freedom Trail? And hiking and science museum and—" She studied the other ideas quietly, then threw the list dramatically into the air. "Oh, *mes amies!* I want to do it all!"

The girls all threw their lists up, and they rained down like paper doves. Charlotte savored the moment. Maybe, just maybe, Sophie's visit would be perfect!

All Grown Up

An hour later, Sophie and Charlotte shared the last of Miss Pierce's tea as they snuggled into their beds in Charlotte's room. "Your friends are *incroyable*." Sophie sighed, looking perfectly stylish even after she changed into pajamas and was sitting on the blow-up mattress Charlotte's dad had set up. "Simply amazing."

"They really liked you," Charlotte replied, setting her teacup on her bedside table.

"I was a little nervous that maybe they will not like me," Sophie admitted.

"Me too." Charlotte smiled. "I mean, I was worried you wouldn't like them! *Everyone* likes you."

Sophie shook her head. "Now," she said, settling back into her bed. "I want to hear all about your boyfriend. Tell me about Nick."

"He's not *really* my boyfriend," Charlotte confessed. "He's more like a boy who likes me."

"But the kiss!"

Charlotte blushed. Sophie had been the first person she'd told after Nick's kiss. Now she felt a little silly about it. Why wasn't he her boyfriend? *Is something wrong with me that I just don't feel ready yet?* Charlotte felt her cheeks burn.

"Are there any boys *you* like?" She turned the questioning back on Sophie.

"There is Adrien. . . ." Sophie sighed, a dreamy look in her eyes. "Remember Philippe's best friend? He got sooo cute! You wouldn't *believe*."

"Mmmm?" Charlotte mumbled, and listened as Sophie

rambled on and on about Philippe, Adrien, and all the other boys. Charlotte had never really noticed any of the boys when she had visited Sophie's school, and she found herself feeling a little bit curious. *I'm so glad Sophie's here!* Charlotte thought. *For the next two weeks, it'll be like an endless sleepover. We'll share all our secrets and crushes . . . just like we used to share our dreams and ideas.*

"Have you seen Orangina?" Charlotte asked during a pause in the conversation. They always used to laugh about the orange cat and pretend he was really a pirate or a wizard in disguise. Charlotte wanted to remind Sophie of their pretend games and tell her about the story she was writing—maybe Sophie would have some ideas.

But Sophie just yawned. "Oh," she said. "I don't worry about that cat anymore! We saw that he is fine on his new boat."

Charlotte sat up, feeling a little confused. *After all we went through looking for Orangina, Sophie doesn't think about him anymore? How could that be?*

"Sorry, but I am so tired!" Sophie stretched out on her mattress, and Charlotte noted the bleary look in Sophie's eyes. They could talk more later. *We have two whole weeks together, after all!* she thought.

"Let's get some sleep," Charlotte suggested. "It's going to be a busy day tomorrow with school and . . ." She couldn't recall what was on Katani's schedule, but it would probably be fun.

"Okay." Sophie agreed and after a quick good night, Charlotte turned out the lights.

Sophie was asleep in minutes, but Charlotte couldn't settle down. She stared at the ceiling for a long time. Charlotte was so thrilled to finally be reunited with her old friend that she could have talked all through the night! *Sophie's had a long trip,* Charlotte told herself. *We'll just catch up tomorrow.*

But after tossing and turning for fifteen minutes, another thought occurred to her. *I wonder if the story I'm writing for Sophie is too silly. If she doesn't think about Orangina anymore, why would she want to read a story about him?* Charlotte sighed, but she just couldn't stop wondering about that ridiculous cat and his adventures. *What if the tiny man needs Orangina's help? But Orangina doesn't want to listen?*

Charlotte couldn't help herself. She quietly snuck out of her bed and booted up her computer as ideas spun around in her brain.

Part 2
Big Bruce Barley

"My name isss Orangina, *mon ami!*" the cat said, lifting his paw to let the strange little man stand up.

"Great! I'll call you Orry." He brushed himself off with a blade of grass, then shook one of Orangina's claws. "I'm Big Bruce Barley."

"*Big* Bruce, did you say?" Orangina growled a little with amusement. "As in *gros*? *Grand*?"

"You got it." Big Bruce ducked as a bee buzzed past. The bug was bigger than his head! "So . . . want to hear my proposal, mate?"

But Orangina was gazing down the riverbank, searching for his boat.

"When they find that I am missing," he purred, "*monsieur* will be *triste*, so sad! He'll say, 'Orangina was the most handsome, skilled, and clever cat I ever knew!'"

"You're clever, Orry?"

"Cleverrrer than you." Suddenly Orangina caught a whiff of barge smoke and took off running down the bank, whiskers twitching.

He didn't see the large, dark hole in the ground until it swallowed him up—tail and all!

CHAPTER

6

Sensei Sensation

Sophie's coming later," Charlotte announced for the bazillionth time after school on Tuesday. A pair of seventh-grade girls Charlotte didn't even know nodded and walked away.

Charlotte had been shocked to discover that her big announcement at Henry Yurt's Bar Mitzvah had created such a buzz! Everyone expected to see Sophie at school, and Charlotte had to keep repeating the same excuse: "My dad stayed home from work today so Sophie could unpack and recover from jet lag."

The BSG giggled as Charlotte rolled her eyes. "What was that, Sophie question number one thousand and forty-two?" Katani asked.

Avery leaned up against the lockers. "QOM alert! Behind you!" she whispered.

"So," Joline started out, "where's this French friend of yours?"

"Number one thousand and forty-three!" Isabel blurted out, and Avery collapsed with laughter.

"You girls are sooo *wacko*." Anna tossed her hair. "I bet *Sophie* didn't come to Boston after all," she added.

"You're right," Avery told Anna. "She heard you were here, and she got right back on that airplane." Avery smirked, and Katani touched her shoulder. "Ave . . ." She always told the BSG it was best to just walk away from the QOM rather than trying to play their game. But this time it was a little too late.

"Whatever," Joline responded.

"Yeah, at least we don't need *imaginary* friends to make us popular," Anna taunted as she walked away.

When they reached the end of the hall, Joline turned back. "Hey, Maeve, let us know where your party is going to be. . . . That is, if it's not an *imaginary* party!" And, knowing they had stung last, the Queens headed victorious to the school exit.

Maeve's mature reply was to stick out her tongue at the girls' backs. She was getting good at this!

Avery gave Maeve a high-five. "The perfect response."

"Anyone up for a snack?" Katani asked. "I'm dying for a Montoya's iced hot chocolate. . . . And we could get croissants in honor of Sophie!"

"Can't." Charlotte reminded them that Sophie was stopping by school. "My *imaginary friend* needs to meet with Mrs. Fields. Dad's bringing her"—she checked her bangly watch—"in about ten minutes."

Katani smiled. "Say hey to Grandma Ruby for me."

"Sorry, I can't go either," Isabel told her friends. "I'm taking a graphic-art class over at the community center today." She grabbed her book bag and headed out.

"Hey, Isabel, wait up," Maeve called. "I'll walk with you. I have Hebrew tutoring again."

Avery was off to run drills with her softball team on the field behind the school, so Katani said to Charlotte, "Montoya's is on Sophie's calendar for later this week, anyway. I can hold off my craving till then." She slung her yellow shoulder bag, accented with little fabric flowers, over her shoulder. "See ya."

Quelle Surprise

The halls were quiet as Charlotte walked to the office. Outside the principal's door, Charlotte paused for a moment, listening closely.

"*. . . premier séjour a Boston?*" Someone was speaking French, asking about a "first stay in Boston," and it wasn't Sophie! Charlotte knocked lightly, and her dad opened the door.

"*Bonjour!*" greeted Mrs. Fields. "I was just speaking with Sophie about her visit."

"In French?" Charlotte asked.

The principal explained that she learned French in college, and even spent a semester at La Sorbonne, the most historic and famous university in Paris!

"*Quelle bonne surprise!*" Charlotte exclaimed. "What a great surprise!"

"*Bien sûr!* I am full of surprises," Mrs. Fields told

Charlotte. Then she explained to Sophie that she was welcome to shadow Charlotte through her whole schedule for the rest of the week.

As Sophie nodded along and asked questions about the different classes and school rules, Charlotte noticed once again how sophisticated her friend looked. She was wearing another very cute legging outfit, this time with a plain white scarf around her neck. Charlotte looked down at her own capris and purple-striped polo shirt. When she'd put it on in the morning, she'd thought she looked cute, but now, next to Sophie, she wasn't so sure.

"Is there anything else I can help you with?" Mrs. Fields asked in English.

"I am just glad to be with my friend!" Sophie exclaimed, putting her arm around Charlotte.

Is that perfume? Charlotte leaned in closer to Sophie's neck. Yes. It was. *Dad says I'm not old enough for perfume,* Charlotte thought. *Sophie's so lucky.*

Sophie gave Charlotte a friendly little squeeze before taking back her arm and putting her hands on her hips.

"Ready to go?" Charlotte asked.

"Wait, *j'ai une idée.*" Sophie explained her idea. "I was thinking. Maybe my classmates in *Paris* can talk to the students here in America over the Internet."

"*Merveilleux.*" Mrs. Fields was clearly excited about the possibility. "How does it work?"

"I might be able to help with the technology," Mr. Ramsey offered. "I used Skype all the time when Charlotte and I lived abroad."

"Terrific. Let's get it done now, while you're here," Mrs. Fields suggested, then turned to Charlotte. "While your dad and I get this set up with Ms. O'Reilly, why don't you give Sophie a tour of the school?"

"I am so glad to be here," Sophie said as Charlotte walked her past the classrooms and the cafeteria. "It's not so different from when we went to school together in Paris, *non*?"

"*Non*," Charlotte agreed. "School is school wherever you go." For a moment it seemed as if they were together again in their old school in Paris, friends for life. Charlotte linked arms with Sophie and smiled.

On their way to see the ball fields, and hopefully, to catch up for a sec with Avery, Charlotte and Sophie passed the gym. They could hear kids' voices inside shouting, "*Kiyap! Kiyap!*"

"What are they doing?" Sophie wondered, pausing by the door. "*Une minute*," she begged, peeking into the room.

"It's only Dillon," Charlotte explained, after a quick look over her friend's shoulder.

"Who is Dillon?" Sophie took Charlotte's arm and led her into the gym. "We can go to the field after—ooohhh!" Sophie got all excited when she saw Dillon in his karate uniform. "I love kung fu!"

Dillon turned from his class of elementary school kids to face the newcomers. "It's not kung fu," he corrected. "It's karate. Kung fu is Chinese martial arts. Karate is Japanese."

Sophie shook her head. "All I know is *j'adore* Jackie Chan movies!"

"That's kung fu." Dillon smiled brightly. "Chan is from China." He didn't miss a beat before adding, "I like his movies too." His class patiently looked on. The kids had been in the middle of learning a new kick, so they were all standing with one leg out.

"Did you see *New Fist of Fury*?" Sophie asked.

"That movie was a flop!" Dillon told her. "His new stuff is so much better." Dillon didn't seem to notice that some of the little ones were starting to fall over onto the mat.

"Ah, but to build on the past," Sophie reflected. Charlotte wasn't sure what that was supposed to mean, but Sophie's French accent made each word sound very important. And man, oh man, was Dillon impressed. In fact, Charlotte had never seen him like this before. Usually he was Mr. Popular, flirting with every girl in sight, but Sophie seemed to have him frozen in place, and his face was cherry red. *I think Dillon's so smitten, he's completely forgotten about his class!*

She was right. A small boy in the front row was the only one left with his leg out. "Master Dillon," the kid whimpered, "my leg's getting tired."

"Oops," Dillon said, quickly ending the conversation with Sophie. "You can rest now, Benny."

"An absentminded sensei," Sophie teased. If it was possible for Dillon to get any redder, he did. Charlotte was amazed at how quickly Dillon started crushing on Sophie. The transformation took less than . . . *une minute*!

"Let's go," Charlotte suggested. "Dillon needs to teach."

The girls turned back into the hallway where there were suddenly quite a few students spilling out of classrooms. After-school clubs were coming to an end.

"Bonjour," Sophie said repeatedly as she took time to greet some of Charlotte's classmates and friends. Betsy Fitzgerald had a dozen questions about the French Revolution, and Sophie answered all of them! Betsy walked off grinning widely.

Sophie's so smooth. Charlotte remembered her own first week at AAJH. Even though she'd lived in Boston when she was little, all the years of traveling had made the city a foreign place, and, of course, the faces at school were all brand-new. On her very first day she was such a klutz that she managed to zip a tablecloth into her pants at lunch!

That would never happen to Sophie, Charlotte realized. *She's never even been to America, but she's so confident, like she owns the country. . . . Or at least the school. Everyone loves her.*

Charlotte especially noticed the way the boys looked at Sophie. It wasn't just Dillon who'd gone all gaga. The Trentinis and even Henry Yurt stared a little longer than normal.

Then she saw Nick coming down the hall, freshly showered from a pickup game of hoops on the outside court. *Oh, good!* Charlotte felt relieved. Nick was one boy who wouldn't fall for Sophie. Charlotte was sure of it!

"Hey!" Nick trotted over and gave Charlotte's hand a squeeze. "This must be the famous Sophie Morel!"

"Bonjour!" Sophie greeted, and gave Nick a warm smile.

He smiled right back. "So, what do you think of America?"

Sophie told him all her impressions—how nice everyone was, but how some people talked way too fast for her to understand. After a few minutes Sophie turned to Charlotte and said in French, *"Il est très mignon! Tu as le bon goût."*

"What? What did she say?" Nick begged.

"Allons-y! We have to go," Charlotte protested, pulling on Sophie's arm. She couldn't believe Sophie had said that out loud! Of course, Nick couldn't understand, but still . . . No way was Charlotte translating for her crush: *He's really cute! You have good taste!*

"T'es folle?!" Charlotte griped—"Are you crazy?!"—as Sophie started laughing.

"What did *you* say?" Nick turned to Charlotte, looking totally befuddled.

Charlotte's escape plan was disrupted by a crash as the door of the gym opened and little Benny from karate careened out into the hall, running at full speed.

Even though Charlotte tried to step aside and avoid getting pancaked by the kid, she didn't have even a smidgen of Avery's agility or quick reflexes. Quite the opposite, in fact. If there was going to be an accident, it was one hundred percent certain Charlotte would somehow be involved.

As fate would have it, Charlotte missed being plowed down by the oncoming freight train named Benny, but lost her balance as she stepped out of the way and crashed right into Sophie! The two of them tumbled to the floor. Benny, unaware of his role in the mishap, giggled and pointed at the jumble of girls.

Charlotte had fallen clumsily a thousand times before, but she never got used to that miserable feeling of humiliation that can only come from lying on the floor, staring up at wide-eyed faces. *Why today? Why now, in front of Sophie? And Nick!?*

"Oof," Sophie said from beneath Charlotte. Somehow Charlotte had managed to get herself tangled in Sophie's beautiful scarf. It made getting up a bit of a challenge.

Billy and Josh Trentini came running around the corner from their lockers, looking for the source of the commotion at the same time as Dillon burst out of the gym.

Billy got there first. "I'll help you," he told Sophie, pulling on one of her arms, trying to get her back on her feet.

"No, I will," Josh said, shoving his brother away and grabbing Sophie's other arm.

"I was here first," Billy whined.

Dillon interrupted their squabble with two quick karate wrist locks, and the twins backed away, cradling their hands. "What'd you do *that* for?" Josh groaned.

"Let *me* help you," Dillon offered, extending one hand.

"You may *all* help me up," Sophie said, raising her hands toward the boys. "*Merci.*" She gracefully got back on her feet.

Charlotte didn't know whether to laugh or cry. She was super embarrassed and at the same time, it was a riot to see the boys acting so insanely! She couldn't wait to tell the BSG. If she'd been Sophie, she'd have told them all to go away. . . . But Sophie handled it so much more maturely. There was a small crowd around her now. Charlotte didn't want to look to see who was over there. She could only imagine all the boys vying for Sophie's attention, making sure she was okay.

Charlotte was just about to get herself up, with no help from anyone, when she felt a warm hand take hers and a small breath near her ear.

"Here, let me help you." It was Nick. *I can always count on Nick to be there for me*, Charlotte realized happily.

"Sorry, Sophie." Charlotte squeezed her way into the crowd around her friend. "That was totally my fault just then."

"It is all right." Sophie smiled. "We are all used to your, how do you say . . . futz attacks?"

The Trentini twins laughed so hard, they nearly fell in a pile on the floor themselves. "Futz attacks!" they chortled, fake punching each other.

"Um, the word is *klutz*," Nick corrected with a side-ways glance at Charlotte.

Charlotte faked a laugh even though she suddenly felt mortified. *Sophie is so perfect. . . . Why can't I be more like her?* Charlotte sighed. *I wish just once I could get through a single day without falling down and being a klutz . . . or a futz, whatever that is!*

BFF = Best French Friend

Sophie and Charlotte didn't talk much on the way home. Or rather, Sophie talked, and Charlotte said things like "mmm" and "yeah." Sophie seemed totally enamored with Boston, American culture, and boys. Also, she wouldn't stop practicing the word "klutz," and Charlotte wished she would never hear that word again! It was almost a relief to sign on to the computer later that evening and find the other BSG already chatting away.

```
Chat Room: BSG                                    _ □ X
File  Edit  People  View  Help

                                        5 people here
flikchic: found perfect                 flikchic
place for bat m prty                    lafrida
lafrida: where?                         4kicks
flikchik: liberty hotel—                skywriter
nice but $$$                            Kgirl
4kicks: coolio!
Kgirl: did u talk 2 parents?
flikchic: not yet. 2mro.
skywriter: hello all!
4kicks: yo wat up! hehe
Kgirl: will sophie b @
school 2mro?
skywriter: yes and shes
here now 2
Kgirl: Hi BFFF (=Best
French Friend Forever!)
```

Charlotte moved over so Sophie could sit at the computer and type.

Charlotte sat in her room staring at the chat screen while Sophie went to help Mr. Ramsey make a special French meal. Neither of them would tell her what they were making, but the two were up to something. They'd practically banished her from the kitchen.

When Charlotte finished her homework, Sophie still hadn't come back, so Charlotte stuck her head out the door and asked, "Now?"

"We are not ready yet!" yelled Sophie. Something smelled wonderful. Like cheese and greens. Maybe it was some sort of fancy pasta?

"Do you need help?" she called.

"No, thanks," her dad replied. "We'll let you know when it's ready!"

Charlotte closed the chat screen and opened "Orangina's Travels." She'd written almost four hundred words, which was about how long her articles for the school newspaper usually ran. But the story wasn't even close to finished.

As Charlotte stared at the blinking cursor, two moments came together in her mind. She remembered how Sophie had said "Oof" when they fell in the hallway, and also her funny idea from the airport about tunnels connecting all the different countries in the world.

"That's it!" Charlotte said out loud, waking up Marty, who'd been sleeping under the desk. Charlotte massaged the dog's tummy with her foot as she typed.

Part 3

Tunnels in the Dark

"Oof," Orangina complained, twitching his sore tail. Cats are supposed to land on their feet, but it never seemed to work out that way. If there's one thing he hated more than being wet, it was being down at the bottom of a dark hole.

"No worries, mate! We'll be out in a jiffy!" sang a happy voice.

So Big Bruce had somehow fallen in the hole too. *Merveilleux!* Orangina knew his barge was up there, moving farther and farther away. Perhaps "Big" Bruce could help him out.

"This is my hole, mate. Leads all over the world. See?"

Suddenly the air flared into light, and Orangina could see his newest "mate" holding up a tiny lantern with a firefly trapped inside.

Around the two of them, tunnels branched off in every direction. A sign pointing up said "Paris." One across the way read "Hong Kong" another "New York" and a third, "Arctic Circle." There were too many signs to pay attention to all of them.

"Care to see the pyramids? A cave full of crystals? What about Mount Fuji?"

"No thank you, *petit monsieur*, I must return to *Parrr-ee!*" Orangina meant "Paris," but he pronounced it like the French cat he was, poking around frantically with his nose for a way back up.

"Wait!" Big Bruce swung his firefly lantern right in the cat's face. "I came to *Par-ee* looking for someone cleverer than I. Will you help me?"

Orangina didn't answer. He was thinking of his comfy home in the captain's cabin of his barge, his *bateau*. . . .

"Ahhh, I think you will." Big Bruce reached into a pocket and pulled out a book that somehow grew three times its size when the tiny man opened it.

Orangina peered at the bookmarked page, and froze, hair standing on end.

7

Global Skyping

Ohhh!" When Katani saw what Sophie was wearing to school, she could barely hold back her excitement. "Your outfit!" Turning quickly to Charlotte, Katani whispered, "How do you say 'magnificent' in French?"

"*Magnifique,*" Charlotte told her softly.

"*Magnifique,*" Katani repeated.

Sophie was decked out in a short khaki skirt over stockings, a warm yellow peasant blouse, and another scarf— this one tan with pale pink roses.

"We say *yafe m'ode* in Hebrew," Maeve said. "I learned that from my tutor. Very pretty!" Secretly, Maeve wished that Sophie's outfit had a bit more color and slightly less beige. Maeve peeked down at her own khaki skirt, which she'd paired with a yellow and pink V-neck and pink sparkling slip-on shoes. *These shoes would look great with her scarf,* Maeve thought.

Isabel told Sophie she looked "*muy bonita.*"

Avery used her own second language: sports talk.

"Score one for Sophie!" she cheered, punching the air.

Isabel and Avery had chosen not to follow the fashion plan for the day—Isabel preferred her own unique look, and Avery didn't own any skirts!

Charlotte had put on a khaki skirt, but couldn't find anything yellow that was clean. *Sophie does look nice,* Charlotte thought. *But the whole scarf-matching thing seems a little over the top for school.* Charlotte touched the collar of her plain white scoop-neck tee, feeling drab and dull next to sophisticated Sophie, fashion-savvy Katani, and colorful Maeve.

"Oooh, and your purse matches, too!" Katani squealed when Sophie took out a rose-embroidered pocketbook to look for her lip gloss.

Katani didn't squeal very often, Charlotte noted as several other girls in the hallway gathered around, exclaiming over Sophie's scarf, purse, and French cosmetics. When the bell rang, the sea of worshipful girls carried Sophie away into social studies.

Maeve was about to follow when Chelsea trotted up behind her. "May 9! I'm saving the date. When are we going to get your Bat Mitzvah invites?"

"Any day now," Maeve replied with a sweet smile. "Just keep checking your mailbox."

Josh Trentini overheard and asked, "Is your party going to be as radical as Yurt's?"

"I got three hats and a T-shirt!" his twin Billy bragged. "Plus I won tickets to a Red Sox game in the trivia room."

"Just as rad," Maeve echoed. "Maybe even radder!"

Henry Yurt popped his head out of a nearby classroom. "Radder than mine?" he asked. "The only thing you can do that might be radder would be to ride around the room on a solar-powered rocket ship! Oh, wait"—he paused for effect—"I did that, didn't I?"

Henry was just joking around, but as the kids all rushed off to their next classes, Maeve just stood still for a moment, shaking her head with the realization: *I seriously need a plan. A grand, stupendous, marvelous plan. And fast!*

Love Struck

"Hey." Dillon walked up to the BSG at their usual seats near the window in Ms. O'Reilly's class. Sophie was sitting next to Charlotte, making last-minute notes for a short presentation about France before the phone call with her Parisian classmates.

"Hey," Avery raised her fist for a knuckle butt, her usual greeting with pal Dillon. *Whoa!* Avery was shocked when Dillon not only didn't knuckle her back, but didn't even seem to notice she was standing there. Avery had never seen *that* expression on her buddy's face before.

"How was kung fu yesterday?" Sophie asked primly, looking up from her notes.

"Uhhh," Dillon began. Avery waved a hand in front of his face, but he didn't even blink. "Karate, you mean?" He was stumbling over his words. *He looks like he needs a round-house kick to knock him back into reality,* Avery thought.

Sophie tipped her head slightly when she added, "But of course. I was only making a joke."

"Oh." Dillon, master of the snappy comeback, didn't have a ready reply.

Isabel gave Avery a wink behind Dillon's back. She'd seen this so many times with Elena Maria and boys, but Avery was pretty dense when it came to romance. "Crush alert," Isabel mouthed. Avery whispered back, "No, he's lost his mind."

Isabel made a little heart with her fingers and flashed it at Avery. "True love," she murmured.

Sophie continued asking Dillon about his karate class; simple questions ranging from "How long have you been teaching?" to "Which master do you follow?" To Avery and Isabel's amusement, Dillon seemed to have been reduced to Neanderthal grunts for replies instead of actual words.

"Okay, class! Take your seats!" Ms. O'Reilly stood up from her desk and clapped her hands. That seemed to snap Dillon back to Earth. He retreated to his crew in the back of the room, but not before Sophie blew him a kiss! Dillon turned redder than a tomato, and his buddies gave high-fives all around.

"Enough, boys," Ms. O'Reilly scolded, then began the morning class by welcoming Sophie in French. It was clear that the young teacher didn't actually speak French, but had someone teach her the word *"Bienvenue,"* because her accent was atrocious.

Charlotte gave Sophie a wide-eyed look, and Sophie winked back at her—wordlessly, they agreed not to correct her. It would be their secret.

"Merci," Sophie replied graciously. She got up from her seat and went to the front of the room to address the class.

"I am so honored to be a guest in your school. This is the first time I have been to America. You know, I met Charlotte when she lived in Paris and we have been, as you say, BFFs—Best French Friends—ever since." She paused, and the laughter came. Charlotte felt proud that her best friend was up there, speaking to the whole classroom. Everyone in class knew this was *Charlotte's* friend, and more people had said hello to Charlotte today than ever had before. It was actually a little overwhelming!

Sophie continued, "Charlotte has introduced me to all her friends. Now I want to introduce you to mine."

Sophie was about to press the button on the computer to turn on the Skype connection to her own school, where an afternoon English class was beginning, when Ms. O'Reilly stopped her. "Sophie," she said. "Can you prepare us a little for the conversation by telling us a few differences between French and American schools?"

"But of course," Sophie replied. "In my school the dress is more formal." She waved a hand around the room. "It is nice here that the students can express their own *mode*."

"Style," Charlotte translated, even though Sophie didn't need her to.

"My favorite *mode* is *à la mode*!" Henry Yurt joked. Then he asked, "So, what about our country has been the most surprising?" The Yurtmeister couldn't resist adding, "I bet you'll say it's our fine American cooking. Just wait until you eat the mystery meat at lunch today!"

Sophie smiled. "I cannot *wait* to go to the cafeteria. Charlotte told me to eat nothing I cannot recognize."

"That won't leave many options," the Yurtmeister warned. "You might starve!" Giggles broke out through the room.

"I doubt that, but to answer your question"—Sophie smoothly came back to the topic at hand—"I am surprised at how casually the boys here dress. At my school, the *garçons*—the boys—wear straight jeans, nice shirts, pointed shoes, and sometimes scarves."

"Sounds suave," Maeve whispered, leaning over to Katani.

"Sounds lame!" Billy Trentini called out from the back. "Shorts and T-shirts. That's the American way." And to prove his point, Billy flashed both hands at Dillon like the MC of a fashion show presenting the top model.

The entire class burst into laughter. Except Dillon.

Katani expected that, after Billy's comment, Dillon would stand up next to his chair and flaunt his very "stylish" American "*mode*." But instead, he just sat there, staring at Sophie like a lost puppy.

What's up with D?

Katani quickly jotted on the corner of a paper. She tore the page out of her notebook and when Ms. O'Reilly wasn't looking, passed it over to Avery.

Avery read the note and wrote back. Then she folded it and had to wait another second for Ms. O'Reilly to look away again before thrusting the paper back to Katani.

Katani peeked at Avery's reply:

I'm monitoring the situation. No worries.

Rock Stars and Pointy Shoes

When the laughter in the room died down, Sophie hit a button on the computer. A camera and microphone were already set up so that the kids could see and hear one another. On two continents, students gathered around their classroom computers and waved to one another. Skype was working!

"Bonjour, mes amis!" Sophie greeted her friends at home. *"Bonjour, madame,"* Sophie said to her teacher.

"Hello," the French students replied, practicing their English. Suddenly everyone in France and Boston was talking at once.

"One at a time," Ms. O'Reilly commanded.

"Un par un," the teacher in France told her own class.

Riley raised his hand. "I have a question." Ms. O'Reilly had to shush the class so Riley could ask, "What kind of music do you like?"

A French boy name Pierre answered. He named five of the hottest American rock stars, including John Thomas!

"No way! JT sang at my party last weekend!" Henry Yurt burst out.

Anna raised her hand. "Don't you have any bands of your own?" she asked.

"Oui," said Pierre. "There are many French singers and bands. But we like yours better!"

The kids in Ms. O'Reilly's class laughed out loud.

Sophie shook her head. "That Pierre, always with the jokes. There are nice bands in France, too." She paused for a thoughtful moment. "Pierre plays drums for a school band named *Clair de la Lune*."

"Moonlight," Charlotte translated.

Riley would have loved to talk about music with Pierre and compare band stories, but it was the French class's turn to ask a question.

Julia, a tall girl with braided hair, asked, "Sophie! Did you see movie stars?"

Sophie smiled when she replied, "Most of the movie stars are in California. I'm three thousand miles from Hollywood." She pulled Maeve over into the camera's view. "But this is Maeve. She will be a BIG movie star someday!"

Maeve beamed.

A boy in glasses named Marc asked, "What do American people like to eat?"

At that, the Trentini twins couldn't help but lean toward the camera and shout out together, "French fries!"

"I read that the students in America, they only eat hamburgers and pizzas," Marc explained after he stopped laughing.

"Yep, all true," Nick confirmed, patting his belly. "And I heard French kids eat frog legs and snails at every meal."

Marc shrugged and joked, "Ahhh. That too, it is true."

Marc and Nick gave each other a cyber high-five. Nick asked Sophie to give him Marc's e-mail address later. They liked each other immediately and wanted to talk more.

"Is it my turn?" Betsy Fitzgerald wanted to know.

"Sure, Betsy." Ms. O'Reilly told Nick to move away from the camera so that Betsy could have a chance.

"In 1793, at the height of the French Revolution, Marie Antoinette was executed for treason," Betsy began. "Modern scholars disagree on how influential she was during the Revolution. Do you believe she was honestly to blame, or was she sacrificed as a martyr?"

The French classroom was so silent, you could hear a pencil drop. Betsy had a way of taking things way too seriously sometimes.

Sophie's teacher broke the silence by recommending a book on the subject for Betsy.

The rest of the class passed by quickly as the students on both sides of the Atlantic exchanged stories, opinions, and jokes.

"Awww, man," Henry remarked when the bell rang. "I wanted to ask the boys to show off their pointed shoes and scarves. I never got a chance to ask for a fashion show. . . ."

"Maybe we can do this again another time," Ms. O'Reilly told him. "We could start a cyber pen-pal program!"

As the American students poured out into the hallway, off to their next class, Sophie took a second to say *"Au revoir"* to her French friends.

"Au revoir, Sophie," chimed the French students. The girls were waving. The boys—blowing kisses.

Avery and the rest of the BSG hung back, waiting for

Sophie to finish the call. Dillon stayed behind too, and he blushed a slight red when all the French boys blew kisses. *Is he jealous?* Avery wondered. She had told Katani that she was "monitoring the situation," but now she wondered if she needed to keep a closer eye on her long-time friend.

If Dillon was falling too hard, too fast—she might need to knock some sense into him. Avery couldn't help smiling as she imagined herself taking Dillon out to the soccer field and getting him to head a few balls into the goal. That would shake his brain for sure! Snap him right back to reality.

The Queens Dethroned

In the hallway the QOM waited in ambush. "Can we talk to you?" Anna asked Sophie.

"Go ahead." Sophie gestured with one hand. "What have you to say?"

"In private." Joline smirked with a head nod toward a nearby empty classroom.

"You can say anything in front of my friends," Sophie indicated toward the BSG. "We have no secrets."

Anna looked seriously at Joline, then said, "Fine. We think you should come hang out with us tonight. Kiki's father got four tickets to see *Rock-a-Do*." Anna glanced at the BSG. "They're VIP passes."

Rock-a-Do was a new 3-D movie about the glamorous life of celebrity hairstylists. It hadn't made it onto Katani's careful schedule, but Maeve especially had been dying to go see it.

"I think we should all go," Sophie replied, indicating herself and the BSG.

Charlotte nearly choked. She'd told Sophie all about the QOM—they even knew some girls just like the QOM in Paris, and called them *Chuchoteurs,* or "Whisperers." Kiki was even worse. In fact, the girls called her the "Empress of Mean."

"I don't think we should all go." Joline sneered. "I mean, it's about *hairstyles.* Have you seen Avery's hair?" She paused while everyone turned to Avery, who, as always, had her hair pulled back tightly in a ponytail. "I didn't think so. That tail hasn't been set loose since third grade."

"We want to invite *you,*" Anna said firmly, placing an arm on Sophie's shoulders. "Only you."

From the blank look on her friend's face, Charlotte wasn't sure what Sophie was going to say. Sophie kept staring at the QOM, and there was a split second when Charlotte thought that Sophie would say, "Yeah, sure, I'll go. Pick me up at seven."

It came almost as a surprise to Charlotte when Sophie said, "You are very unkind." She put her hands on her hips. "Why you say these most terrible things?" Head held high, Sophie led the BSG down the hall toward the math classroom. "*Au revoir.*"

Charlotte gave a quick glance back to see that Anna and Joline were stunned at how their invitation backfired. They stood, jaws dropped, staring after Sophie and the BSG.

Later, Charlotte heard it from Chelsea, who heard it from Betsy, that the last thing anyone heard from the QOM that morning was Joline turning to Anna and asking, "What can I do to make my hair *chic*, like Sophie's?"

CHAPTER
8
Spinning Out of Control

Hey, Avery," Dillon mumbled, head hanging low and feet shuffling as they walked off the soccer field after a quick pick-up game. "I have a favor to ask."

"Yeah?" Avery switched her soccer bag to the other shoulder.

"It's kinda embarrassing."

"More embarrassing than my team beating yours ten to five just now? Really, Dillon," Avery continued with her teasing, "what could be worse than being crushed by a GIRL?" She laughed, recalling how she'd headed the ball into goal, and Dillon hadn't even seen it coming! "It'll be weeks before you can raise your head high at school."

Dillon sighed. He shook his head and looked up at Avery seriously. "Yup, it's *more* embarrassing. Believe it or not."

"No way!" Avery was still smiling, but she was beginning to get the idea that Dillon wasn't joking around.

"I need a big favor." Dillon paused at the intersection

at one end of the school parking lot, where Avery usually turned off to walk home.

"Okay." Avery decided to use this moment to her advantage. "I'll do you a favor, but you have to do me one first. I'm headed to Charlotte's, since it's my turn to walk Marty. So, you carry my equipment." She thrust her soccer bag at him.

It was so weird! Dillon didn't fight the demand. He just took Avery's bag and slung it over his shoulder with his own bag. "Let's go, then," he responded.

"What's up with you?" Avery asked him as Dillon sulked along silently beside her. "You are definitely not acting yourself!"

"Hey, keep it down. No one can know!" he replied.

"Know what?! What?!?" Avery practically yelled at him, although she had a pretty good guess what this was all about.

Dillon looked around and over his shoulder. "*Shhh,*" he warned. "Okay, here's the thing." He took a deep breath. "I want you to find out if Sophie has a boyfriend in France. Maybe that Pierre dude? Or someone else?"

"Have you gone nuts?!" Avery was yelling at him now. "Do you *remember* what happened when Maeve liked you? I played matchmaker, and it was a huge mess!"

"Maeve and I are still friends," Dillon said calmly.

"Yeah, but the whole thing was a disaster! I swore I'd never do anything like that again."

"But, Avery," Dillon pleaded, "this is really important."

Avery searched his face carefully, considering his

words and earnest expression. "Okay," she begrudgingly agreed. "Gimme my stuff. We're almost there." Avery glanced up at Charlotte's house, looming in front of them. "I'll see what I can find out."

"Say nice things about me, too, okay?" Dillon put in.

"Who do you think I am, Cupid?" Avery retorted, jabbing Dillon playfully in the stomach. "Don't push your luck."

As they took the last few steps toward the house, Avery was excited to see Charlotte, Sophie, and Mr. Ramsey outside, loading a few bags into Mr. Ramsey's car.

"Dillon!" Avery pointed. "There's Sophie now. Go talk to her. Start a conversation." She turned her head toward him, adding, "It's your big chance!" But Dillon had suddenly disappeared. She was talking to herself.

"Avery!" Charlotte called out as she carried a small basket to the car and put it in the trunk. "We're going into the city. Want to come?"

"They're going where?" the tree behind Avery whispered.

"Just a sec, Char!" Avery shouted up the driveway, then darted behind the tree. Dillon was hiding up in the branches! "*Chillax*, Dillon." Avery tried to persuade him. "You don't have to hide!" She gestured impatiently for him to come out, but he just shook his head vehemently.

"I just dropped something . . . ," Avery yelled back to Charlotte with a sideways glance at Dillon that said, *I have no idea why I'm covering for you.*

"We're going to the Common!" Sophie called out. "Isn't it exciting?"

"Boston Common?" Dillon whispered.

"Ummm, be there in a sec!" Avery shouted, then whispered to her friend in the tree, "You're hopeless."

"I know," was the tree's response. "Just find out if she's got a boyfriend, okay?"

"Ooookay!" Avery replied with a snort. She took a few steps toward Charlotte when she realized she had one more thing to say to Dillon. She turned back to the tree. "You know that you are acting like a complete doofus," Avery said.

There was no reply. Avery hurried back to the tree to see what was what. *Bummer*, Avery thought. *My best line completely wasted—the doofus ran away!*

Head in the Clouds

Maeve was sitting at the kitchen table with her math tutor, Matt, when the phone rang. Her mom answered.

"Sorry, Charlotte, but unfortunately Maeve can't go with you to Boston Common today," Ms. Kaplan said. "She's working with her tutor on math."

"But Mommm," Maeve started, mega-bummed that she couldn't hang out with Sophie and Charlotte.

Maeve's mom put her hand over the receiver. "You have too much studying to do. Plus Hebrew to memorize."

Maeve sighed as her mom told Charlotte to have a nice time, and hung up. Images drifted through Maeve's mind of strutting next to Sophie in the park, wearing her favorite pink skinny jeans and white scoop-neck sweater. *Every cute boy we pass stops us to say hello. . . .*

"Earth to Maeve." Matt tapped the math book with his

pencil. "Answer to number twelve? What are you going to multiply this by?"

It was hard. Maeve's dyslexia slowed everything down, and she had to work more diligently than other kids to get the same grades. The numbers sometimes floated around the page or appeared backward to her. Today it seemed even harder to concentrate than usual. It wasn't just the dyslexia that was muddling her brain. Maeve couldn't keep her mind off that pink dress at Think Pink. The gown kept popping up in her thoughts, along with dancing tunes and Hollywood-themed party favors.

"Your head is in the clouds today," Matt told Maeve half an hour later as he packed his things to go. Maeve apologized, but Matt replied, "That's okay. Some days are just like that. Even Albert Einstein was a big daydreamer."

Maeve smiled warmly. She liked her tutor. "Glad we got all my homework done! I feel totally prepped for this week's test." She handed Matt his calculator, and he tucked it in the outside pocket of his messenger bag.

"You'll do great. Just remember to take things one step at a time and check your work."

To her surprise, just as Matt was about to open the door to leave, her father walked in with Sam.

"How's my little math scholar?" Maeve's father asked, kissing her on the forehead before shaking hands with Matt.

Maeve blushed. "I'm no scholar," she told her dad.

"Don't say that, Maeve," Matt chided. "She's doing great," he told Mr. Taylor before heading out.

"My teacher said I'm a genius," Sam announced when Ms. Kaplan came into the front hall.

"I'm sure she did." Maeve rolled her eyes.

"That's nice," their mom said to Sam, leaning down and giving him a hug. "But we already knew that." She winked. "What else did your teacher say?"

Sam thought for a second, then said, "Nothing. That was all."

Ms. Kaplan looked up inquisitively at Maeve's father.

He laughed and shrugged. "Yep, that about covers it."

"Short parent-teacher conference, eh?" Maeve's mom said with a warm grin.

It's nice to see them getting along, Maeve thought. Even though she knew that her parents were separated, she still had her hopes. Sometimes they went a whole evening without fighting. Maeve promised herself to do what she could to make this one of those nights.

"How's the Hebrew going, my almost-adult Jewish daughter?" Her dad ruffled her hair.

"I know my part!" Sam bragged. "I know it all. Want to hear? Want to hear?"

Sam had a small Hebrew sentence that he was going to say during the service. Most siblings only read something in English, but Sam insisted he could handle the Hebrew, and, true to character, Sam had it nailed. Maeve, on the other hand, was still struggling to get the foreign words memorized.

"I'll hear your part later," Mr. Taylor said to Sam. "But I'm glad you know it already."

Sam smiled and dashed off to play with his armies.

"Maeve," her mom suggested, "why don't you grab your Hebrew notebook and read through your parts for your dad right now? It would be good practice."

"But . . . ," Maeve started to protest, then remembered her goal to help her parents get along.

"Oh, all right," Maeve responded, hurrying off to get the notebook. She grabbed the white binder and came back to meet her dad at the dining room table. She sat down next to him, so he could look over her shoulder. Even though her dad wasn't Jewish and didn't know Hebrew, he liked to look at the words while she recited them.

Maeve opened to the first page and read slowly, *"Baruch ata . . ."* They sat together for a few minutes, and Maeve felt the foreign words flowing off her tongue more easily than they ever had before. Her many hours of practice were finally paying off.

Ring, ring! The phone rang, interrupting the quiet peace of the moment.

"Go on, Maeve," her mom told her. "I'll get it." But the call was distracting and Maeve couldn't focus. She could hear everything her mom was saying, and her ears perked up when she heard a few choice phrases.

"No, that can't be right" and "We didn't inquire about rates for a DJ." Then "The Liberty Hotel? I don't think so. I'm sorry for the confusion. Good-bye!"

Maeve gripped the edge of the table as the Hebrew vanished from her memory. By the time her mom hung up, Maeve knew she was in *ginormous* trouble. Her world was suddenly spinning out of control.

"Did you bring Happy Lucky Thingy?" Avery asked from the backseat of the Ramseys' car. Marty was sprawled on her lap, licking her hands. They'd decided to drive to the Commons so they could bring Marty, a whole picnic dinner, and a huge tote bag full of Frisbees, Nerf balls, decks of cards, and who knows what else!

"I packed HLT in the picnic basket," Charlotte replied. "You know how wacko Marty gets when he sees that toy."

Sophie turned from the front seat where she was sitting next to Mr. Ramsey. "Marty's *wack-o* all the time! *Il est un joli chien*," Sophie gushed about Marty's adorableness. "I'm sure you don't even miss Orangina anymore, Char, now that you have such a cute puppy!" she added with a laugh.

Charlotte sighed to herself. She was still working on Orangina's story. Ideas just kept coming, and she couldn't have stopped writing if she tried. Charlotte wanted to say, "Sure, Marty's cuter, but Orangina had the spirit of adventure!" Maybe if Sophie started reading the story, she'd remember all the fun they used to have with Orangina when they lived in Paris.

While Charlotte worried, Avery was retelling the Franco-and-Marty cookie disaster—making Mr. Ramsey laugh so hard he had to pull the car over for a second to get himself together!

"We need to do something to make that parrot and dog be friends," Sophie stated between giggles. "But I think maybe it is not possible!"

"What if Marty brought Franco a present?" Avery suggested. She rubbed the dog's head. "What about pine-apple? Franco loooves pineapple, Marty-man!"

"Woof!" Marty barked.

"What an idea! Pineapple is *magnifique!*" Sophie agreed.

Avery took a deep breath and decided that now was as good a time as any to start spying for Dillon. "What kind of presents do your boyfriends give you, Sophie?" *That was a good one.* Avery gave herself a mental high-five. *If Sophie answers the question, I'll know for sure that she has a boyfriend!*

"Oh, Avery, you know boys," Sophie said dismissively. "They think if they blow a kiss in the hall, they gave you a great gift. What boy needs to bother himself buying choco-lates and flowers if he can give a nice smile and a wave for free?"

The girls all laughed.

"Should we teach Marty to wave, then?" Mr. Ramsey asked, oblivious to what Avery was trying to do.

Avery was into it now, so she plowed forward. New tactic. *I tried to find out about the boyfriend. Now I'll start drop-ping hints and find out what Dillon and Sophie have in com-mon.* "So, Sophie, do you like World Cup Soccer? Dillon loves soccer."

"It's okay," Sophie replied.

"How about Olympic basketball? Did you watch France play? Dillon likes basketball, too."

Sophie turned her head to look over the seat at Avery.

"I am getting a thought," she mused. "Do you have special feelings for this Dillon? You talk about him forever—"

"Oh, no!" Avery practically shouted. "Not Dillon. Ewww." She stopped herself. That wasn't the right thing to say to get Sophie to like her buddy. "I mean," she said, digging deeper and making a mess of things, just like always. "He's nice and funny and everything, but nope, not my type."

"Who's type, then, is he?" Sophie asked.

"Umm . . ." Avery blushed, embarrassed that she had even tried to play matchmaker again. She couldn't just say, "Yours," could she? It was on the tip of her tongue.

"Ahhh, it is okay, I understand," Sophie turned around from the front seat and winked.

Avery's mouth hung open as she realized that her silence, combined with the pink flush in her cheeks, added to the evidence that Avery had a little thing for the sports star.

"Drat," Avery grumbled to herself as Mr. Ramsey pulled into a parking spot not far from Boston Common.

Thankfully, the subject was dropped as Charlotte played tour guide. She pointed out the historic features of Boston's oldest community park, including the beginning of the famous Freedom Trail, as they carried the picnic basket and blanket to a wide grassy area near the pond.

"The Freedom Trail," Charlotte explained, "takes you past all these different historic sites in Boston. Like churches, graveyards, and an old ship. It's pretty cool."

"Can we go?" Sophie asked. "I love a walking tour."

Mr. Ramsey cut in. "We'll do it in a little while. Let's just enjoy the Common for now." He unfolded the blanket and spread it out on the grass.

"Hey, ladies." A familiar voice cut the silence. It was Dillon tossing a Frisbee with his older brother, Gabe. "What a coincidence, seeing you here!" Dillon grinned at Avery, who shot him a you-big-fat-liar look.

Sophie caught the silent glances between the two and elbowed Charlotte. "How do you say, *flirter*?"

Charlotte was tugging Marty away from a trash can and had missed Dillon and Avery's exchange. "Oh, it's the same. Flirt, or flirtation."

Sophie nodded knowingly, then got distracted by a strange vehicle driving down the street nearby. *"Qu'est-ce qui se passe?!"* she exclaimed, jumping up and pointing at the strange neon green, boat-shaped truck.

Charlotte looked up. "Oh. It's just a Duck Tour."

"What does this mean?" Sophie asked, repeating the phrase. "'Duck tour.' Duck is *canard*, *non*?"

"You got it. A Duck is a special kind of vehicle that goes on land and in the water, just like the animal. These ducks are retired war vehicles, and now they drive tourists around Boston," Mr. Ramsey explained.

"Yeah, and after all the historic stuff," added Dillon's brother, Gabe, "the jeep drives right into the Charles River! It's rad." He tossed his Frisbee in the air, and Marty shot off after it.

"You'd like it, Sophie," Dillon added.

Sophie's expression brightened. "Can we go? Please?"

CHAPTER

9

Dillon and the Duck Crew

The Prudential Center was crowded for a weekday afternoon. Avery, Charlotte, and Sophie linked arms and stayed close behind Gabe and Dillon as people pressed around them. Mr. Ramsey had decided to let the kids go on the tour together while he watched Marty in the park.

Their Duck wasn't leaving for another twenty minutes, so they hung out in the mall, checking out the nearby vendors' carts. While Sophie tried on a midnight blue scarf, Dillon sidled over to the Red Sox booth.

"I'll take that one," Avery overheard him say, pointing to a stylish red and blue cap.

He walked up behind Sophie and held out the small gift bag they'd packed the hat inside. "Here." He thrust the bag at her. "For you."

Sophie obviously wasn't sure what to make of the gift. "Thank you," she said politely, tucking the hat into her tote bag. Avery sighed to herself. *Here I go to Dillon's rescue!*

She took Sophie aside. "You should wear the hat. It's, like, the dress code in Boston. You'll look like you were born here!"

"Okay, I am Boston native for the day!" Sophie exclaimed, and with a grand movement, she swept the hat out of the bag and put it on her head. She tucked her bangs under and pulled down the brim.

"*Très chic!*" Charlotte exclaimed, thinking, *Only Sophie could pull off a combo of a baseball cap and a trendy scarf.*

"MAKE WAY FOR DUCKLINGS!" a short woman in a black and yellow polka-dotted raincoat burst into the lobby. "Duck Tour number 34, we're ready to mooove on out!"

"That's us!" Dillon jumped up. Charlotte followed, wondering where she'd heard someone say "mooove" exactly like that before. But she was soon distracted by the sight of their sunshine yellow, boat-shaped vehicle. The guide vaulted her tiny self up the steps and ushered everyone in.

"My name's Mandy, and I'll be your *ducky*—oops, I meant *lucky*—guide today. Did you know there's a statue of the ducklings from the famous book *Make Way for Ducklings*, right on the Boston Common?" Mandy twittered as Sophie and Charlotte climbed onboard.

"We missed it!" Sophie sounded disappointed.

"I'll show you after," Dillon offered as they sat down.

"Look over there!" Dillon tapped the window as the Duck began to move. "That's the Boston Tea Party Church. They all had to wear big white wigs to get in. This one time they snuck out to the harbor with tea bags all stuffed under their wigs and—"

"We are now coming to the Old North Church!" Mandy chirped. "Oldest standing church in Boston." She indicated the same building that Dillon had pointed out.

Dillon shrugged as a way of saying "Oops." Then he jumped up, waving at a statue.

"Hey! Check it out. That dude was my grandfather, mayor of Boston."

Gabe rolled his eyes, and Avery tried to hold in a laugh as Sophie's eyes widened.

Sandy gestured toward the statue as they rolled past. "Check out this tribute to good ole Benjamin Franklin—on your left."

"Dillon!" Sophie shoved him playfully. "He is not your *grandpère*!"

Sandy continued, "Born in Boston, buried in Philadelphia, this founder of our country thought the turkey would make a stellar national bird . . . but I disagree."

"Bet she votes for the duck," Avery quipped to Charlotte, who had pulled out her journal and was making notes about something.

"Bet y'all think I'd vote for the duck." Mandy smiled and whipped off her raincoat. Underneath, she was wearing a yellow dress over bright-red stockings, and the dress was covered with tiny chickens and roosters! Then she reached under her seat and pulled out a hat with a chicken head and wings that flapped up and down by pulling on a cord!

"Actually, I'm all for chickens, ladies and gentlemen!"

The Duck Tour howled with laughter. Charlotte looked up from her journal, where she was jotting down notes for her story. Mandy's lopsided grin looked kind of familiar, too. Did she know her from somewhere?

"Hey. Why did the chicken cross the road?" Dillon poked Sophie in the shoulder.

"Why?" she answered innocently.

"It was a Duck Tour disguised as a chicken!"

"Oh, Dillon," Sophie gasped to Charlotte in between laughs. "He is *trés amusant!*"

"What did she say?" Dillon asked Avery. "I heard my name and then something French."

"I don't know French!" Avery replied.

"But you're friends with Charlotte, and she knows French! Come on, what did she say?"

"She said, 'Dillon is a huge doofus.'" Avery gave Dillon a punch in the arm, satisfied that he wouldn't ask her to translate French ever again.

The Whole Truth

Above the Movie House, Maeve was feeling like a huge doofus. In fact, she felt like the world's biggest, most gigantic doofus for thinking she could get away with a fancy party, just because she really wanted one.

It wasn't Maeve's mother's style to yell when she got angry. No. Instead, she got really quiet. And direct. "Maeve, you need to explain the phone call I just took. Now! What *exactly* is going on?" Maeve's mother sat down with her arms stiffly crossed, waiting. Maeve gulped. The expanse of table between her and her mom felt like a desert wasteland. Impossible to cross.

Maeve glanced at her father. By the look on his face, she knew he wasn't going to protect her.

"Umm." Maeve didn't quite know where to begin. There was no use trying to make up excuses; Maeve had learned that lesson the hard way earlier in the year when she lied to both her parents *and* her friends when she went to a basketball game with Dillon. *The beginning*, she decided. *That's always the best place to start.*

Her mom was still waiting, only too patiently. Maeve took a deep breath. "Well, at Henry Yurt's Bar Mitzvah party I might have told—I mean, I *definitely* told—a few kids from school that I was going to have a party. Ummm, sort of like Henry's."

Maeve's parents both knew all about the extravagant party the Yurtmeister's parents had thrown. Mr. Taylor's eyes grew huge and wide, then he rested his forehead on his hand.

"Go on," her dad prodded.

"So then, my friends got involved in the planning, and we came up with a theme and then, I had this idea to arrive in a limo, and . . ." She told them all the details, including her dream to own the dress hanging in the window at Think Pink. "I thought that if I called some places and asked about prices and reservations . . ." She hesitated, knowing by her parents' expressions that this wasn't going as well as she'd hoped. "Ummm, I thought you'd be super impressed that I was being incredibly responsible and"—Maeve looked from her pale mother to her head-holding father—"well, I kind of, sort of, figured you'd let me have the party that I really want." *Whew.*

"I can't believe it," Ms. Kaplan said softly, so softly that Maeve knew she was in really, really, *really* big trouble. "I thought you understood, Maeve." Her mother gave her father a look that Maeve couldn't decipher. "We cannot afford this party you are imagining. And more important, we've already said NO. But here you go, acting on your own, against our wishes."

"But, Mom," Maeve practically whined. "I'm trapped. All the kids are expecting a huge party. I even told Henry it was going to be radder than his!"

"Rad-der?" her father repeated. "That's not even a word."

"Don't joke, Ross." Maeve's mom was glowering at him. "This is partially your fault."

"Huh?" Maeve's dad looked stunned. "I'm not even Jewish—I know nothing about how Bat Mitzvahs are supposed to be done. How can this possibly be my fault?!"

"You are always encouraging Maeve to dream big! Too big!" Maeve's mother stood up from the table and huffed around the dining room, pacing. "Now Maeve's gone and told her friends that she's going to have some celebrity-style bash. Well"—Maeve's mom turned back to Maeve—"you're just going to have to go back and tell all the kids you were wrong. You need to learn that no means *no*. We are having a small family luncheon as planned, and that's it!" Just when Maeve thought her mother was done with the lecture, she added, "And you will wear the dress we bought you for the school Valentine's Day dance."

Maeve shrieked. She couldn't help it; the scream just burst out of nowhere, and she hid her face in her hands. *"No! It's not fair!"* she wanted to shout, but couldn't find the words.

"Carol." Maeve's dad was now on his feet too. "I think you're being a bit unreasonable." He stepped toward Maeve's mom. "I know the Movie House is losing money, and the economy is bad for everyone, but maybe we—"

Did he say "maybe"? Maeve couldn't believe her ears! Hope, a tiny seed that sprouted quickly, rose within her.

"No!" her mother retorted. "No, no, no." That seemed to be all she could say. "This is bad parenting, Ross! If we give her everything she wants, she'll never learn the value of money, and it's more than the party, anyway. . . ."

It was over. Maeve plugged her ears to drown out the bickering. There would be no limo, no red carpet, no famous DJ, and no new dress.

Hope was destroyed.

Writing Sleuth

On the Duck Tour, Sophie looked out at the approaching river with increasing alarm on her face. "Are you sure this car can float?" she asked Charlotte.

"I hate to get my tail feathers wet. . . ." Their goofy guide, Mandy, ducked down, pretending to hide. "But it looks like we're heading straight for the water!"

Sophie let out a little yelp as the amphibious vehicle dropped into the Charles River, but they didn't even get splashed. Charlotte rolled her eyes at Mandy's antics and snuck out her journal. Floating down the river on the Duck reminded her of the houseboat that she'd lived on in Paris with her father.

"Sophie, do you remember that time Orangina saw a fish in the water and—," Charlotte started, but Sophie had turned around in their seat so she could talk to Dillon and Avery. They were all laughing at something Sophie had said.

"No, no," Dillon was instructing. "Not a quick 'dud,' but a longer sound. Like this." He cleared his throat. "Duuuuude."

Sophie imitated him, but with her strong accent it sounded more like "Duuud" than "Duuude." Everyone laughed again, and Charlotte, who had been lost in memory when the English lesson began, felt left out. While the others taught American slang to Sophie, Charlotte retreated back into her journal and began shaping some ideas for part four of Orangina's story.

Charlotte's Journal

Ideas
Orangina gets lost in a crowd of foreign tourists all hurrying through the tunnels. Think about description! The colors in the river all swirl together. . . . Maybe Big Bruce's book is full of colors? Or cats? Maybe there's one special cat. . . .

Charlotte wrote until her pen ran out of ink. As she was digging through her purse for another one, a voice interrupted.

"Taking notes?"

Charlotte looked up, surprised to see Mandy's chicken hat flapping at her! Then she looked around. They were back at the Prudential Center and the Duck was empty. *Sophie and Avery left without me?* she worried, then saw them waiting on the sidewalk.

"Sorry," Charlotte mumbled.

"No problemo!" Mandy winked, and Charlotte noticed that she was wearing tiny, dangly cow earrings. Suddenly she knew why Mandy seemed so familiar!

"Um, do you by any chance know Mr. Moore? He teaches science at my school in Brookline."

Mandy broke into a huge grin. "My, you're quite the sleuth! Charlie Moore is my very own dear brother. How did you ever guess?"

Charlotte hopped out of the Duck, hugging her journal to her chest. "The cows gave it away!"

Gabe and Dillon had to take off after the tour, but Sophie wore the cap Dillon gave her through their picnic dinner on the Common *and* for the whole car ride home. Every once in a while Avery overheard her practicing quietly, "Dud. Duuude. Dood."

When they got to Avery's house, Sophie jumped out too, to give Avery *bisous* good-bye. "You are so lucky," Sophie gushed as she turned to get back into the car. "You have the nicest boyfriend."

It took Avery a second to understand what Sophie had just said. "Huh?" she sputtered. Her mind was spinning. *How did it all go so terribly wrong?*

Avery finally pulled herself together and shouted, "He's not my boyfriend!" But it was too late. Mr. Ramsey had already driven away.

In the car, Charlotte was writing furiously with a pen she'd found in the glove box, groaning in frustration when the car's bumps messed up the letters. She'd felt kind of lonely all day long, even though she'd been with her friends, but now that the story was flowing, she felt like Orangina and Big Bruce were sitting next to her, cheering her on.

What If?

Maeve wished for the millionth time that she'd gone to the Boston Common with Charlotte and Sophie. Maybe then her parents wouldn't have had this fight. Maybe then this whole mess would have just blown over. But it hadn't happened that way. Everything had gone wrong, and her parents were arguing around her, as if Maeve weren't even there. *I really messed up,* she thought, feeling tears well up in the corners of her eyes. *My parents were getting along so well and now . . . now . . . I wish I'd never even gone to Henry's party!*

"A Bat Mitzvah isn't about the party, Ross, and Maeve knows that!" her mom snapped.

"I don't understand why this is such a big deal. Maybe we can work it out," her dad argued, his voice louder than usual.

"Who's paying for the lunch?" Maeve's mom demanded. "Even without a party, we've already committed to a family lunch. Grandma and Grandpa Kaplan are flying in. So are your parents, Ross."

"Aren't we splitting the lunch costs, Carol?" Maeve's dad asked.

"Yes," her mom said firmly. "And that leaves no money for a party. None. *I* certainly have none to spare."

Maeve used a stray napkin on the table to rub at her tear-streaked cheeks as guilt ate her up inside. *I just wanted that gorgeous dress and a fantabulous party for my friends. Was that so bad? Am I really a responsible and grown-up young woman now, like Rabbi Millstein says?*

Maeve put down the napkin and swallowed hard. "What if . . . ," she started, and both parents turned to glare at her. "What if I help pay for the party myself?" Maeve finished.

"Just how are you going to do that?" her mom asked suspiciously.

"Let the girl talk," her dad countered in a defiant tone.

"Yeah, let the girl talk," Sam imitated, coming into the room, carrying his own Hebrew binder. Apparently he was planning to show off how well he knew his part after all.

"I'll babysit for Sam's friend Austin," Maeve said emphatically, emboldened by her own idea. "Then I can help you pay for everything."

Maeve's mom shook her head. "Do you have any idea how much a hotel costs? A DJ? Not to mention your grand plans for butterflies and limos?"

"I . . . ," Maeve began, but stopped. In truth, she really didn't have a clue.

"Sorry, darling." Her father was obviously exhausted from the fight. He explained to Maeve that with the luncheon and the problems at the Movie House and supporting two households, there was no way they could afford a big party. "Babysitting money would cover the cost of only one or two centerpieces—"

"Your Bat Mitzvah has to be about tradition," Maeve's mom interrupted. "It simply can't be about money. Or about a party."

Sam, in a sweet moment, came and took Maeve's hand. He could tell she'd been crying. "It's okay, Maeve-y." Sam squeezed her hand in his. "You probably don't want to babysit Austin 'cause he's a pain. Even though his parents are rich and they probably pay a TON."

Maeve perked up a little, instantly regretting that she hadn't called Austin's mom over the weekend, when her mom first told her about the job. "Would . . . would a TON of babysitting money buy one dress?" Maeve wondered out loud, but her dad wasn't listening anymore. He was ragging on Maeve's mom for interrupting him.

There was no way Maeve would wear an old dress to her Bat Mitzvah, even if it was just to the boring family luncheon. While her parents returned to bickering about the lunch costs, Maeve's imagination was wrapped around the dress with its glittering sequins.

TON, she said over and over in her mind. *They pay a TON. I can show my parents how responsible I am by making enough money to buy that dress! Once they see how I did it all by myself, they'll stop fighting. Maybe they'll even be friends.*

"I'll do it!" Maeve said suddenly, her voice rising above the din.

"What? Do what?" her mom asked, cut off from whatever she'd been saying to turn to Maeve.

"I'll take the babysitting job."

For a second her mother looked confused, like she had no idea what Maeve was even talking about. Then she gathered her thoughts and threw her hands in the air in defeat. "Maeve, you haven't even called the family back yet. They probably found someone else! And honestly, I don't know how you are going to fit it into your schedule, anyway."

"But, Mom, if I'm going to be a responsible young woman, I can—"

"I'd be happy to help rearrange her schedule," Mr. Taylor offered.

"You do understand, Maeve," her mother warned with a sideways glare at her former husband, "that taking a job doesn't mean you get a party. It just means that you'll be showing *some* responsibility and independence if you follow through."

Her father nodded. "I agree with your mom—this doesn't mean you get a party."

Finally, Maeve's parents were a united front.

"Okay," Maeve agreed, fighting against more tears. "I just want to show you that I'm responsible and independent." *At least I'll get the dress I want*, Maeve thought, but somehow it didn't help shake the lump of sorrow inside her. *I wish I hadn't told so many kids about the party and passed out those cards. What am I going to say to them now? How will I show my face at school? Maybe I should just stay home sick the rest of the week. . . .*

Maeve did the only thing she could think to solve her problem: She retreated to her room and turned on the computer, hoping for some support from her friends, the BSG. Thankfully, Katani was there!

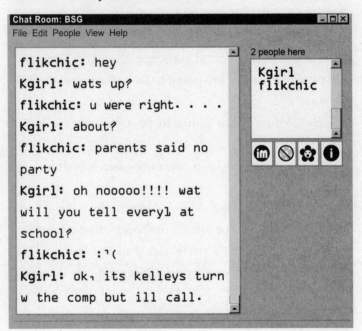

Chat Room: BSG

File Edit People View Help

2 people here

Kgirl
flikchic

flikchic: hey

Kgirl: wats up?

flikchic: u were right. . . .

Kgirl: about?

flikchic: parents said no party

Kgirl: oh nooooo!!!! wat will you tell every1 at school?

flikchic: :¬(

Kgirl: ok, its kelleys turn w the comp but ill call.

Future Famous Author

As soon as Charlotte got home, she rushed to her computer, the words for the next part of her story hanging on the tips of her fingers.

Part 4
Magic and Mystery

There in Big Bruce's book was a simple watercolor painting. Orangina blinked his yellow eyes and looked again at the most beautiful cat he had ever seen in his entire life. Her eyes were luminous green, her fur was deep and dark as the river Seine, and her whiskers curled delicately at the ends.

"Who isss she?" Orangina purred, all thoughts of the barge forgotten.

"A witch," Big Bruce explained. "Ahhh, I mean, the *good* kind. And a good friend, until . . . See, I wasn't *always* this size. There was an accident involving a beehive, three butterflies, some pumpkin seeds, and a shooting star. . . ." As he spoke, Bruce led the way through the twisting tunnels. Orangina followed, in a daze. The book had shrunk again and was tucked away in Bruce's pocket, but the cat-witch's face was burned in his memory.

"So you see," said Bruce, and Orangina realized he'd missed most of the story, "all we need to do is get past the butterbees and choose the right pumpkin."

Butterbees? Orangina wondered. They passed a sign reading "Danger!" and Orangina kept walking. Soon after, were three signs: "Turn Back!" "Not One Step Farther!" "We Mean It!" After a lot more twisting and turning, a final sign was posted on a small wooden door: "Don't Tell Us We Didn't Warn You."

Big Bruce reached for the doorknob.

CHAPTER

10

The Party Goes Poof

Maeve could not stop crying. As hard as she tried to stem the flow of tears, she just couldn't seem to pull herself together.

It had all started innocently enough. The girls had gathered for a quick breakfast at Montoya's Bakery before school. Maeve wasn't very hungry and already felt down in the dumps, knowing that she'd have to tell her devastating news first to the BSG and then to the rest of the world, but she quietly ordered a bran muffin and a cup of iced hot chocolate.

Nick was there, behind the counter, helping his parents serve breakfast to the early crowd. "How are the plans for your Bat Mitzvah going?" he asked innocently. And that was all it took. The floodgates, which had held all morning, started to split open as the first tears trickled out.

"Fine." Maeve's chest tightened and she couldn't say any more. *Don't cry don't cry don't cry*, she repeated to herself, but it was already too late. Maeve practically threw her three dollars at Nick, grabbed her breakfast, and ran to the BSG table where Avery, Katani, Charlotte, and Isabel were already hanging out. With Sophie.

Her friends' faces blurred through a curtain of fresh tears, and Maeve knew she'd completely failed to keep it together. *If only I had a handkerchief to dab at my eyes . . .*

"Qu-est que c'est?" Sophie was the first to respond, handing Maeve a stack of napkins from the table dispenser. "What has happened? Someone has died?"

Maeve shook her head no as she blew her nose loudly into a napkin. *Sophie is so nice,* Maeve thought. *She might be the coolest person in the whole world. I bet* her *parents would let her have a party. . . .* This thought set off a stream of fresh tears, and the Beacon Street Girls hovered around Maeve, asking questions she couldn't answer: Is this about Riley? Or your parents? Are you sick? Is it the math test?

Katani was the only BSG who stayed quiet. She knew what this was about from their phone conversation the night before, but she wanted to give Maeve a chance to tell everyone herself.

"Give her a second," Sophie said calmly, one hand on the pretty pink scarf wrapped around Maeve's neck.

"You'll be okay," Charlotte reassured her upset friend, but in the middle of her deep concern, she felt something else. Something uncomfortable. Maeve and Sophie weren't the only ones wearing scarves. Katani had a thin, black strip of cloth tied around her neck, too. It went perfectly with her trendy patterned shirt and brick red skirt.

Strange. Is it my imagination, Charlotte wondered, *or is everyone trying to become more and more like Sophie?*

I wish I was more like Sophie, Maeve said to herself at the exact same moment, grabbing another pile of napkins. Sophie was fantabulous, and Maeve felt small and completely embarrassed that she'd broken down in Sophie's presence. And she hadn't even told one person her devastating news yet! *Pull it together,* Maeve told herself.

"S-s-sorry," she choked out. "I—I—I . . ."

"Hey," Avery suggested. "Try doing that breathing thing from your yoga class."

The first breath whistled in and out too quickly.

"In. Out. In. Out," Avery guided Maeve. "Breathe slowly through your nostrils."

"I—I—I can't," Maeve stuttered through her tears. "I'm all stuffed up!"

"Then breathe through your mouth," Katani put in.

Charlotte stroked her back. "We're here for you."

"Just pretend you're in a calm blue space," Isabel suggested.

Maeve forced herself to focus on her friends' words. *Breathe in. Breathe out. Calm blue space.*

It was working. Her breaths came more slowly, and her tears began to dry. With one last nose blow, Maeve found the strength to joke, "Does anyone have some mascara? I cried mine all off."

Isabel rummaged through her book bag until she found a tube, and handed it to Maeve. "Happy early birthday," she said. "Never been used. It's all yours."

"Thanks." Maeve took the mascara, and a tube of lip gloss from her own purse, and Katani handed over a mirror. It took the rest of the napkins in the dispenser to clean up the mess of tears and black smears on Maeve's face. Afterward, she still had red circles around her eyes.

Charlotte handed Maeve her mug of iced hot chocolate. "Chocolate," she reminded Maeve, "solves all the problems in the world."

Maeve took a long sip and then, finally, smiled.

"So, what's wrong?" Isabel asked, lightly touching Maeve's shoulder.

Maeve looked over at Sophie and asked, "How do you say 'Bat Mitzvah' in French?"

Charlotte answered. "Since it's a Hebrew word, just 'Bat Mitzvah.'"

Maeve pinched her lips together and groaned. "Figures. It's a dumb word in any language."

"What's the prob with the Bat M?" Avery sat on her chair backward, talking through bites of yogurt. "I thought you were wicked excited about your party."

Maeve sighed, and, although it felt like nails on a chalkboard, finally admitted to everyone, "There won't *be* a party."

Katani nodded. "Tell them the rest," she urged. "You can do it!"

"There never was going to be a party." Maeve took three more deep breaths and a big gulp of iced hot chocolate before continuing. "I just wanted one so badly, I told everyone they were invited. And when my parents said no, I thought I could still pull it off anyway. But I can't."

"We are all sorry," Sophie said kindly. "But what is the big, how you say, deal?"

Maeve felt the tears welling up again. She swallowed hard to hold them back. "How am I going to tell the kids at school?"

Everyone was quiet with sympathy. This was the real issue. Of course the BSG felt a little let down that the party had never been real, but they cared more that Maeve was okay. But Anna, Joline, and Kiki certainly wouldn't feel that way.

"No worries," Avery piped up. "They'll just have to deal."

Katani nodded. "Maeve and I talked last night, and I thought the best thing to do was just apologize and say that her parents want it to be just family."

"But they're going to be so *disappointed*." Maeve moaned, not quite realizing that deep down, she was the most disappointed of all. Disappointed that she couldn't have her party, but also disappointed that she'd let her best friends down.

"I've got it!" Sophie snapped her fingers. "We will send, how you say, little cards to all your classmates to explain."

Charlotte caught onto the idea. "They'll be unvitations! Like invitations, only the opposite."

"I'll personally deliver unvitations to Anna and Joline," Katani offered, which broke the ice, making everyone laugh . . . except Maeve, who smiled thinly.

"Thanks, guys." Maeve drained the last of her iced hot

chocolate and glanced in Katani's mirror. The red circles were almost gone.

"Of course!" Sophie put an arm around Maeve. "This is not a *problème* at all. Poof!" she waved her hand. "No party. Too bad for those duuuuds."

This made Maeve laugh for real.

"Duuuudes," Charlotte reminded Sophie.

"Too bad for those duuuuudes," Sophie repeated, satisfied that she'd said it right.

Maeve sighed. "Those *duuuuudes* are going to be mad at me. I promised them the raddest party ever."

"They won't be mad," Isabel promised. "Anyway, if they are, that's their deal. Everyone knows that these things really aren't about the party. Like my own confirmation. It was more about the prayers and the promises than anything else."

"You sound like my mom," Maeve grimaced, rolling her eyes. "Ugh." Then a glimmer came into Maeve's eye and she added, "You're right, Isabel. Being a Bat Mitzvah is not about the party." She wrinkled her nose. "But it's not *all* about the service either."

"It's not?" Charlotte asked, and the other BSG echoed with, "Huh?"

"It's about the dress . . . right??"

Ping-Pong

Maeve, back to talking a million miles a minute, explained her master plan. "There may not be a party, but that dress will be my consolation prize. You guys would not believe how *fabulous* it is! There have to be a million sequins, and I totally think I could get away with wearing it to the Academy Awards! Thing is, I only have about forty dollars saved, so I'm gonna have to earn, like, a hundred and fifty dollars. I'm not going to be able to hang out as much with you all and Sophie," Maeve apologized. "I'm sitting for this kid named Austin today and tomorrow after school."

As she said it, Maeve wondered, *Did I do the right thing, taking this job? I mean, I still need to practice my Hebrew and prepare for the service, and Sophie isn't here much longer, and I am giving up two whole afternoons. I'm not so sure. . . . Then again, Sam said they pay a TON of money, and the dress costs a TON!*

Sophie gave Maeve's hand a squeeze. "I wish you luck in buying the dress! It sounds *très* chic. Maybe I can help you pick out the shoes?"

Maeve jumped up and draped her arm over Sophie's shoulders. "I have the best friends ever! Thanks so much, and *merci beaucoup*, Sophie."

"I think—" Charlotte wanted to let Maeve know that maybe she shouldn't get so excited about this dress, especially since it cost so much, but Maeve was still gushing to Sophie.

"I can't imagine how life will be without you here! We'll all miss you so much when you go back to Paris . . . ," Maeve went on dramatically.

Charlotte quietly pushed herself back from the table, trying to put a finger on her feelings. It was like Maeve didn't even see her sitting there. Everything was Sophie, Sophie, Sophie. She wasn't really angry or sad. So, what was she?

Oh, no, Charlotte realized as an unsettling feeling took over. Maeve's arm was around Sophie's shoulder instead of hers. *What's going on?* Charlotte wondered. *Have I been replaced?*

At that exact moment, Nick showed up, carrying a platter.

"Special delivery," he said, setting a plate of French pastries in front of the girls. "Made by my mom in honor of Sophie's visit."

"Merci, merci," Sophie gushed.

"Hey, do you guys want to go hiking with me this weekend? It'll be fun," Nick asked with a glance in Charlotte's direction.

"That's rad, duuud!" Sophie said, making everyone at the table laugh.

"Merveilleux!" Charlotte replied, imitating Sophie as if it was a joke, but deep down, Charlotte felt uneasy. No one heard her anyway. Nick's sister had called him away, and everyone else was wrapped up in a new American slang lesson with Sophie.

"Repeat after me: awesomicity," Maeve lectured, spreading her elbows out on the table so Charlotte had to shift over to make room.

I'm the only one who feels left out, Charlotte realized, heart sinking as the conversation shifted to the subject of French fashion. It was like she was on the outside, looking in. Not really part of the action. Just an observer. *What's wrong with me?* Charlotte wondered. *Why does everything feel so awful right now?*

"Hey." Dillon came by the table just before everyone had to head out to school. "'Sup?"

"Nothing, dude," Sophie replied, finally getting the inflection correct, which somehow made everyone laugh even harder than when she got it wrong! She gestured across the table at Avery, "Come sit down."

Dillon grabbed an empty chair from the next table over and started to push it toward Avery.

"There's more room over there," Avery replied, kicking Izzy under the table. Isabel nodded, trying not to laugh outright at the stunned expression on Dillon's face, and pushed over, leaving an open space next to Sophie.

"No, no, Isabel." Sophie waved her hands graciously. "Dillon should sit by Avery. *Parfait.* Perfect. He'd be more comfortable by the window." In a quick move, Sophie rearranged the mugs and plates on the table to leave a crumbless, open spot next to Avery. "There," she told him. "All set."

Dillon pushed his chair toward the window.

"No, there." Avery pointed in the other direction.

He pulled the chair back.

"Oh, the poor boy!" Sophie exclaimed. "He is like a Ping-Pong ball!"

Dillon stood statue still, his face turning stoplight red. Isabel's laugh finally escaped as she realized he probably had no idea what was going on. Seeing that Charlotte didn't seem to be following along either, Isabel whispered in her ear.

"*Soap Opera Digest* update: Dillon likes Sophie. Sophie thinks he likes Avery. Avery wants to help Dillon, and Sophie wants to help Avery."

All Charlotte heard was "Sophie this"and "Sophie that" and "Sophie, Sophie, Sophie . . ." This was just too much. Her friend was constantly in the spotlight, and she was invisible.

"I don't want to hear any more," Charlotte mumbled, watching Dillon give up and sit at an empty table to chat with Nick. Were *they* talking about Sophie too?

Maeve chimed in, "But it's a dramatic love triangle! Intrigue and romance!" She clutched at her heart.

Charlotte simply shrugged. "Not interested."

"You okay?" Isabel asked, sensing something was troubling Charlotte.

"I'm fine," Charlotte told her, symbolically brushing the conversation away with a sweep of her hand. "Never been better." But inside, she was all torn up. There was no reason to be upset—Sophie was one of her closest friends. Or was she?

Charlotte finally got a chance to take out her journal during free writing in English class.

Charlotte's Journal

What's wrong with me? One second I'm worried Sophie won't get along with my friends, but then when she does, I'm suddenly jealous! I don't understand how someone could be your BFF when you live in her country, but when they come to yours—it could go so horribly wrong. I wanted everyone to love Sophie, and they do, but way too much! And now I wish they didn't. She's forgotten all about me.

Have I lost my friend? How is that possible? We've always been there for each other. Why can't she see that I need my old BFF back?

I feel lost.

This must be how Orangina felt when he was lost in the tunnels, unable to get back home. I don't know how he's going to get out yet, but at least he has a magic book.

If I had a magic book, what would I use it for? Maybe I'd become more stylish and cool like Sophie. I mean, Anna and Joline even want to hang out with her! Not that I care what they think, but I was never cool enough for them. Also, Nick and Dillon are so weird around her. All the boys follow her around with big puppy eyes.

I'm so confused.

I want everything back the way it was, when we were BFFs. That's what I'd use the magic book for. But I guess that won't happen, and there's no way I can just tell her how I feel. And I can't tell the BSG, either. They all love her so much. So what do I do? Just wait and hope it gets better? But what if it doesn't? And what if I lose the BSG, too???

She didn't know how to answer her own questions, so Charlotte drew a line at the bottom of her journal entry signifying that she was done thinking about the Sophie problem for now. She turned the page and wrote: "Orangina's Travels: Part Five. IDEAS" across the top.

Charlotte tapped her pencil on the journal. Orangina was in a tricky situation, about to open a door when he had no idea what was behind it and lots of warning not to. But he was an adventurer, so of course he had to keep going. *Maybe I could learn a few things from that silly, brave cat.* Charlotte smiled to herself.

Part Two
French Mania

11

Queen of Chic

Charlotte walked into the lunchroom with her journal clutched tightly in one hand and a bag lunch in the other.

"Hey, Char!" Avery and Isabel waved her over from their usual table . . . but Sophie was sitting in Charlotte's spot.

Everything's going to be fine, she tried to tell herself, placing her stuff in front of the wiggly seat across the table. Usually no one sat there, but there wasn't another free seat. Maeve and Katani sat on either side of Sophie, sipping juice while they laughed together.

As if they'd planned it, all three girls suddenly flipped their scarves the exact same way over their right shoulders. This was way too much! It reminded Charlotte of Anna and Joline—who always dressed and acted identically, like they alone knew anything about style.

As if the freaky scarf thing wasn't enough, a tall girl Charlotte recognized from music class stopped to ask Sophie, "My friends and I wanted to know . . . are there any stores in America that sell shoes *just* like yours? Or can you only get them in Paris?"

How many Sophie clones are there? Charlotte wondered, trying to get comfortable in her wobbly seat.

Avery opened her lunch bag and bent in toward Charlotte to whisper conspiratorially, "Maybe I should make a sign: 'Sophie Advice: one dollar.' I'd make a killing."

Normally, Charlotte would have chuckled at Avery's remark, but not today. She was completely overcome with the feeling that Sophie was growing larger than life, while she was shrinking into the background.

And things were about to get much worse.

"QOM alert," Avery announced in the middle of a long slurp of milk.

Charlotte wondered if her thoughts had somehow summoned Kiki, Anna, and Joline. They hovered just far enough away to make it clear that they pitied Sophie for sitting at this unfortunate, totally uncool table.

"Hey, Sophie. Missed you at the movie," Anna chirped, completely ignoring Charlotte and the BSG.

"My dad got us VIP tickets," Kiki bragged. "We sat in the same section as JT." Kiki shot an aren't-you-jealous look at Maeve, who tried to pretend her square of cheese pizza was much more interesting than sitting with celebrities.

Kiki smiled at Sophie. "Next time, maybe you'll come with us."

Sophie clicked her tongue. "If you invite my friends too, but of course!"

Kiki rolled her eyes disdainfully, as if she were preparing

to make a great sacrifice. She sighed loudly, then pouted. "If Sophie comes, I suppose you all can tag along too."

"Your enthusiasm is *sooo* welcoming." Katani's voice dripped with sarcasm.

Avery let out such a huge snort of laughter that milk came spurting out of her nose! Some of it splattered onto Kiki's jeans, and the Empress of Mean left in a huff.

But Anna and Joline didn't follow. "We just love the way you dress," Anna remarked to Sophie.

"L-O-V-E, love!" Joline spelled out.

"We're going to the mall this weekend," Anna added, her voice syrupy sweet. "Madame Brusie has a satellite store here in Brookline. Her boxy jackets are TDF! To die for!"

"*Oui, oui!* I have the green coat from her last collection," Sophie replied. It was clear to Charlotte that she was impressed anyone in America knew about the French fashionista Madame Brusie. "I was very lucky to get it."

"Oooh," Joline gushed.

"You know, you could come with us." Anna glanced over at Charlotte and the BSG, smiling as she extended the invitation to them all with a regal wave of her hand.

"Perhaps we will." Sophie nodded and bit into her apple.

"See you!" Joline squealed, and they sauntered away, whispering to each other at top speed.

Katani pushed her tray to the side and folded her hands together. *Sophie doesn't know any better,* she told herself. But it still made her uncomfortable to think about doing anything with the Queens. "Something smells fishy," Katani spoke up.

"And it's not the cafeteria's mystery meat," Isabel added with a chuckle.

"Not to worry so much!" Sophie brushed away Katani's suspicions. "They are trying to be nice. Maybe they are changing their ways? *Oui?* Relax and enjoy."

Charlotte couldn't possibly "relax and enjoy." It was all too weird. The QOM probably didn't even know the *meaning* of nice. They just wanted a piece of Sophie's popularity! *Why doesn't Sophie get it?* Charlotte thought. But she couldn't bring herself to say anything, because her "famous" friend was smiling widely and describing Madame Brusie's spring line to Katani and Maeve.

Didn't Sophie understand that the only reason Anna included the BSG was so Sophie would go? Charlotte felt like it was a little too late to explain her worries, but she truly wished that Sophie had just said no. It seemed like Sophie was the new Queen—not of mean, but of what? Charlotte thought about it. *Queen of Fabulosity? No. Queen of Cool? Maybe. Queen of Chic? Definitely.* That was it! Sophie Morel was the newly crowned Queen of Chic. But where was Charlotte in her realm?

How to Defreakify

Maeve was actually relieved that the Queens of Mean stopped by during lunch. Not a single person had asked her about her Bat Mitzvah party that morning, and her luck held as Maeve trailed Sophie through their afternoon classes. The spotlight stayed firmly on AAJH's newest French celebrity. In the hallways everyone was whispering,

"Have you seen Sophie Morel? She's amazing! Totally stylish. Where can I get a scarf like that?"

Right before science, the last class of the day, Betsy Fitzgerald mentioned something about Maeve's party. But thankfully the bell rang, and Betsy hurried to her seat before Maeve could cough up her disappointing answer: "There's no party. You'll be getting an unvitation any day now. Sorry."

As Sophie described her science class in Paris to a room full of rapt admirers, Maeve couldn't pay attention. No matter how hard she tried to listen, her fight with her parents kept sneaking into her mind. She recited a little wish: *Please, everyone, just pay attention to Sophie and let me conveniently forget to talk about the nonexistent party.* If everything went right, this whole Bat Mitzvah disaster could disappear into the day-to-day drama of AAJH!

While Maeve was daydreaming, Avery swiveled her chair around to keep an eye on Dillon. Instead of flicking paper footballs with the Trentini twins, he was hanging on Sophie's every word. "Crack a joke or something, dude, don't just stare like that!" Avery wanted to shout at him.

After class the girls gathered at Charlotte's locker while Sophie chatted with Mr. Moore about meeting his sister on the Duck Tour.

"Did Dillon come out yet?" Avery asked.

Isabel shook her head. "He's still lurking in the science room with Sophie."

"He's been so . . . like, sort of sad and strange. . . . What's the word?" Katani paused, searching for an appropriate adjective.

"Forlorn," Charlotte offered.

"What's that mean?" Maeve asked.

Charlotte, ever the writer, answered, "Lost, abandoned, lonely—"

"Okay, Word Nerd," Avery cut her off affectionately. "Got it. Forlorn is the right word."

"Shhh." Isabel stopped the conversation. "Here they come." By "they" she meant Sophie and Dillon, who seemed to be chatting like old pals.

As they got closer, though, Avery could see that Sophie was doing most of the talking and Dillon was having a hard time walking straight. But at least he was smiling.

"Hey, ladies," Dillon greeted the BSG.

"Dillon was just telling me about his favorite French soccer players. I don't even know all of them!" Sophie laughed and put a hand on Dillon's shoulder. "Avery is so lucky to have a friend like you."

"Um, yeah, thanks," Dillon sputtered, and grabbed Avery by the arm, insisting, "I . . . um . . . need to talk to you." He yanked her down the hall.

Avery clearly heard Sophie say, "Ahhh, now that's *l'amour*!"

"No, it's not!" Avery called back over her shoulder, but her words were lost as Dillon led her into a corner by the drinking fountain.

Avery shook her head at her forlorn friend. "What's up with you?"

"What do I talk to her about?" Dillon demanded. "I tried tennis, soccer, kung fu"—he leaned against the wall, ticking sports off one by one on his fingers—"skate-boarding, basketball, and baseball. What am I missing? You're a girl. You've got to know!"

"Dude, *chillax*." Avery backed away a few steps.

Dillon threw up his hands. "Come on! Help me out here."

"Oookaaay," Avery began. *I may know next to nothing about romance,* she told herself, *but I know Dillon has to stop acting like such a freak around his crush.* "First, stop following Sophie around. You're acting like an escapee from a mental hospital. Second, go back to being your charming, arrogant self. Third of all—"

Dillon raised his hand to stop her. "Got your point," he said.

"No," Avery told him. "I don't think you do." Avery poked Dillon in the chest. "Sophie will like you better if you defreakify."

"I'm not a freak!" Dillon protested.

Avery poked him again, this time in the belly. Hard. "Yes, you are. You're being super freaky."

"You'll eat those words!" he challenged. "Soccer fields: one on one. First to five goals wins. Loser buys iced hot chocolate at Montoya's." Then Dillon grinned—his usual, charismatic grin.

"See!" Avery cheered. "I knew normal, old Dillon was still in there somewhere!"

Dillon's grin immediately faded back to . . . forlorn. "I'm too *normal* for her, huh?"

Shoot. Avery shook her head vehemently, thinking, *I'll*

have to beat him silly on the soccer field. That'll bring the old Dillon back. If not, I'll call a basketball free-throw contest tomorrow. That boy needs serious sports therapy!

Dillon leaned against the wall again. "Why doesn't Sophie wear the Red Sox hat I gave her?" There was a slight whine to his voice that Avery had never heard before.

"Oh, come on, Dillon," she said, exasperated, wanting desperately to throttle him. "You're smart enough to know that hats aren't allowed at school. Anyway, since they don't have pro baseball, caps aren't very fashionable in France. They just wear scarves and pointy shoes and other weird things over there."

Dillon's face suddenly lit up. His third mood swing in five minutes. "Sweet idea!" And he was off, dashing down the hall.

"Hey, where are you going?" Avery called out to his rapidly retreating backside. "I thought we were heading out to the fields."

"No can do," Dillon called back, his voice echoing off the lockers in the hall. "I've got to go shopping."

The World's Cutest Monster

Ding-dong! Maeve rang the doorbell at Austin's house that afternoon feeling like the world's most-prepared babysitter. She went through the list in her head one last time: *comfy pink workout pants, check. Kid-friendly cartoon T-shirt, check. Crayons and granola bars and coloring books, check.* Isabel had shared some of her best babysitting advice earlier today, and Maeve had actually taken notes.

Remember to ask for the emergency phone numbers and if he has any allergies. Maeve felt in her book bag for the things she had thought herself to add at the last second: a few of her favorite kid movies and some dance CDs. *MKT is ready to take on the world!* she thought as the door swung open.

"Good to see you, Maeve," Mrs. Franklin greeted. "Come on in." She showed Maeve into the kitchen and pointed out the emergency numbers on the fridge before Maeve could ask for them.

"Is Austin allergic to anything?" Maeve asked.

"No, but thank you for asking, dear! Just make sure he has a *healthy* snack and finishes his homework." She patted her son's head.

"Mooom!" Austin had black hair, adorable blue eyes, and a cute, goofy smile. He sat quietly on the living room floor with a bucket of LEGOs while his mom showed Maeve the rest of the house.

Finally Mrs. Franklin picked up her purse and paused at the door. "I'll be back at seven. Be good!"

Austin gave Maeve an angelic smile, and she smiled back. "We'll be fine!"

Five minutes later she wished she hadn't been so confident. Things weren't going fine at *all*. How could a kid who was so quiet and nice suddenly morph into a monster?

All Maeve did was ask if he wanted carrot sticks or string cheese for a snack.

Austin ignored her and pulled a chair up to the counter. Standing on his tiptoes, he pulled a bag of M&M's out of the top cabinet.

"Um, what did your mom say about a snack?" Maeve asked cheerfully.

"I'm having M&M's. I *always* have M&M's." Austin's goofy grin suddenly didn't seem so cute.

"How about you have some carrot sticks, *then* a few M&M's?" Maeve deftly snatched the bag of chocolate from his hands, and the kid screamed!

"Nooooooo! I want M&M's!!!!!"

While Maeve stood there, too stunned to move, he went into a total freak-out mode, thrashing around on the floor and sobbing.

Maeve took a deep breath. If she could handle Sam, she could handle Austin, right? She poured a few M&M's into her hand and started eating them. "Yum! These are good. Too bad Austin can't have any. I'd be *happy* to share if he calmed down and tried some carrots."

This tactic worked for a little while. At least it got him off the floor! But Monster Boy reappeared when Maeve tried to make him eat two carrot sticks between each handful of candy.

He dropped the carrots on the floor and did the cha-cha on them, clearly enjoying the crunching noise as much as the horrified look on Maeve's face. Then he ran into the living room and started throwing LEGOs in all directions!

"I hate carrots!!!" he shouted.

Maeve managed to hold it together. *That yoga breathing sure is helpful,* she thought. *In. Out. In. Out.* Somehow, as if by magic, she managed to clean up the smashed carrots, hide the bag of M&M's, gather up the LEGOs, and get Austin settled into a chair.

But the instant she opened his backpack to get out his homework, the little wacko went nuts again! Austin jumped out of the chair, screaming "You aren't the boss of me!" and ran straight to the bathroom, where he locked himself in.

First Maeve asked him nicely to come out. Then she waited for fifteen minutes to see if he would get bored. He didn't. So she pleaded with Austin.

"I'll give you the whole bag of M&M's. Just come out of there, please?"

"No."

"You can have a soda, too. I won't tell your mom."

"No. I hate you!!!"

Tears burning at the corners of her eyes, Maeve ran to the phone. *Mom will help me!* But when the answering machine picked up after the fourth ring, she remembered that her mom was at a meeting all afternoon. There was only one option left. Maeve needed the BSG!

CHAPTER

12

Invites and Unvites

Up in the Tower the BSG couldn't hear the phone ringing. Katani had called an emergency meeting, and everyone was sitting on pillows with notebooks and pens spread out around them.

"Maeve is so bummed out about canceling her party," Katani pronounced, stretching out her legs and leaning back on her elbows. "I wish there was something we could do to cheer her up."

"Maeve wanted that party *sooo* much." Charlotte sighed. "And now she has to tell everyone it's not happening! She must feel miserable."

"Why does she need to cancel?" Sophie asked. "Making a party is not *difficile*. In France we have *fêtes*"—she snapped—"like a, how do you say? Like a piece of pie."

The girls all laughed.

Isabel corrected Sophie. "The saying is 'it's a piece of cake,' but we all understand perfectly!"

"Ah, yes, cake," Sophie repeated the phrase a few

times to remember it. Then she smiled over at Isabel. "*We* can make a *fabuloso* party for Maeve."

Isabel nodded happily, confirming that Sophie had used "fabuloso" correctly.

"Awesome idea, Sophie! Why not?" Avery jumped up and danced around with Marty, singing "It's party time!" while the dog barked excitedly. They all missed the phone ringing yet again.

Katani jumped up too, her sad, concerned face replaced by one with purpose. "A surprise Bat Mitzvah party! Great! Or, as you say"—Katani gestured to Sophie—"*merveilleux!*" Katani gave Sophie a hug. "But how do we begin?"

Charlotte watched her friends surround Sophie, gushing about her great idea, and wished she could just be happy for them all. But a dark, secret part of her kept getting more and more jealous. Did they even remember that she had been saying "*merveilleux*" long before Sophie got here?

"What kind of party should we have? A dinner party?" Isabel brainstormed. "I could make invitations."

Charlotte hated to be negative, but . . . "This is kinda last minute. I mean, the Bat Mitzvah is next Saturday! Where are we going to get enough plates and cups and silverware?" she asked.

"Hmm." Sophie pinched her lips together. "We could borrow from people's houses."

"But then the plates and silverware wouldn't match," Katani replied. "For Maeve, it should be glamorous. . . . And that means matching." She held her breath for an instant, then let it out, saying, "I can make decorations. I can sew a red carpet out of some leftover fabric."

"What about the photo booth and stuff like Yurt had?" Avery sat down, dangling Happy Lucky Thingy for Marty to play with.

"That's probably too expensive," Katani cautioned.

The room grew silent for a few minutes, then Isabel suggested, "Instead of catering the party, maybe Elena Maria and Scott could help us cook!"

At that, everyone began to laugh, remembering the cake and cookies from Sophie's welcome party. "Let's not invite Marty and Franco this time," Avery quipped.

"We need to know how many people are coming," Katani broke in. "How much food can only two cooks make?"

"A lot more if they don't have a parrot helping them!" Isabel laughed.

"Charlotte! Girls!" Mr. Ramsey's voice echoed up the tower steps. "I just got back with dinner!" He somehow managed to carry a pizza box, a container of salad, and a canvas grocery bag of root beer and ice cream up the narrow stairs to the Tower.

"Thanks, Dad!" Charlotte set out the make-your-own root beer float ingredients on the floor, and the BSG dug in.

Rhythm to the Rescue

Maeve sighed. *Where are the BSG when I need them?* She was desperate for some help with this monster child, and no one had answered her phone calls or texts.

Maeve knocked on the bathroom door once again with

no success. Austin was one stubborn, aggravating, impossible kid! Then she went outside to see if she could climb in the bathroom window from the outside. But Austin just stuck his tongue out at her from behind the locked window, laughing hysterically.

Maeve sank down on the front steps, ready to dissolve into a puddle of tears right there on her very first baby-sitting job. She simply couldn't take it anymore! *Austin will be stuck in the bathroom forever, and I'll never earn enough money to buy my dream dress*, she thought. But as the first tears slipped out, she saw a familiar-looking guitar case turn the corner.

"Riley?" Maeve managed to call out. She knew he didn't live on this street. What was he doing here?

"What's up? I just finished band practice." He picked up the pace, the black case covered with stickers swinging at his side.

"N-n-n-nothing . . . ," Maeve stammered. She couldn't decide whether she was overjoyed to see a friendly face or mortified that her number-one crush had caught her in such an embarrassing situation.

"Doesn't look like nothing." Riley put his guitar case down next to Maeve, then a set of bongos he'd been carrying under the other arm. "Who's that kid?" He pointed up at Austin, who was making gross noises through the window.

"He's the most awful, spoiled brat in the whole *universe*!" Maeve exclaimed, and spilled the entire babysitting saga, from carrot sticks to flying LEGOs.

As Riley listened, he absently tapped out a rhythm on his drum. Riley had played drums long before he took up the guitar.

Rat-a-tat-tat. Rat-a-tat-tat. One minute passed. *Rat-a-tat-tat.* Two. *Rat-a-tat-tat.* The face disappeared from the window. *Rat-a-tat-tat.* A few seconds into the third minute, a little dark-haired boy poked his head out the front door.

Maeve stopped talking and held her breath.

"You must be Austin. I'm Riley," Riley introduced himself. "Like to drum?"

That was all it took. For the next two hours, Riley and Austin played the drums outside, first on Riley's bongos and then moving to pots and pans that Maeve grabbed from the kitchen. They even managed to squeeze in a homework break during intermission before they went back for another set. This time Maeve stuck one of her favorite dance CDs into the kitchen stereo and left the front door open. Soon, they had their own little rhythm section going on the front steps: Maeve banged along on an upside-down stew pot while Riley strummed his guitar. Austin giggled hysterically, trying to keep up on the bongos. Maeve was having a blast! With every whack of her makeshift drum, she felt some of her frustration and disappointment about the babysitting disaster and her soon-to-be-officially-cancelled party fading away.

Location, Location

"We need a location," Katani announced, after taking a long sip of her root beer float. "I think everything else will fall into place if we know where we're having the party."

"How about the Museum of Science?" Avery suggested in the middle of a mouthful of pizza.

Katani held up one hand. "Expensive. And probably not available. . . . But hold that thought," she said and climbed down from the Tower, leaving behind her unfinished dinner.

Katani still hadn't come back by the time the other girls were finished eating, so they went to find her. Katani was sitting at Charlotte's computer, pencil in one hand, telephone in the other. She looked like she was already CEO of Kgirl Enterprises.

"I understand," she said into the receiver. "Thank you for checking, anyway." Katani hung up and swung around in Charlotte's chair, facing her friends.

"I did an Internet search for nearby hotels and called the closest three." She held up the notepad she was using. There were names and numbers written on it. "Everyone is booked up that night already." Katani pointed to a column labeled "$$" next to the hotel names. "And even if they had a room, everything's too expensive."

"Is there anywhere else to have this party?" Sophie asked quietly.

The girls fell silent, thinking hard.

Boy Alert!

By the time the Franklins arrived home, Maeve was happy and relaxed and overflowing with positive energy.

But Mrs. Franklin wasn't impressed. She stood in the kitchen with her arms folded, glaring at Riley, while her husband put away the scattered pots and pans. "I am so disappointed, Maeve! You should never have invited a boy over without my permission."

"Oh—she didn't. It was my idea," Riley apologized. "I was just trying to help because Austin—"

"He locked himself in the bathroom," Maeve quickly explained. "And I didn't know what to do!" She could see by the look on Mr. Franklin's face that she wasn't the first babysitter to give this kind of report. "I was desperate, and I thought he might get hurt. I called my mom and my friends and then Riley was just walking by with his drum—"

"Riley's so cool!" Austin chimed in, hugging the bongo drum. Riley had said he could keep it, and now the little boy looked at his new friend with hero worship.

"You really should have called us first," Mr. Franklin reiterated to Maeve.

"I'm sorry," Maeve replied. "It's just that I'm really, really trying to be more independent and responsible. I mean, that's what my parents keep telling me to do," Maeve rambled on, hoping she wasn't digging herself deeper into a hole. "And I thought if I could just fix things myself, it would be better. . . . Then Riley showed up and Austin calmed down, so I thought everything was okay. . . ." She wondered if this was the last time she'd babysit here. *I just have to earn enough to buy that dress! And it all turned out okay in the end, didn't it? Austin got his snack, and he finished his homework. Isn't that what matters? We had a great time!*

Mrs. Franklin leaned down and had a quiet conversation with Austin.

"*Please* can they come back?" Maeve overhead the little boy say.

When Mrs. Franklin stood up, she said to her husband, "I think we'll let Maeve come back. Austin promises to behave better next time."

Mr. Franklin assented, but stressed again that Maeve needed to call one of them immediately if things got out of hand. Then he handed Maeve an envelope with fifty dollars inside!

Is that ten dollars an hour? Terrif! Maeve practically skipped out the door. Then she realized Riley was following her. "Um, here, you should get paid too." Maeve handed him a ten, calculating in her head that Riley was only there for about an hour and a half, and she put up with the monster on her own the rest of the time. . . . She'd never been that great at math, so ten sounded about right. Besides, this was her dress money!

"Thanks." Riley stuffed the money in his jeans pocket. "See ya tomorrow. . . ." He shuffled off with his guitar.

On her way home, Maeve found herself in front of Think Pink. Her feet must have brought her there on their own accord. Maeve looked up to the window, taking in the pink fabulousness of her dream dress. *That's my Bat Mitzvah gown!* Maeve pictured herself at the synagogue, stunning in pink and sequins while her friends and family congratulated her on her beautiful speech, her perfect chanting, and her thoughtful community service project. *Riley will be there to take my hand and lead me to the limo. . . .*

Suddenly, Maeve's dream fizzled and died. There was no party, no limo, and the dress's tag said $190. She only had $40 from today, plus $31 saved up. Maeve had thought it was more, but she'd forgotten about a couple of breakfasts at Montoya's and emergency stops at Irving's Toy and Card Shop for Swedish Fish. Maeve was good enough at math to know that she needed to babysit more than just one or even two more afternoons to earn enough for the dress.

As much as she wished she could, Maeve realized that she couldn't avoid the truth forever. Thinking about Swedish Fish had given her an idea. *I think I'll make an important stop on my way home*, Maeve decided with a long sigh. *Mrs. Weiss will know what to do about all this.*

Swedish Fish for Free

Mrs. Weiss owned Irving's Toy and Card Shop. When Maeve turned onto Harvard Street and spotted the friendly red and white awning above the shop, she broke into a run. Mrs. Weiss was like Maeve's personal Yoda. Wise counsel and a good friend. Maeve couldn't wait to see her.

"Good evening, Maeve," Mrs. Weiss greeted from behind the counter, where she was ringing up an older man's sale.

"Hi," Maeve responded as she bee-lined for the Swedish Fish and used the candy scoop to put a bunch into a small plastic bag.

After the old man ambled out, Mrs. Weiss took a long look at Maeve's face. "The fish are free to all troubled girls today." She winked. "Special deal."

"Do I look that bad?" Maeve asked sadly.

Mrs. Weiss pulled a stool up next to hers behind the register and told Maeve to sit. "All bad days have a good, long story. Let's hear it."

Maeve fought back her tears as she confessed everything to Mrs. Weiss, from the Yurtmeister's Bar Mitzvah to the conversation with her parents about her own party and the save-the-date cards she'd handed out to absolutely everyone. She ended with how much better she felt while drumming, and then, how reality came crashing back when she saw *her* dress in the window. The one she would never wear in a limo on her way to a fancy bash.

"What should I do?" Maeve asked as she practically melted into the stool with exhaustion, confusion, and sorrow.

Mrs. Weiss patted her hand and sat silently for a while. When Maeve was breathing steadily, calmly again, Mrs. Weiss quietly said, "I'm proud of you, Maeve. You've already taken the first step to solving your problems."

"I have?" Maeve didn't understand and thought that all she'd really done was complain.

"Yes, you have. You are taking ownership for what you did."

Mrs. Weiss and Maeve talked for nearly an hour, right up until closing time, about what Maeve could and should do next. Maeve was there so long, she called her mom to say she'd be late.

By the time she left the shop, Maeve knew exactly what she needed to do.

Taking Control

Maeve rushed home, tired from such an emotional day, but feeling like maybe, just maybe, she had everything under control for once. She carefully stepped over the battle of Bunker Hill and found her mother at the kitchen table, reading a new business management book.

Maeve took a deep, yoga breath and said, "Mom, I *have* to talk to you."

Ms. Kaplan lowered her book and looked up at Maeve.

"I made a huge mistake." Maeve brushed a tear off her cheek. "I'm going to fix it, though."

"I'm listening." Maeve's mother stood up and came to put her arm around Maeve.

Maeve leaned into her mom's warm comfort and went on, "I ignored you and Dad. I know we can't afford a big party, but I thought I could have one anyway. I thought I could get what I wanted and have things my way if I kept bugging you about it. I thought I needed a fancy party just like Henry Yurt's. But that isn't what it means to become a Bat Mitzvah." Maeve sniffled. "I'm sorry."

Her mom pulled a tissue out of her pocket and handed

it to Maeve. "*This*," she said, hugging her daughter tighter, "is what being a Bat Mitzvah is really about." She tipped her hand under her daughter's chin, pulling Maeve's eyes up to hers. "It's about taking adult responsibilities, understanding what is and is not important, and knowing when you can't change things. *That* is what you are doing right now! I'm so *proud* of you, sweetie."

Maeve nodded. "I'm going to make unvitations, so everyone knows there will be no party." Maeve paused, then added, "I want to celebrate by having lunch with just my family. Really. That's what I want." When Maeve smiled, she felt a tingly warm current course though her veins. It felt great. "And if I can earn enough babysitting money, I think I still want to buy that dress," Maeve added quietly.

Ms. Kaplan kissed her daughter firmly on the forehead.

"Good for you! I love you" was all she said. And that was plenty.

Tower Power

It was time for the BSG to go home, and they still had no idea if they could pull off a party for Maeve. They figured they could handle invitations, decorations, entertainment, and probably food . . . but they were still stuck on a location. They'd already gone through everyone's houses and found reasons why none of them would work.

"The Movie House?" Avery brainstormed.

"How can you have a party in a room full of seats?" Isabel asked.

"What about the stage?" Charlotte suggested.

Katani shook her head. "Too small. And too hard to keep secret! Maeve would find out about it in no time."

"Mr. Summers is here to take Katani home!" Mr. Ramsey called up the stairs.

Charlotte jumped up. "Dad?" she shouted. "Could you come here a sec?"

There wasn't much room in the Tower with five girls, a dog, and their dinner leftovers spread out everywhere, but somehow Mr. Ramsey fit himself on one of the window-sills. "What's going on, girls?" he asked.

Charlotte quickly summarized their party problem, with Katani adding in the details.

Mr. Ramsey nodded. "Well," he said, "it's wonderful that you want to do something for your friend, but a party like this is a big undertaking. I'd say, start small. Why not a sleepover to celebrate?"

Charlotte shook her head. "Maeve deserves something more."

Isabel agreed. "We want to invite everyone *she* invited."

"Which is, like, the entire seventh grade," Avery explained.

Mr. Ramsey raised his eyebrows. But he didn't say no. He didn't say, "This is impossible!" He was willing to let them try, and Charlotte loved her dad at that moment.

"I think this will be quite the challenge for you girls,

but I believe you can do it, if you work hard," he answered. "But you have to promise me that you'll clear your plans with Ms. Kaplan. We don't want to do anything that she doesn't agree with."

"Yes, yes, yes, yes," four girls sang out in chorus together. "We promise."

"*Oui!*" added Sophie.

As Katani started down the stairs to meet her dad, Mr. Ramsey added, "Money does not grow on trees. By that I mean, you have to watch what you spend, and you can't ask anyone for money. That would just make Maeve's family uncomfortable. Everything you do and everything you get has to be given freely or done by volunteers."

"Sure thing, Dad," Charlotte readily agreed.

"I mean it, Char," her father said seriously.

Charlotte realized, then, that her father had just challenged them to pull together a top-notch party with no resources. Could it be done?

After Mr. Ramsey and Katani had left, Sophie stood up. "We will have a party for Maeve," she concluded. "We will make one easy as cake."

"Easy as pie," Isabel said with a smile.

Sophie paused. "But you said it was cake, not pie?"

Charlotte laughed, the first one to figure out what had happened. "Sophie, it's 'a piece of cake' *or* 'easy as pie.' They mean the same thing."

Sophie rolled her eyes. "Your language is impossible as . . . as . . . *cookies!*"

Kgirl™ *Things to Do for Maeve's Party*

1. Must stop Maeve from handing out unvitations
2. Invitations: Isabel
3. Food: simple: easy to cook. Spaghetti and salad?
4. Supplies: Ask Patrice/Scott/Elena Maria to pick up groceries for us
5. Movie star theme: make red carpet. research movie stars
6. Chairs and tables: can we borrow from school?
7. Dishes: Avery thinks they have enough
8. Music: ask Mustard Monkey
9. Clean up: make a list of volunteers
10. LOCATION. location. location????????????!!!!!!!

CHAPTER

13

Paris à la Mode

I sn't it too hot for those thingy-ma-bobbers?" Avery
asked Isabel as they walked into school together the
next morning. Nearly every girl they passed had a chic
French scarf around her neck! "I mean, who wears scarves
in May?" Avery continued.

Isabel twirled a strand of hair around a finger, then
reached into her shoulder bag. "Well . . . they are a brilliant way to express yourself!" She pulled out a tropical
bird-themed silk scarf and draped it over Avery's shoulders. "Ta-da!"

"No way!" Avery tossed the scarf right back at Isabel.
"Am I the only person in the whole school who hasn't gone
French Mania Crazy?!"

Pushing through a gaggle of seventh-grade girls, all
wearing scarves, Avery made her way to her locker. She
flipped the combination lock open and was about to grab
some books when Maeve, Katani, Charlotte, and Sophie
arrived.

"Phew! I'm not alone in the world!" Avery cheered, slapping Charlotte a high-five.

"Huh?" Charlotte looked around at her friends' faces, trying to figure out what was going on.

"You're the only two girls in the whole school who aren't wearing scarves!" Isabel explained, pointing at Charlotte's naked neck, sticking out from the collar of her T-shirt.

"Here, you can borrow one of mine." Isabel pulled out a trendy black-and-white silk scarf. "Turns out my aunt has a whole scarf collection! She said I could borrow them anytime."

The truth was, Sophie had already offered Charlotte one of her scarves that morning. But Charlotte just didn't feel like herself with such a dressy accessory. And besides, none of her clothes matched the muted colors and sophisticated designs of Sophie's scarves. Today Sophie had picked out a gray skirt and black shirt, paired with a colorful designer scarf and matching shoes.

While Charlotte stood speechless, unsure whether she should go with the fashion flow or not, Maeve jumped right in front of her!

"Oooh! Can I wear that one? Please, Charlotte?" Maeve pleaded, fingering the black and white scarf.

Charlotte nodded, giving in to Maeve's enthusiasm.

"It's sooo much more cute, chic, and ooh la la—more French than *this* one." Maeve pulled off the same fuchsia scarf she'd worn the day before and stuffed it in her book bag, right on top of a pile of unvitations. Maeve didn't really want to think about those.

"Doesn't your neck get sweaty wearing those things?" Avery asked incredulously.

Sophie smiled. "Not if the scarf is silk! A good scarf is refreshing, in fact. Like a colorful breeze." She turned to Maeve. "Here, I will help you tie this on, the French way!"

Charlotte backed out of the way, leaning up against the wall, right beneath a sign announcing "French Club! First meeting after school."

When did this French thing get so out of control? Charlotte wondered, feeling helpless and an outsider as girls she didn't even know flocked to watch Sophie's scarf-tying lesson. *A scarf looks right on Sophie,* Charlotte thought. *But she should be the only person wearing one. Now everyone thinks it's cool.* With every scarf-clad girl who joined the crowd, Charlotte felt more and more drab, boring, and uninteresting. The phrase "wallflower" came to mind and seemed to fit.

"We should form our own club!" Avery leaned up against the wall next to Charlotte. "The Scarfless Wonders. Members, two."

Charlotte cracked a smile. At least her best friends didn't care if she followed the whole scarf fad. In fact, there was a Tower rule that stated: We will dare to be fashion individualistas—we're all different, so why should we dress the same? *Maybe I need to make a sign with that rule and post it next to the French Club poster,* Charlotte thought.

Then she saw Nick coming down the hall, and waved. "There's the third Scarfless Wonder!"

"Hey, boys don't count." Avery elbowed Charlotte.

"What boy in his right mind would tie some flowery thing around his neck?"

Fashion Police

Ten minutes later Avery had an answer to her question. Not all boys at AAJH were in their right minds. One, in particular, was quite definitely freakified, off the deep end, and completely insane.

"Is that . . . Dillon?" Katani whispered as they took their seats in social studies class.

"Yep." Avery shook her head, trying to erase Dillon's new image from her brain.

"What the . . . What happened to him? When? How? But most of all, *why*?" Isabel stammered.

Avery wasted no time. She marched over to where he stood at the back of the classroom and punched the shoulder of the boy she thought she knew. "Just how thoroughly have you lost it?"

"Huh?" Dillon turned around, all smiles and sunshine. "What's up?"

"What's up?! Look at yourself!" Avery poked her finger at Dillon's clothing, first jabbing at his pointy shoes, then flicking his fancy pants, and finally nearly strangling him with his new gray scarf! "Where are your sweatpants? Your jersey? Your scruffy sneakers?" Avery interrogated him as if she were a detective. "Okay, stranger, where did you put my friend Dillon? Is this your evil twin who's come to torture us?"

Dillon simply laughed. "Oh, Avery, vat is ze *problème*?" he said, with a fake French accent and a phony European air that choked off any further taunts from Avery and made Sophie perk up.

"*Bonjour*, Dillon!" Sophie sauntered over. "You look *magnifique! Incroyable!* Awesome!" Sophie was full of kind words in both French and English. "*Très français!* Very French!" Sophie smiled warmly and Dillon turned beet red. "Oooh, Dillon, you have been to Paris, *non*?"

"Just the mall," Dillon replied, blushing even more deeply. "It took forever to find these clothes, though. Had to go to that special French store, and, man, was that something else. This lady there said . . ." Dillon cut his story off in the middle when Sophie stepped closer to him and unwound the scarf from his neck. With Sophie standing just a hand's-length away, Avery could see that Dillon was forgetting how to breathe. He was turning from blushing red to an oxygen-deprived shade of blue.

Sophie shook out Dillon's scarf and slid it back around his neck, tying it in a simple knot with the ends flat against his shirt, not off to the side like her own. "There," she said. "Fabulosity complete. That is how the boys wear scarves." Sophie kissed her fingers and gestured like a chef who'd made the best meal of her life.

Dillon muttered something unintelligible, something that sounded a little like "Thhnnnks." By the look on Dillon's face, Avery knew that he was close to passing out. Thankfully Sophie stepped back just in time. "Let's go sit down," Sophie suggested.

As they took their seats Sophie smiled brightly at Avery and whispered, "Isn't it wonderful when a boy dresses to impress a girl?" She winked at Avery as if this was their special secret.

Avery slammed her own forehead with her hand. "It's not me he's trying to impre—," she began, but was interrupted by the teacher.

"Sophie, thank you for showing everyone how to wear a scarf the French way," Ms. O'Reilly began. "However, a scarf can be tied many different ways, depending on the local fashion." Then, to everyone's surprise, their teacher took a silk scarf out of her desk, twisted it up, and wrapped it around her waist like a belt! Charlotte couldn't believe it! First it was just the BSG who wanted to be like Sophie, but now it had spread throughout the school—to the girls, the boys, and now even the teachers! Who was next?

Chase Finley gave Dillon a sideways glance. "Yeah, and some dudes have the local fashion all wrong."

"Chill, man. A scarf is kinda like a necktie," Nick defended Dillon.

Betsy Fitzgerald waved her hand frantically in the air. "Neckties come from France!" she informed everyone. "During King Louis XIII's reign, soldiers wore cravats, which were basically fancy scarves, and—"

"Thank you, Betsy." Ms. O'Reilly cut her off. "That's very interesting!"

"France can have them back!" Henry turned to Sophie. "All neckties do is choke you and fall in your soup."

"I'll make a petition to our prime minister!" Sophie joked.

"Fashion has a very interesting role around the world." Ms. O'Reilly smoothly transitioned the class into a talk about cultural and global clothing trends, calling repeatedly on Charlotte for her opinion since Charlotte had lived in so many places.

"Tell us what you might wear to a party in Africa," Ms. O'Reilly prompted her.

"A dashiki shirt over American jeans." Charlotte explained how she used to wear the African designed multicolored blouses with her own pants. "Or if it was a more formal party, a sarong. That's a special kind of dress you can wear in different ways by wrapping it around yourself."

Charlotte perked up a bit as she answered the teacher's questions, but after every one, the class always asked about France.

"How do you pick what to wear at home in Paris?" Joline asked.

"Well, I usually picked out a color that fits my mood, first—," Charlotte started.

"In Paris," Sophie explained, inadvertently cutting Charlotte off before she was finished, "we are inspired by what we see on television or in the magazines, but sometimes I get ideas just from people I pass on the streets!"

Charlotte's spirits fell as hands waved in the air. No one had wanted to ask *her* about fashion in Paris, Tanzania, or even the Great Barrier Reef.

"All the top designers come from France," Katani added.

"Except for *you*, Katani," Isabel noted.

Sophie smiled. "I am certain you will be at the top one day, Kgirl!"

Ms. O'Reilly cleared her throat. "Fashion is also

important in many different cultural traditions. Can anyone think of an example?"

"I wore a sweet crown at my Bar Mitzvah!" Henry Yurt broke in. He leaped up from his desk and held out his arms. "All hail King Yurt!"

The Trentini twins bowed, and the class broke into laughter.

The Apology

As the class compared what they all wore to birthday parties, dances, Easter services, Bar Mitzvahs, and even Halloween, Maeve slumped down in her seat. Her unvitations seemed to burn through the pink canvas of her book bag. She'd printed out more than a hundred copies last night on her computer. Enough to pass out to the whole seventh grade.

Maeve tried to imagine herself handing out the papers, and failed completely. With a sigh, she opened a new text file on her laptop.

♡...

Maeve's Notes to Self
1. *In the future, never EVER invite people to a party that doesn't exist.*
2. *Leave the unvitations in the cafeteria and hope people find them.*
3. *Move to France until this whole thing blows over.*
4. *Buy the Think Pink dress first. I bet they* adore *sequins in France!*

Maeve leaned back in her desk, visualizing her dress. . . . Well, the one that *would* be hers if she could just handle Austin for a few more afternoons.

When the bell rang, Maeve jumped, slightly caught off guard, then asked Isabel what the homework assignment had been.

"Didn't you hear?" Isabel wondered while the group walked out of the classroom.

"No, I was thinking"—Maeve reached into her backpack and slowly, painfully withdrew a stack of papers, which she then sadly handed to Isabel—"about these. I think I'll just leave them somewhere in the cafeteria."

Isabel nodded and gestured for the BSG and Sophie to follow her off to one side of the hallway where they could talk without anyone, especially not Anna and Joline, hearing.

Isabel thrust the unvitations out toward the others. "Maeve . . . made these . . . to . . . hand out." Isabel said loudly, over-pronouncing everything. The rest of the BSG got her secret meaning immediately. They had to stop Maeve from handing out the apology notes!

Katani took one of Maeve's unvitations and held it up.

"Very nice!" she complimented Maeve. "I like the fancy border, and the font makes it so classy."

"I figured if I was going to have to apologize," Maeve said with a small shrug, "I should do it with ultimate style and grace."

The girls passed one of Maeve's notes around.

MKT Productions Presents:
An Un-vitation

Starring: *Maeve Kaplan-Taylor!*

On May 9th, a celebration was
declared. A day of rejoicing and
festivities in honor of

Maeve's Bat Mitzvah

Although it was to be a party beyond
compare, tragically, due to unforseen
circumstances, we regret to inform you
that the party has been cancelled

Maeve offers her most sincere
apologies to all who are
hereby and forth with
un-vited

C'est la Vie!

"Wow! If I ever have to make unvitations, I'm putting you in charge!" Avery exclaimed.

"The French is a very *classique* touch," Sophie noted.

Charlotte put an arm around Maeve's shoulders. "You managed to write it so graciously."

Maeve smiled at her friends' approval. The cards *were* elegant. Just like something Scarlett O'Hara from *Gone with the Wind* would have written. So why did the mere thought of handing them out make Maeve's heart race and her palms go all sweaty?

"There are just a couple of, ummm, problems with the unvitations," Isabel said out of the blue.

Behind Maeve's back, Isabel opened her eyes wide, silently begging her friends for help.

"Um, yeah," Charlotte put in. "The borders are . . . black-and-white!" She groaned slightly at her own lame suggestion.

"They really should be in color," Sophie smoothly amended.

"I can help with that!" Isabel quickly offered. "I have colored pencils in my bag."

"And you spelled 'forth with' wrong. It's actually one word," Charlotte pointed out. "I can fix it without you even reprinting anything. I'll just write a dash in there on the copies."

"We can take care of these little fixes and hand them out for you later," Katani offered.

"Yeah," Avery put in. "So you don't have to just leave them in the cafeteria."

On the sly, Isabel winked at Katani while saying, "Don't worry. We're going to take care of all of it for you, Maeve!"

Maeve almost threw the entire stack of invitations in the air, like confetti, she was so happy! "You are the greatest BFFs EVER!" she gushed. "Thanks so so so so so much!" She hugged each of them in turn, then hurried off to switch her books for the next class.

"We'll be the greatest BFFs *if* we can pull off this party!" Isabel mentioned to the group once Maeve was out of hearing range.

"That's for sure," Avery agreed.

"Do you really think we can organize a surprise party in just one week?" Katani worried.

"We also have to figure out where to hide her unvitations," Charlotte put in.

"*C'est la vie!*" Sophie said with finality.

CHAPTER

14

Sophie Mania

When Charlotte and Sophie walked into the lunch-room, they were greeted by walls plastered with bright red and blue French Club posters and a surprising lunch menu.

Charlotte stared at the menu. *Whose idea was this?* She had planned to make *croque-monsieurs* for Sophie over the weekend! It was her specialty, and she even had all the ingredients already.

"Over here!" Avery waved from a spot near the end of a very long lunch line where she, Isabel, Maeve, and Katani had saved a spot. It seemed the entire school wanted to try the French food!

"I brought my lunch today, but I think I'd rather try that salad nick-oise thingy!" Avery announced.

"It's sah-lad nis-wahs," Sophie corrected. "And it's *délicieux*! But I will have a *croque-monsieur*, my favorite!"

Charlotte's mood sank. Would Sophie want to have the same lunch *again* this weekend?

Soupe à l'oignon
French onion soup

&

Salade niçoise
Salad with tuna and egg

&

Quiche du jour
Quiche of the day

&

Croque-monsieur
Hot ham and cheese sandwich

Betsy Fitzgerald waltzed into line behind the BSG. "What do you think?" she asked, eyes glittering. "I spent *hours* after school this week, talking to Mrs. Fields and the cafeteria staff. They finally agreed to kick off AAJH's very first French Club with a Parisian luncheon!"

"It's . . . ," Charlotte started.

"Fantabulawesome!" Maeve finished, making up a new word on the spot.

"I am feeling right at home!" Sophie smiled, and Charlotte sighed. Suddenly it felt as if the whole world were conspiring to tear Sophie away from her. *What happened to our friendship? It lasted even when there was a whole ocean between us!* Now Sophie was standing right next to Charlotte, but she might as well have been across the world. Charlotte shrank back against the wall as Sophie's fans crowded around, chirping with excitement about the menu and Betsy's new club. If Sophie was BFFs with everyone in the entire school, was there any room for Charlotte?

When the BSG finally got through the line, lunch was half over. Charlotte plopped down on the wiggly seat next to Avery, setting down a tray with a slightly soggy *croque-monsieur*. Sophie was lagging behind. Of course, everyone wanted her to sit with them. Right now Anna and Joline had her cornered by the snack machines.

"No, thank you, I already have a place to sit. Maybe next time?" Charlotte overheard Sophie say.

Help! I'm losing my oldest friend, and I don't know what to do, Charlotte cried out inside as Sophie seated herself across the table, between Katani and Maeve. There was a group of scarf-clad girls forming a sort of line, waiting to talk to her. *What happened to the special week we were going to spend together, just us? Like it always was before?* Charlotte smooshed up her face and stared at her lunch.

"Char, what's bugging you?" Isabel asked, taking a bite of her quiche.

"Nothing," Charlotte grumped, poking at her soggy ham and cheese. If she'd made *croque-monsieurs* for everyone, they would have been perfect.

"Doesn't seem like nothing to me," Katani prodded, worried.

I didn't know I was so transparent, Charlotte thought. "It's nothing, really." She couldn't tell them how neglected she was feeling with Sophie sitting right there!

"Okay." Avery shrugged. "Just tell us when you're ready. No frowns allowed in the Scarfless Wonders Club!" Avery stood up in her seat and leaned over the table to tap Sophie on the shoulder. "Speaking of eating, are you going to finish the rest of your croak-monsore?" Avery was obviously never going to learn the intricacies of French pronunciation. She rubbed her belly. "It looks yum."

Charlotte noticed that Sophie was having trouble eating anyway, what with so many admirers gathered to speak to her. Her lunch had barely been touched when Sophie passed it over to Avery.

"Did you see my posters? I have handouts, too." Betsy had made it through the lunch line, and now cut into the Sophie line, balancing a bowl of soup on her tray with one hand as she passed out papers with the other. She looked even more serious than usual, wearing a dark blue silk scarf with a button-down shirt.

Katani managed to snag one of the papers and read it out loud to the BSG. "'Come learn the language of love! AAJH's first official French Language Club begins at three o'clock today in the social studies room. Hosted by club president Betsy Fitzgerald, with special guests Mrs. Fields and Sophie Morel.'"

"I thought we were going to the art museum after school today?" Isabel glanced at Charlotte, who nodded. It was written in on Katani's schedule.

Sophie didn't even bat an eye. "There will be time!" she said cheerfully.

"First, we *all* have to learn the language of love!" Maeve gushed. "There are sooo many fabulous old movies in French. Have you guys ever seen *La Belle et la Bête*, the first and greatest *Beauty and the Beast* film?"

The BSG shook their heads at Maeve's movie obsession. This happened almost every day, and they'd never once heard of any of the movies she mentioned, unless she'd brought one to a sleepover.

"*I'll* be in your club, Fitzgerald!" Dillon tossed in. He'd been hovering near the Sophie line, as if trying to get up the courage to talk to the Queen of Chic. "I can't wait to speak-a-ze French," he said in the nutty accent he'd somehow acquired during social studies.

"You can't wait to *parler français*," Sophie gently corrected Dillon, causing him to blush yet again.

Avery swallowed the last bite of Sophie's abandoned

lunch and thought, *If Dillon doesn't get control of himself soon, his face might turn red permanently.* She laughed to herself, picturing his face like a tomato.

"Oh, no you don't, Betsy!" Anna came rushing up. Joline was hot on her heels. They pushed and shoved their way through the crowd to get to Sophie.

"Joline and I already started a French club. Ours are the *red* signs. We're meeting after school today, and Sophie is coming to *our* meeting!" Anna gave Sophie her sugary-sweet smile.

"*S'il vous plaît,*" Joline added with wide puppy eyes directed straight at Sophie. "It's a French fashion club!"

With a small spin, Joline showed off the paisley-patterned yellow and beige scarf she was wearing. Anna had on the exact same one, and they were both tied off to the side, exactly how Sophie had taught Maeve to tie hers.

"*Très chic?* Don't you think?" Anna asked, flipping the end of her scarf over her shoulder.

Sophie paused, as if mulling it over, then declared, "Yes, very nice."

All the girls in the crowd murmured in agreement, as if they'd been waiting for Sophie's reaction . . . not hanging on Anna's every word, like usual.

"Come *on.*" Betsy turned around and threw up her hands at the crowd. "Sophie is way too smart for you. She would rather be involved in instructing linguistics than presenting fashion to a bunch of copycats."

Charlotte wondered which club Sophie had agreed to be involved with. Or had she agreed to both? The look on Sophie's face was fading from permanently cheery to something more worried as the push and pull escalated.

"You stole our idea," Anna accused Betsy. "We had our French fashion club going before you started your lame language one."

"Linguistics," Joline mocked the word that Betsy used. "What does that even mean?"

"It's the study of language," Betsy replied. "Not that the two of you even know English very well!"

"You are *so* not invited to our fashion club," Anna snipped.

Betsy stepped closer to Anna. "You couldn't make me join your club if you begged."

"Paix!" Sophie clapped her hands once and stood up between a serious-looking Betsy and the pouting QOM. "That means 'peace' and is the first word we learn today." Sophie put her hands on her hips. "There is no reason to argue. *Non.* We will have both. Fashion club and *Français* club! Today after school, okay?"

Betsy and Anna glared at each other for another long moment, then stalked away. But the buzz in the crowd was palpable. Everyone wanted to know who was going to which club! And how would Sophie come to both?

"She'll have to switch back and forth," one girl said to her friend.

"Or maybe they'll have the clubs back-to-back," the friend answered.

Katani mouthed to the BSG, "No time for the art museum?"

Isabel nodded. "It's okay," she mouthed back. She could go to the museum any old day, but Sophie was only here to teach them French and fashion for one more week!

Charlotte sighed. She'd much rather head on over to a museum with her friends than hang out in the background at school while everyone worshipped Sophie. But what could she do? It looked like the BSG had made their decision. Katani was even debating with Maeve whether they should go to the fashion club! *How could they even think of joining a club that the QOM started? That's just asking for trouble!* The whole world seemed to be turning inside out and upside down.

Sitting at the table, head in hands, Charlotte began to wonder if anyone remembered her existence at all. *I could lead a French club,* Charlotte thought. *I'm fluent, just like Sophie. But no one ever asked me.* It was so confusing. One minute Charlotte was worried about Sophie fitting in with the BSG. The next . . . Sophie was taking AAJH by storm and leaving the BSG and her in the dust.

One Rare Tulip

Charlotte cleared her lunch tray, alone, feeling her throat tighten. *I won't cry,* she told herself. *I feel absolutely miserable, but I won't!*

"Charlotte," Ms. O'Reilly called her name as she set her tray down at the window. "Have a moment?"

Charlotte shrugged. "Sure."

Ms. O'Reilly, who was on lunch duty that day, brought

Charlotte to a quiet corner of the cafeteria and said, "So, your friend has become quite popular, hmmm?"

Charlotte shrugged. "I know."

The kind social studies teacher patted an empty on-duty teacher seat. "I've been watching you and Sophie, and I have a story you might like to hear."

A story? Charlotte's mind instantly raced to Orangina's story. He was still stuck at the end of a dark tunnel, about to open a mysterious door. Hopefully Ms. O'Reilly's story was happier than that. "Okay," she said, although she felt a little like a teacher's pet sitting over here. *Not that anyone would notice. . . .*

"Sometimes," Ms. O'Reilly began, "people go crazy over something because it's new and different. But then, when the craze is over, everyone is left wondering what happened."

It didn't take a brain surgeon to realize that this was no random story Ms. O'Reilly was telling. *She's talking about Sophie,* Charlotte realized. She recalled her own first days in Australia, Tanzania, and Paris. She'd been new and different and sort of cool for a little while . . . until she ruined everything with the inevitable klutz attack.

Charlotte was drawn out of her thoughts when Ms. O'Reilly's story took a strange turn into world history. "In the early seventeenth century, the tulip was new to Holland. It didn't take long, though, before everyone saw how pretty and wonderful and *chic* the flower was." Ms. O'Reilly smiled warmly at Charlotte. "Suddenly the flower became very, very popular. So popular, in fact, that bulbs sold for incredibly high prices—thousands of florins."

"What's a florin? Their money?" Charlotte asked.

"Yes. And a normal yearly salary in Holland at the time was only three hundred florins! But the fancier and rarer bulbs you owned, the more you could sell them for and the better your status was in society."

I get it now. Charlotte considered. *Sophie is a rare tulip.* "So is that all? Everyone just bought more and more tulips?" *I wonder how the roses felt. . . .* Charlotte thought.

"Well," Ms. O'Reilly went on. "By the end of 1636, there was total tulip mania in Holland. Traders earned more money than they ever imagined. People all over were clamoring to get better and fresher and brighter flowers. But fads don't last forever."

Ms. O'Reilly paused dramatically.

"There were too many tulips?" Charlotte guessed.

"Exactly. And Charlotte, what happens where there are too many of the same thing? Too many copycats?"

"Ummm . . . ," Charlotte replied. The bell rang, and kids flooded around her, out of the lunch room. Scarves of all shades and patterns fluttered past like tulip petals.

"Crazes never last," Ms. O'Reilly finished her story. "Tulip prices fell, and people lost their entire savings. It was a horrible tulip crash."

"Thanks for the story, Ms. O'Reilly."

Charlotte left the cafeteria feeling a bit lighter and more at peace with the whole situation. Sooner or later, the Sophie mania would die down. *And I'll be there for her when it's over,* Charlotte thought. She had a quote above her writing desk at home: "A real friend is someone who walks in when the rest of the world walks out.—Walter Winchell." And Charlotte intended to stay Sophie's real friend, no matter what happened.

As she made her way to class by herself, Charlotte felt freer than she had in days. She loved her friends and would always be there for them if they needed her, but right now no one really did, and that was okay. A little extra bounce snuck into her step as she realized exactly what *she* needed most: a place to be just by herself.

I'm not going to go to either of Sophie's clubs, Charlotte decided. *She can handle this on her own, and I'd like some time to curl up with Marty, a good book, and maybe work on "Orangina's Travels."* She had a new idea now, inspired by the tulips.

Overbooked

After school Maeve met up with Katani, Avery, and Isabel by her locker. Sophie was busy arranging things with Betsy and Anna for the clubs, and no one knew exactly where Charlotte had gone to. *She's probably with Sophie,* Maeve decided. *They are such cute friends! I love it when they speak French. . . .*

That reminded her.

"Um, I can't go to French club," Maeve said.

"Ohhh . . . right! The monster child," Isabel sympathized. Maeve had IM'ed the entire horrifying story the night before.

"Well, he's not so bad now. I think we're kind of

friends." Maeve grabbed her babysitting stuff out of her locker. "Plus I brought a whole bag of M&M's to bribe him with! If it goes well, they might want me to sit again next week."

"Ahhh, very interesting." Katani gave the others a look that meant that this was very good news.

Maeve was oblivious to the glances her friends were passing behind her back and over her head. "Well, have fun at the French clubs!" She pranced toward the door, then turned around.

"Hey, no one's said anything about my unvitations yet," Maeve stated. "Do you think they're mad at me?"

"No!" Isabel barked, a little too abruptly. "I mean, not at all. We haven't handed them out yet."

"We will at the clubs," Avery added.

"And we won't let *anyone* get angry!" Katani finished.

Maeve shrugged and dashed out the door. She wanted enough time to make a very important stop on her way to Austin's house—a stop at Think Pink.

Pink Panic

The dress looked even more gorgeous on than it had in the window! Ms. Rose, the saleslady, held both hands up with thumbs circled into the A-OK symbol. Ms. Razzberry Pink made all her associates change their names to something pink-related while they were working. Maeve thought that was one of the most fabulous ideas ever! *When I'm a famous actress, I might go by Ms. Magenta Kaplan-Taylor sometimes, just for the glamour!*

"I love it!" Maeve announced, spinning around in the pink sequined gown. With this dress on, she figured she could go by any name in the world and she'd still turn heads.

"Shall I box it up for you?" Ms. Rose asked, and Maeve turned the shade of the saleslady's name. All she had in her pocket was the $40 from yesterday's babysitting, plus the $31 she had saved up. She still needed to earn $118!

"Can I put it on hold?"

The saleslady shook her head. "I'm sorry; it's the only dress we have left in this style! They've practically flown out of here. Perhaps you could come back later with your mother? When she sees how beautiful you look, I'm sure she'll want you to have it!" Ms. Rose smiled.

Maeve nodded, a lump rising in her throat. "Okay. I'll come back."

"We'll just put it back in the window, then," Ms. Rose cautioned. "Hurry back! And have a nice day." Ms. Rose waved as Maeve ducked out the door, clutching her babysitting bag with white knuckles. She *needed* that dress, and time was running out!

CHAPTER
15

Sworn to Secrecy

"Come on, Austin, it's homework time." Maeve carried Austin's backpack to the dining room table where she'd already laid out pencils, a glass of water, and some M&M's to use as rewards.

"Awww, Maeve, do I have to?" Austin grumped, dragging his feet as he entered the room. "I was practicing a hip-hop beat on Riley's bongo."

Even though Riley had given Austin the drum, he still insisted that he was just borrowing it and he'd give it back soon.

"Sorry, Charlie." Maeve ruffled Austin's hair. "You can go back to playing drums after homework."

When Maeve first brought up the idea of a designated half hour for homework, she'd offered to do her own work at the same time. Austin seemed to like that idea— especially when Maeve groaned about how long homework always took her and how hard math was. It was like they had something in common.

"But I hate reading," Austin complained.

"And I don't like math at all." Maeve pouted like she was also in second grade, then brightened up. "But we're both going to try!"

Maeve pulled out her math book and stared at the page. Because of her dyslexia, it took a lot of time to figure out word problems. So she started with a worksheet of simple calculations.

"Maeve, what's this say?" Austin asked, looking up from the story he was reading.

"Read me the sentence," Maeve instructed, not knowing what he meant.

"The . . . bird . . . fway . . . few . . . flew? . . . far away," Austin read slowly.

Maeve took a look at the sentence he was pointing to. He'd totally skipped over the word "orange," then tripped over "flew." Maeve's eyes grew wide. She thought about Austin's completely out-of-control behavior the last time she babysat, especially when it came time for schoolwork. *Could it be?* An idea was forming, but Maeve wasn't sure.

Maeve wrote a line of words in her math notebook. Some were real words, but others were made up.

"Austin, try reading these," she instructed.

He did okay with most of the real words, but when it came to the fake ones, his face got all red and he jumped up from the table. "No! No! No!" he shouted.

Maeve quickly closed her notebook and held out a handful of M&M's. "It's okay! We won't do any more right now," she soothed him.

Maeve had Austin read the rest of his book out loud, and at the end, asked him a few questions about what had happened. He couldn't answer. Maeve remembered when she was in first grade, struggling to make it through pages and pages of letters. It used all her energy to sound out the words, leaving her no extra brain space to understand the story.

The way Austin was acting was painfully familiar. *What if Austin is dyslexic too?* That would explain his problems with reading. And it might even explain some of his behavior: If he acted out, his teachers and parents would focus on dealing with that before they'd make him read.

When Maeve's parents finally got her tested for a learning difference, she'd gone through hours of special education and tutoring—in fact, she *still* had tutors. But finally she'd gotten to a point where she at least knew what her strengths and weaknesses were and how to approach her homework without completely shutting down.

I've had dyslexia my whole life, and I'm okay! Maeve realized. *It may take me a little longer to do my homework, but I've figured out how to get by. I bet I could help Austin figure it out too!*

"Hey, Austin," she said, playfully snagging his book away. "Let's play a game." She pushed her own homework aside. "You read a sentence, then I'll read it back to you, and you'll repeat it one more time. And after that, we'll act it out together. We can make up funny voices or actions, or even wear costumes if you want."

"Yay! I'm coming right back!" Austin jumped up and

disappeared for so long, Maeve was worried he'd locked himself in the bathroom again. But finally he returned with a pile of silly hats.

Maeve plopped a plastic fireman's hat on her head and Austin put on a Darth Vader mask. He was supposed to be a cat, not Darth Vader, but Maeve wasn't about to get picky! Austin tripped through the first sentence, and Maeve read it back patiently. "The chestnut tree in the front yard was Terrance the cat's favorite place."

By the time the Franklins came home, Austin understood the whole story, he had answered all his workbook questions about it, and he'd had a wonderful afternoon. In fact, "homework half hour" lasted nearly two hours!

"Mom! Dad! Guess what? I know the whole story—by heart! Want to hear it? Want me to read it to you?" Austin was beaming.

After promising Austin they'd be right back, the Franklins walked Maeve to the door. "I've never seen him so excited about homework. And he's never wanted to read me *anything* before," Mrs. Franklin commented with a smile as she paid Maeve.

"I think," Maeve began tentatively, "well, that is, from my personal experience, Mrs. Franklin, I have the feeling that just maybe Austin might have a learning difference."

The Franklins' faces changed from overjoyed to confused. Maeve hurried to explain. "I'm dyslexic, see, and it seemed like Austin might have more fun if I made reading into a game. Like a play. That's how I always have to do it. And it worked!" Maeve was beaming.

Mr. Franklin nodded thoughtfully and turned to his wife. "The school did recommend testing. . . ."

"We'll discuss this later," she shushed him. "Maeve, dear, whatever you did worked wonders. Would you be interested in tutoring and babysitting next week?" Mrs. Franklin asked.

Maeve was thrilled. For the first time in her life she could be the tutor instead of the tutee. "Coolio!" she said, in way of an answer.

"Is that a yes?" Mr. Franklin asked with a warm smile.

"I'd love it!" Maeve agreed.

I can't believe MKT, the girl with the most tutors in the universe, is going to BE a tutor! Maeve thought excitedly. She skipped happily the rest of the way home, touching the money in her pocket. She'd counted all the money six times already: $121 total. As she passed her dream dress in the Think Pink window—the only one left in that exact style—Maeve blew it a kiss.

The Secret Committee

While Maeve was babysitting, Avery, Katani, and Isabel were headed to Maeve's house on a secret mission.

"Quoi de neuf?" Isabel practiced her French.

"What's that mean?" Avery tried to remember.

"'What's new?'" Katani swung her orange scarf over her shoulder and picked up the pace to keep up with Avery. She may have been almost a foot taller than Avery, but her legs weren't nearly as fast!

"*Bien sûr.* Of course," Isabel agreed. The first meeting of Betsy's French Club had been productive and fun, especially with Mrs. Fields there helping out. Katani's grandmother had a knack for keeping kids focused. Sophie had bounced back and forth between the two clubs, and so had Katani.

"I hope Charlotte's okay," Katani remarked. She had noticed Charlotte was missing the first time she switched clubs. She tried to tell Sophie, but it was impossible to talk to her with everyone clamoring for her attention.

"Char's pretty bummed about Sophie mania," Avery put it bluntly.

The other BSG nodded. They had called Charlotte from Katani's phone as soon as they realized she was missing, and she'd told them the whole story. But none of them really knew Sophie well enough to confront her about what was going on, and Charlotte didn't want them to, anyway. She was hoping it would all "crash like the tulips." Whatever that meant.

"They're going out for Mexican tonight, right?" Isabel remembered telling Sophie about her favorite restaurant in the Boston area—the only one that made tortillas that could even measure up to her mother's cooking.

"Yeah, I think that's right." Katani nodded. So far, Sophie and the Ramseys hadn't followed her detailed schedule at *all*. It annoyed Katani's sense of organization, but she told herself it would all work out in the end.

"I wish they could have joined our secret mission." Avery kicked a stone along the sidewalk as she pulled ahead of the group again. The Movie House was just ahead.

Katani sighed. "I'm beginning to think this is mission: impossible. How can we pull this off without asking anyone for money?"

No one got a chance to answer because Ms. Kaplan turned into the driveway and stepped out of her car with her briefcase. Sam hopped out of the backseat, hugging a brand-new plastic soldier set.

"Hi, girls," Maeve's mom greeted, and turned back to get some groceries out of the car.

"We'll help you," Isabel offered. The girls each picked up a canvas bag and followed Ms. Kaplan upstairs into the duplex.

"Maeve's babysitting right now, but I appreciate the help," Maeve's mom thanked them as she started putting away the groceries.

"We actually came to talk to you," Katani said.

"Look out troops, bombs away!" Sam shouted, disappearing into his bedroom with his new toy.

"What's going on, girls? Is there a problem?" Ms. Kaplan folded her arms, waiting for an answer.

"Well . . ." Isabel twisted a strand of hair around one finger, hoping Sam was distracted enough by his soldiers that he wouldn't listen in.

"We want to throw a party," Avery blurted out. "For Maeve."

Ms. Kaplan nodded curtly and sat down. Katani explained the whole story—how Maeve broke down in tears at Montoya's, how hard she'd worked on Project Thread and on learning her Hebrew; and how much they all wanted to honor her on her special day.

"I know you and Maeve agreed to have just a luncheon with family," Katani finished. "But our party would be *after* that. It wouldn't be super fancy. And we'd take care of everything ourselves." She crossed her fingers behind her back.

"I don't know," Ms. Kaplan said, looking at the faces of the three eager girls. "It is so kind of you to think of such a thing, and I'm touched that you would do this for Maeve. But I already told her no. I think it would cost more money than you realize. And even if that weren't the case, I'm afraid there isn't much time to pull something like this together."

Katani's heart sank. That's what *she* was afraid of too.

"But we already have all these plans!" Isabel thrust out a notebook full of Katani's lists of things to do. "And I know lots of people would want to help out."

Ms. Kaplan looked through the notebook, and made a *hmmm* sound. "You know," she said. "I told Maeve she couldn't have a big party for two reasons. One, I wanted to teach her that becoming a Bat Mitzvah isn't about huge, fancy, glittery parties. It's about community service and tradition. Second, there seem to be a lot of people who spend a tremendous amount of money on the party." Ms. Kaplan paused. "I personally can't afford or support such an extravagant show of wealth. And sometimes I worry that it sends the wrong message to the kids and takes the focus off of the ceremony. *That* should be the focal point of the experience. I mean, when else does a thirteen-year-old get the opportunity to show how hard she has worked and to display her knowledge of her own religion in front of her community?"

The girls stood stunned for a moment, not entirely sure how to respond to this lecture. Was it a yes or a no? Avery fidgeted, shifting her weight from one leg to the other.

Finally Isabel spread her hands in front of her. "Maeve keeps talking about how much work she's doing and how responsible she feels about everything."

Katani added, "And we're really happy that the work Maeve started at Jeri's Place is going to count for her community service project."

"And we want to celebrate all this with a surprise party, community style!" Avery cheered. "You know, with everyone pitching in."

"It'd be a kind of potluck after-party party," Katani explained.

Ms. Kaplan nodded. "Believe it or not, you're beginning to convince me. But *where* are you planning on—"

"Sam!" Isabel suddenly cried out. "We have a spy!" Sam was peeking from behind the partially opened door into the living room with a plastic soldier clenched in one hand.

"Oh, dear." Maeve's mother sighed. "Sam isn't very good at keeping secrets, but . . ." Just then, the phone rang. "Hold on, girls, I'll be right back." Ms. Kaplan picked up the phone and wandered off into her office.

"Sam, come here," Katani ordered.

"No way!" Sam yelped, running down the hall toward his room. "Retreat, troops!" he shouted as he dashed away.

But Avery was faster than a retreating soldier. She quickly caught up, gently tackled Sam to the floor, and tickled him. He giggled as he struggled to get away again.

"I'll let you up," Avery said, "as soon as you promise you will keep this a secret."

"I will *not* promise," Sam declared, squirming around, trying to get up.

"Then I can't let you go," Avery said with a sinister grin. She tickled him some more.

"Okay, okay!" Sam begged to be let up. "I'll keep your stinky secret. But I get the biggest piece of cake at the party."

"Pinkie swear?" Avery made him link pinkie fingers and shake on it.

"I promise." Sam shook eagerly.

Multitalented Multitasking

Ring! Ring!

Charlotte leaped up the stairs two at a time. They'd just gotten back from the Mexican restaurant, and the phone was ringing upstairs. She kicked off her fancy shoes— they'd been squishing her toes all through dinner—and picked up the phone. *Maybe it's Nick!* She could really use a friendly voice after her long day at school. Sophie hadn't said anything about Charlotte skipping out on the clubs, and she wasn't sure what that meant.

"Hello?" Charlotte answered as her dad and Sophie came into the kitchen, chatting with each other in French.

"It's Betsy Fitzgerald! Did you get my e-mail?"

"No, not yet. We were—"

Charlotte's cell phone buzzed. She flipped it open to look at the text message.

Kgirl: need u on IM asap!!!

"Just a sec," Charlotte told Betsy and carried the phone into her room, where a scattering of IM windows and a "you have new mail" message greeted her.

"I'd like to take Sophie into Boston tomorrow to see the USS *Constitution* museum," Betsy chattered. "I think the history and atmosphere . . ." Charlotte spaced out Betsy's next few sentences as she opened up her e-mail and gasped at the number of messages in her in-box. Seventeen! And they'd only been gone for two hours! "Okay," Charlotte answered a question Betsy had just asked, even though she wasn't entirely sure what it was. Her IM windows were all flashing!

Charlotte clicked on the top one. It was from Chelsea.

shutterbug: Want 2 go hiking 2mro w BFF?

Charlotte looked around for Sophie. *She must still be in the kitchen.* Oh well, Charlotte had already planned on hiking with Nick. Chelsea could just come too.

skywriter: you can join nick and us

shutterbug: gr8

"Hello? Hello?" Betsy's voice crackled out of the receiver. "Is that okay?"

"Yes! Sounds great. Bye," Charlotte clicked the phone off and looked in her e-mail in-box. Over half of the messages were from kids she didn't even *know*.

Sophie wandered in from the hallway with two bottles of nail polish. "Pink or gold? What would your friend Katani say?"

Katani! That reminded Charlotte. She needed to talk to Kgirl on IM!

"Ummm . . . gold?" Charlotte answered Sophie as she clicked through the IM windows. Finally she found the right one.

> **Kgirl:** u back yet?
> **Kgirl:** i have secret party-planning
> committee news!!!

Charlotte was about to type "what?" but Chelsea's window flashed and popped on top of Katani's.

> **shutterbug:** where r we hiking? mom
> wants 2 know
> **skywriter:** 1 sec need to ask nick

Charlotte quickly typed in Nick's IM name and clicked in the box to type her question. Just after she hit enter, she realized she was in the wrong window!

> **skywriter:** where r we hiking 2mro?
> chels wants to come with
> **Kgirl:** ??? schedule says horseback
> riding 2mro! i called the stable
> already
> **skywriter:** Right. brb.

Then Charlotte realized the problem. Nick wasn't

online! She opened up her e-mail, ignoring the pile-up of unread messages, and began to type.

She'd only made it halfway through the first sentence when the phone rang.

"Hello?" Charlotte held the phone on her other shoulder—her neck was getting sore! But she actually managed to finish typing her e-mail to Nick and press send while she was talking.

"Is Sophie there?"

Oh, great. It was Joline Kaminsky. Charlotte could have recognized her voice anywhere. "It's for you." She held out the phone, but Sophie just lifted one freshly nail-polished hand helplessly. *Oh, great. Now I get to chat with the QOM . . .,* Charlotte thought, starting to get annoyed.

"Who is it?" Sophie asked.

"Joline. She wants to meet you at the mall tomorrow." Charlotte passed on the message.

"Magnifique!" Sophie exclaimed.

Joline overheard. "Great!" she squeaked.

Charlotte could hear Anna giggling in the background. "Ummm—," Charlotte started, realizing that they now had some historical thing with Betsy, hiking, horseback riding, and the mall scheduled all for one day! But Anna and Joline had already hung up. Things were getting way out of control! *I wish the two of us could just spend time together,* Charlotte bemoaned. *She was my friend first, wasn't she?* She sighed and clicked on her e-mail. *What else can go wrong?*

The first four messages were all from Julie Faber, the

girl who hadn't invited Avery to her birthday bash back in the fall. Now Julie wanted Sophie to come to a pool party this weekend. She didn't say anything about whether Charlotte or the other BSG were invited. Charlotte was speechless! *Does anyone even remember that I'm the reason Sophie came to Boston? That I've been her BFF for years?* She didn't know how to reply to Julie's request, so she didn't.

The e-mails were endless—one was from a shy girl Charlotte barely knew, written in butchered French, and then there was a message from Jennifer, the newspaper editor, requesting that Charlotte write an article on "Paris Fever" for the school paper. Personally, Charlotte thought "French Mania" was a better title, but she didn't have time to reply that she'd rather write about mold growing than cover "Paris Fever" because *all* of her IM windows were flashing again! This was crazy!!! Riley's IM was on top, so Charlotte clicked on it first.

> **GuitarRockStar:** band needs BFF's
> help tom
> **skywriter:** ???
> **GuitarRockStar:** need 2 work on new
> french lyrics
> **GuitarRockStar:** k?

Charlotte glanced over at Sophie, who was blithely applying a second coat of gold polish. "Mustard Monkey needs your help with lyrics. They're this band at school," Charlotte reported.

"But of course I will help!" Sophie answered.

Charlotte shrugged and typed "ok."

It was like she had lost her own identity! *Sophie, Sophie, Sophie! Everyone wants Sophie! What am I, her social secretary?* Charlotte griped to herself.

Just then, an e-mail arrived from Nick to brighten Charlotte's mood a little bit.

```
To: Charlotte
From: Nick
Subject: RE: Hiking


Psyched to hike!!! I'll stop by in the
a.m. Need sunscreen, hats, bottles of
water. Planning to take the skyline
trail.
See ya,
Nick
```

"Nick's coming over in the morning," Charlotte told Sophie. "So, we've got hiking, the mall, band lyrics, and what am I forgetting?"

"It all sounds *magnifique*." Sophie smiled, then yawned.

Charlotte suddenly wanted to leap out of her desk chair and run out of the room, leaving Sophie to handle all her obsessed admirers on her own! *Aughhh! This is ridiculous!* Charlotte shouted inside. Then she saw that Katani was still waiting on IM to hear back. She took three deep breaths. *Okay. Calm down. You can handle this.*

Ding-da-ding-dum-dum . . . A tinny version of JT's

number-one hit song played from inside Charlotte's jacket pocket.

Her cell. Charlotte took it out and stared at it for a second, like it was poisonous, then answered. "Hello?" she snapped.

"Uhhh . . . I think I have the wrong number."

"No, Dillon. This is Charlotte."

There was a long pause on the other end of the line, and finally Dillon said, "Uhhh . . . Is Sophie there?"

Charlotte handed the phone over as her calm disappeared and she started to seethe. No way was she taking another message for her popular friend! Especially not from a boy. Thankfully, Sophie was done with her nails and took the phone carefully.

"You want to invite me to play soccer?" Charlotte overheard. "Ahhh, but I have not the right shoes!"

This better not be another Saturday activity. . . . Charlotte winced. She couldn't believe it. The way things were going, they'd have to literally make a hundred clones of Sophie to get through the weekend! Charlotte, for one, couldn't handle so many people and plans crammed into two very short days. *But if Sophie wants to do all of it, let her figure it out,* Charlotte thought bitterly. Sophie was the Queen of Chic. A rock star. A tulip.

The "tulip" laughed with a musical, cheery sound. "Ahhh, but of course! See you!" And she hung up.

"Okay, that's it," Charlotte announced.

"That's what?" Sophie answered, stretching out on her cot.

"I'm not answering the phone, writing e-mails, or IMing for the rest of the weekend!" Charlotte proclaimed. "You're totally booked, and we haven't even made it through Saturday night! Ugh!" Spontaneously, Charlotte reached over and shut down her computer. The monitor went dark and all the flashing IM windows disappeared. The sudden black emptiness of the screen somehow made her feel a little better.

"This will, how do you say, work itself out in the morning," Sophie promised.

Charlotte wished she could believe her.

16

Too Many BFFs

The slam of a car door made Charlotte roll over in bed. *Am I still dreaming?* she wondered as voices drifted up from the driveway.

"What are *you* doing here?" There was no mistaking Anna's shrill tones.

"Sophie's going to the USS *Constitution* with me," Betsy responded, keeping her cool.

"No, she isn't!" Joline scoffed. "She's going to the mall. With *us.*"

"That can't be right. Sophie's going hiking!" Charlotte recognized Nick's voice and started to realize that maybe this wasn't just a weird dream. She sat up slightly, blinking the sleep out of her eyes.

"Hiking? You've got to be kidding. That's sooo lame. Sophie is totally too cool for that." Anna didn't sound impressed.

"What?" Nick countered. "She said she'd go a couple days ago. And Charlotte e-mailed me a definite yes last night."

"That's weird," Betsy retorted. "I *called* Charlotte, and she said Sophie was free."

Uh-oh. Charlotte glanced over at Sophie, who was still fast asleep on her cot. The Queen of Chic was curled up in a ball with her dark hair sticking out wildly in all directions. *If her admirers could see her now,* Charlotte thought. *It would be really embarrassing!*

Outside, a new voice joined the conversation. "What are you all doing here?!"

It was Katani. Charlotte tiptoed to the window and looked out. Cars were lined up and down the street, a few idling and sending up plumes of exhaust. Kids from school swarmed the front lawn, like locusts. *Or maybe a bouquet of tulips,* Charlotte mused. Her still-tired brain imagined them all instantly transformed into flowers. Maybe then they'd quiet down and quit all the arguing.

"It's all set. Sophie's going horseback riding with me," Katani told the crowd. "Look, it's on the schedule!" She held up a copy of her detailed itinerary that Sophie hadn't followed at all, and Charlotte felt a stab of guilt. Katani had worked hard on that schedule, but so far the only thing they'd actually done on it was the welcome party in the Tower!

"Umm, she's supposed to help Mustard Monkey with some lyrics, too." Riley joined the fray.

"And she's coming to my party!" Julie Faber hopped out of her mother's convertible.

"This is ridiculous," Betsy started. "Absolutely ridicu—"

Anna cut her off as she marched toward the door. A QOM on a mission. "Why don't you all clear out?"

Inside, Charlotte rushed over and shook the lump named Sophie. "Sophie, your, um"—she searched for the right word—"your *BFFs*, I mean, uhhh, all of them, are here."

Sophie sat up, eyes wide. "*Combien?* How many?"

"Oh, not too many." Charlotte couldn't keep the sarcasm out of her voice. She had held it in so long. "Remember all those people calling and IMing last night? Well, they all showed up. All thirty of them."

"Thirty?! What do they want?" Sophie looked ready to panic.

The voices outside combined with Anna's insistent knocking on the door created a cacophony of noise, and Charlotte lost it.

"I can't handle this!" she shouted. It was totally unlike her to yell, and Sophie shrank back. "*Everyone* is here to do a million different things with you, so go, have fun." Exasperated and overwhelmed, Charlotte collapsed back onto her bed.

Sophie drifted over to the window and put a hand to her mouth when she saw the crowd outside. "But this is crazy! I cannot do this!"

"Sooophie! Where are you?" A voice called from outside. At that point Charlotte didn't even care who it was.

Sophie backed away from the window and put her hands over her ears. "Please, Char. Make them go away! I don't want to disappoint anyone, but I am at my ends."

"What?" Charlotte got up and pulled the shade down over the window so hard, the cord snapped back up like a snake striking. "I thought you *liked* all this attention."

Sophie's voice was very small. "I just wanted to make everyone happy and be nice to all your friends so they would like me. Wasn't that what you wanted? And now, *c'est une catastrophe! Aide-moi*, Charlotte, you have to help me! I'm so sorry for everything, *mon amie*."

For the first time since Sophie arrived, the French fashionista wasn't dressed up, surrounded by look-alikes, or trying to impress anyone. She was sleepy and had a terrible case of bed head. Right then, Charlotte realized that her friend was still the Sophie she'd always known.

And she's even more upset than I am about this insanity! Charlotte thought, finally understanding what was happening. It wasn't totally fair for her to get so mad at Sophie because it really wasn't her fault. "It's okay, Sophie. I *knew* this was coming. And I think tulip mania is about to crash."

"I do not understand. Tulip mania? Is this a special phrase, like 'easy as pie'?"

Before Charlotte could explain, her dad knocked on the door. "Umm, Char? There are quite a few people here to see you. Were you planning something? Because you know, I'd like to hear about these things ahead of time."

Charlotte took a deep breath, telling herself, *I made this mess by not dealing with things yesterday. It's my responsibility to clean it up.*

"Charlotte?" her dad repeated. "Please explain. Now."

"I'm just getting dressed, Dad. I'll be right out." Charlotte pulled on a pair of jean shorts and a T-shirt, and slipped her bare feet into a pair of fuzzy purple slippers.

"I'll take care of everything, Sophie," she promised. Then she ducked out the door and down the stairs.

But when Charlotte grabbed the knob to swing open the front door and face the tulip swarm, she was yanked swiftly forward. Anna had given up waiting for someone to answer her knocks and had pulled open the door with such force that Charlotte went flying!

"Auuughhh!" Charlotte yelped as she fell forward, crashing right into Joline, who teetered into Katani, who toppled over onto Isabel, Avery, Chelsea, Julie, Nick, Riley, and Dillon! It was like the world's strangest game of dominoes, and for once in her life, Charlotte wasn't the only one lying on the ground, feeling like an idiot.

Anna McMasters, the only one still standing, surveyed the scene with her usual haughty air. As she came running down the steps, probably to make some final biting remark, she was suddenly yanked to the ground by her fancy peach-colored scarf, which had somehow managed to get snagged on the metal railing!

Charlotte couldn't help it. She started laughing and couldn't stop. Somehow she managed to get up and shout in a voice loud enough for everyone to hear, "Due to unforeseen circumstances, Sophie Morel is closed for the day." And with that, Charlotte stepped back into the house and slammed the door shut.

Secret Messages

Oh. Wait . . . the BSG! Charlotte turned back around, staring at the door for a second. There was no way she could open it again. Not without inviting the swarm inside.

Then she had an idea.

Charlotte peered through the mail slot. Everyone was shouting at one another while Katani struggled to get things organized. Anna was sulking off to one side, Julie's mother had dragged her back to the car, and Betsy's dad was trying to get Katani's attention.

The only person close enough to notice a spy in the mail slot was Nick.

"Hey," Charlotte whispered. No response. A little louder, "Nick!"

He turned around, unsure where the voice was coming from.

"Over here." Charlotte flipped the small metal door back and forth a few times so that it clanged softly.

"Charlotte?" He walked up the steps to the door, bent down, and peered into the slot.

Her eyes met his. "Ummm. Sorry this is such a mess. Could you tell the BSG I'm sorry? And I'll call?"

Nick nodded, but he looked hurt. "What about hiking?"

"I still want to go. Tomorrow?" Charlotte hoped that was okay. "I think Sophie'll be up to it first thing in the morning. It'll just be you, me, Sophie, Chelsea, and—" Charlotte heard someone coming up the steps, and when

Nick turned his head, Charlotte could see whoever it was had on a soccer uniform.

"Is that Dillon?"

"Uh-huh," Nick said as Dillon elbowed him aside to look in the slot.

"Dude, what's going on here? Secret messages?"

"Come hiking with us tomorrow?" Charlotte whispered loud enough for Dillon to hear. "Sophie would love it if you came."

At that, Dillon's face glowed. His smile filled the whole mail slot.

"See you tomorrow," Charlotte told the boys. "And don't forget to tell the BSG I'll be in touch!" Then she headed upstairs to take care of her frazzled French friend.

Sophie was fast asleep. Charlotte decided to let her be and signed onto IM to explain the whole mess. After ten minutes or so, all the BSG were there.

Chat Room: BSG ___ □ ✕

File Edit People View Help

5 people here

skywriter
flikchic
lafrida
Kgirl
4kicks

skywriter: Sry about this morning.
lafrida: np
Kgirl: . . . u owe me 1!!!
skywriter: i know :(
Kgirl: its ok.
flikchic: sophie's too popular

skywriter: yeah . . . we're hiking 2mro. plz DON'T tell the whole school!

flikchic: k

4kicks: Ill b there

Kgirl: no you wont

4kicks: huh?

lafrida: other things 2 do

4 kicks: oh, right. have fun

flikchic: whats going on?

skywriter: nothing.

lafrida: nada

Kgirl: unimportant

flikchic: oooookkkk . . . u guys r weird!

skywriter: gtg miss u all

5 people here

skywriter
flikchic
lafrida
Kgirl
4kicks

Charlotte had to go because her mind had wandered back to tulips and all those kids swarming her front porch. Suddenly she knew exactly what should happen next in Orangina's story!

Part 5
Attack of the Butterbees

On the other side of the door a field of brilliantly

colored tulips basked in the warm sunshine.

"What is so *dangereux* about flowers?" Orangina sniffed at a red and orange tulip.

"Shhh!" Big Bruce held a finger to his lips. "The butterbees'll hear you!"

But it was already too late.

The air filled with angry buzzing. The creatures had colorful wings, like butterflies, but stingers, like monster bees. They swarmed the travelers in a cloud bigger than Orangina's lost barge!

Big Bruce cowered behind one of the cat's legs. "Let's scram! Otherwise, we'll never make it."

"Neverrr say neverrr." Orangina batted at the bugs with his paws and tail as the wheels of his clever brain turned.

"Can you chirp *comme un oiseau*, like a bird?" Orangina asked.

"What kind of a mad, larky idea is that?" Big Bruce's voice shook. "Owww! It bit me!"

Orangina smacked three more butterbees away from his little friend and growled. "Take out the book! How big can it grow?"

"Not sure . . ."

Big Bruce took out the book, and Orangina caught a glimpse of the beautiful cat's face peering out from between the pages. "Ah, *ma chérie,* I will rescue you!" Orangina purred.

As the cat and the tiny man cowered, swatting away stingers and colorful wings, the book swelled in size, until it was big enough to hide underneath.

But Orangina's plan wasn't to hide. He had a much more interesting idea.

Friends Forever

"Qu'est-ce que c'est?" Sophie asked quietly from over Charlotte's shoulder, causing the writer to jump with surprise.

"Uh, nothing." Charlotte tried to cover the computer screen with her hands and glanced at the clock. She'd been writing for more than an hour, so absorbed that she hadn't even heard Sophie get up!

"Can I see?" Sophie asked.

Charlotte was suddenly very nervous. She could feel her heart beating hard in her chest. "Ummm," she sputtered. "You might think it's silly."

"What is it?" Sophie asked, trying desperately to look past Charlotte. "It is about Orangina?" Sophie actually sounded curious.

"It was supposed to be your welcome gift," Charlotte admitted. *What's the harm in letting her see?* Charlotte steeled herself, then stepped away from the computer. "But I haven't finished it yet. . . ."

"'Orangina's Travels!'" Sophie exclaimed as she read the title. *"Magnifique!"* There was that word again, "magnificent." But this time, the way Sophie said it was full of real excitement, completely different from the night before.

Sophie eagerly sat down at the desk and began to read. Charlotte leaned back on her bed, waiting to hear what Sophie thought of the story.

She has to like it, the optimist inside Charlotte whispered. *I wrote it for her.*

But she doesn't think about Orangina any more, her own brain countered. *Only clothes and boys.*

She's still reading! argued the optimist. *Wouldn't she have stopped if she didn't like it?*

Maybe she's just being polite, the worrier responded. *Wait and see.*

Sophie's reaction when she finally spun around in the chair was better than either side of Charlotte's brain ever could have hoped for.

"Fantastique!" Sophie leaped up and hugged Charlotte. "It's so good. You are a writer, just like your father!"

"Really?" Charlotte asked, breathless. "You really liked it? But you said you didn't think about Orangina anymore . . . and that Marty's cuter . . . and I thought . . ."

"Oh, *mon amie!* I didn't mean it that way. Of course I still love that cat. And this story . . ." Sophie beamed. "It is just how I imagine Orangina talking! And I feel so worried for him. Will he ever find the cat from the book?"

"Of course he will! But I haven't decided yet if she should be good or bad." Charlotte felt all her anxiety and insecurity melt away as Sophie nodded enthusiastically.

"Good, of course!" Sophie paused. "But maybe . . ."

They talked about the story until Charlotte had a whole

five pages of new notes and ideas to sort through. It was so wonderful to just talk to her friend Sophie, without a million other people around.

During a pause in the conversation, Charlotte realized they'd lapsed into speaking French and not even noticed. It was almost just like before, when they'd been best friends in Paris, making up adventures for the orange cat while he sat by the window of Charlotte's houseboat, tail twitching and ears perked.

"I'm sorry if I've been acting funny," Charlotte blurted out, then rushed on before she wimped out and never told Sophie how hurt she'd been feeling over the past week. "It's just that . . . well . . . at school at least . . . you're so popular and cool now."

Sophie nodded, waiting for Charlotte to continue.

"It's weird, but I was even feeling like maybe you didn't want to be friends with me anymore, because everyone at school was, like, your instant BFF, and no one seemed to notice me. I'm sorry, I just—"

"Oh, Charlotte! Do not apologize!" Sophie exclaimed. "*Ma cherie! Mon amie!* How could you ever think I didn't want to be your friend?! We are, like you say, BFFs! The extra F is not really for French like we pretend, but for '*forever,*' yes?"

Charlotte nodded. *Why didn't I tell Sophie how I felt sooner?* she wondered, but it was too late for regrets. *Better late than never!* she told herself.

"So we're really still friends? Even though I look

terrible in designer scarves, I can't get you VIP passes, and I didn't come to either of your clubs?"

Sophie smiled and said, "You are my best friend ever. You know the most important thing: *Chacun doit midi à sa porte.*"

The actual French words meant, "everyone sees noon from their own door," but Charlotte recognized the phrase. "Be true to yourself," Charlotte translated out loud.

"And true to your friends!" Sophie added.

Charlotte grabbed a piece of paper and jotted down the French idiom. "I'm adding that to my quote board right now!"

After she had pinned up the words, Charlotte sat back and hugged a pillow to her chest. "I told Nick we'd hike with him tomorrow. And I invited Dillon. I hope that's okay?"

"Of course!" Sophie was still sitting in Charlotte's computer chair, and her hands hovered over the keyboard. "Should I tell him so? Is Avery coming?"

"Wait a sec." Charlotte remembered Dillon's hopeful face through the mail slot, and wondered if Sophie realized how far he'd fallen for her. Now seemed to be the time for coming clean, so . . . "You know Dillon likes you, right?"

Sophie laughed. "Me? *Non!* He likes Avery. Is it not obvious?"

"Ummm . . . actually, he likes you," Charlotte repeated. "He and Avery have been friends since, like, kindergarten.

So sometimes they seem flirty, but believe me, they'd never go out." Charlotte waited for that news to sink in, watching Sophie's expression.

Sophie smiled, then frowned, then smiled again. "You are sure?" Sophie spun slowly in Charlotte's desk chair, understanding dawning on her face. "Ahhh . . . now that you say this, I see it is obvious. He buys me the cap, changes his clothing, invites me to play soccer. . . ."

"Mmm," Charlotte agreed. "So, do you like Dillon?"

Sophie got up from Charlotte's desk chair and joined her on the bed, sitting with her legs crossed. "I am confused about him. He is very cute, and he knows kung fu! But I will leave in one week, and I still like Adrien too." Sophie got a dreamy look in her eyes and sighed. "But right now, Adrien seems so far away. Dillon, he is . . . koa-lio."

Charlotte giggled at Sophie's new American slang word. "Dillon's definitely *coolio*," Charlotte corrected her pronunciation.

"What will I do?" Sophie asked. "You are the boy expert."

"Me?!" Charlotte almost fell backward off the bed. *Sophie's asking me for boy advice? Wow!*

"Yes. Ummm . . . you know, I still have not kissed a boy," Sophie said shyly.

Suddenly Charlotte realized something ironic. *What if this whole time while I was worried that Sophie was way ahead of me, she was thinking the same thing?* It had seemed like Sophie knew everything about clothes, boys, and how to be cool. But now Sophie was asking Charlotte for advice, and she actually had some good advice to give!

"Well, if your stomach feels all funny when you think about him, it's definitely a crush. And also, I think it's like what you were saying before: *Chacun doit midi à sa porte.* Be true to yourself."

Sophie smiled and jumped up from the bed. "How about we spend the day together?" she suggested. "Take me to your favorite place here in Boston. Just the two of us—like when you lived in Paris. That is what I want to do today!"

"Okay!" Charlotte's heart felt lighter as she leaped up next to Sophie.

Then her BFF wrapped Charlotte in such a huge bear hug that the two of them fell back onto the bed giggling, just like old times.

Castle Island

"Maybe Orangina should visit a castle," Sophie suggested.

"Oooh . . . a castle by the sea!" Charlotte replied as she looked out over the ocean from the beach walk around Castle Island.

Mr. Ramsey had agreed that Charlotte's idea of spending the day at the historic fort located in the Boston harbor was a wonderful idea, and they'd left immediately after a late breakfast of yogurt parfaits. Marty wanted to come, too, but Avery and Isabel had offered to take him to the park instead.

It was windy on the beach outside the fort, but neither

Sophie nor Charlotte seemed to mind the cool breezes. They were so happy just to be together on an outing—no pressure, no other obligations, no being pulled in a million different directions by a million different people.

"Can Orangina swim?" Sophie wondered.

"No, he doesn't like being wet, remember?" Charlotte replied.

Sophie ran up to the very edge of the surf, jumping back playfully when the waves came reaching for her bare toes. "It's all so different here than Paris!" Sophie shouted as Charlotte joined the game. "The ocean is freezing! And everything is bigger. The streets, the cars—everything."

"I like it here, though," Charlotte replied. "Sometimes I miss the Seine, but who needs a river when you have a whole ocean?"

Just then, a roaring sound distracted them; an airplane had come in to land at Logan Airport. Both their feet got soaked by the next wave.

Soon, Charlotte thought, *all the drama of this past week will be a distant memory. A plane just like that one will carry Sophie back to Paris. . . .*

"We need hot cocoa!" Charlotte announced to get her mind off that sad thought. "There has to be a café some-where close. . . . Come on!" She linked arms with Sophie, and the girls skipped off laughing.

"Sophie?" Charlotte asked when they were sitting together, sipping hot chocolate. "Do you want to help me with my story when we get home?"

"Bien sûr," her friend replied. "I'd love to!"

Part 6
Into the Pumpkin Forest

Orangina flipped open the book so the pages fluttered, then poked his head under to lift it onto his back like a pair of strange-looking wings.

"Chirp!" Orangina ordered as the storm of colorful, buzzing butterbees dove for his back, screeing in surprise when they landed on paper instead of fur.

"Tweet. Tweet. Tweet," said Big Bruce.

"Louder, *petit monsieur*!" Orangina yowled as he arched his back, making the "wings" flap like a bird.

"Tweeeeet! Tweeeeet!"

Flap, flap.

Butterbees scattered every which way, hovering just out of reach. Then when the flapping and tweeting didn't stop, they buzzed off into the bright blue sky.

"Whooop!" Big Bruce cheered. "We got 'em! Orry, you really are the cleverest bloke I ever did see."

"Wherrre is she?" Orangina asked with a faraway look in his eyes. He had shrugged the book-wings off his back and stared into the beautiful painted cat's green eyes.

"Ahhh, right this way, mate."

Past the field of tulips, the cat and tiny man found a cobbled path leading into a dark, mossy forest. Curling and twisting around the ancient tree trunks were bright green pumpkin vines and huge pumpkin leaves. Here and there, pumpkins the same shade as

Orangina's fur grew bigger than the large dogs that
sometimes chased cats through the streets of Paris.
Orangina was safe from them on his barge, though.
Safe and happy.

But he realized then that he was feeling pretty good
even here in the dark forest, because he had his new
friend, Big Bruce, by his side. They'd made it through
the tulip field and out of danger, together. All he had to
do now was find the beautiful cat from the book, and
his adventure would be complete. . . .

CHAPTER
17

The Chipmunk Ninja

Sophie, let's go!" Charlotte burst into her bedroom, wearing shorts and a sweatshirt. Her long hair was pulled into a ponytail through the back of an AAJH baseball cap. "My dad's waiting downstairs. We gotta go pick up Nick, Chelsea, and Dillon for the hike."

"I need *une minute*," Sophie told her.

"Umm, Soph, I'm thinking you need more than one minute." Charlotte surveyed the scene in the room. Sophie stood in her bathrobe in the middle of a maelstrom of clothing. Her suitcase lay upside down on the floor, shoes were scattered out onto Charlotte's desk, and there was even a pair of discarded brown leggings hanging over the computer monitor!

Charlotte snagged the leggings and tossed them to Sophie. "Put these on, we need to hit the road."

"*Non!* They are not right." Sophie flipped through a pile of clothing on the bed. "I want to look nice today."

Charlotte knew why. "We're going *hiking*, Soph. Dillon

won't care what you wear. And trust me, you'll be happier if you're comfortable."

"But what will he think if I don't look like myself?" Sophie held up a short skirt, a short-sleeved sweater, and a silvery scarf.

Charlotte shook her head no. Sophie grabbed a different pair of leggings, with a little lace around each ankle, a thick belt, and a midlength shirt dress.

"Hiking," Charlotte said, shaking her head no again. She could hear her father calling from the front hall. "Think dirt and bugs and rocks."

"Ugh." Sophie grimaced. "Maybe this?" She held up a pair of light khaki pants and a silk blouse.

"*Non!* Nothing light colored or dry-clean only." Charlotte knelt down and dug through Sophie's suitcase, finally locating a pair of blue jeans and a button-down shirt. "Wear these."

"Girls?" Charlotte's dad called up. "Chelsea's mom just called. Are you almost ready?"

"We'll be right down!" Charlotte answered.

Sophie reluctantly slipped into the clothes Charlotte had picked out. She went to the mirror and turned this way and that, trying to decide if she liked the way the outfit looked.

"Dillon likes you for you, not your clothes." Charlotte reassured Sophie. "But he might change his mind if you don't hurry up," she teased.

"Okay, this is the outfit, then." Sophie grabbed a thin sweater and tied it around her waist. Then they both stared at her pile of shoes.

Charlotte saw the problem straightaway. Sophie had no good hiking shoes!

"Here, you can wear these." Charlotte handed over a pair of beat-up old hiking boots that had carried her through many adventures in Australia.

Sophie's feet had always been a size smaller than Charlotte's, but now Sophie could just barely squeeze her toes through the opening of the old shoes, and Charlotte's extra pair of sneakers were also too small!

There was no choice. Sophie slipped on her ballet flats, and then chose a matching scarf to twine around her neck. As a finishing touch she put on the Red Sox hat Dillon had given her.

"Done," Sophie announced, taking one last glance in the mirror.

"It'll work—I hope," Charlotte agreed, hustling Sophie outside and into the car.

Along the Skyline

Hiking, biking, and dog-walking trails crisscrossed the Blue Hills Reservation. As Charlotte, Sophie, Chelsea, Nick, and Dillon piled out of Mr. Ramsey's car, he pointed to their location on a well-worn trail map.

"The skyline trail makes an eight-mile loop around the whole reservation," Mr. Ramsey explained. "If you think you can make it the whole way, I'll meet you back here. But there's another parking area on the other side where I can pick you up if you get tired. Got your cell phones?"

Charlotte held up hers. Chelsea had one too, and Dillon had borrowed his dad's.

"Okay, kids. Call and tell me when and where you need to be picked up. I won't go far!" Mr. Ramsey waved and got back in the car. He had offered to hike with them, but Charlotte wanted a day with just her friends. Thankfully, her dad understood and trusted her enough to make good decisions. Also, Nick had completed a hiking safety course at camp the summer before and had brought along a first-aid kit, flashlight, water purification tablets, and a multitool. Mr. Ramsey had double-checked that they each had two bottles of water, a bag lunch, and an extra jacket.

"Are we ready?" Charlotte asked the group, unable to keep the excitement out of her voice. She loved the smell and taste of the air out in the woods!

"All systems go." Nick patted his backpack full of supplies.

"Sunscreen or bug spray anyone?" Chelsea passed around the bottles and hung her camera around her neck.

"Is this the place with that sweet view of Boston?" Dillon asked Nick.

"Totally, but it's near the end of the loop." Nick glanced at Sophie's shoes. "Think you can make it?"

"*Totally.*" Sophie confidently tossed back her shoulders and led the way onto the trail.

The path started out straight and flat. Sophie was entertaining everyone with a story about a science experiment at school that went terribly wrong, until a rock got stuck in her shoe. Everyone stopped while she fished it out.

"The school smelled like stinky socks for two weeks!" Sophie finished her story and got up to lead the way once again.

The path was rising slightly now, and Sophie stayed in the lead, slipping this way and that on the loose rocks strewn across the trail. Her little shoes didn't offer much support, and Dillon hovered right behind her, as if waiting to catch her if she fell.

"Has she ever been hiking before?" Chelsea whispered to Charlotte.

"I thought so . . . ," Charlotte pondered.

"Oh!" Sophie yelped as one of her shoes flipped off for the dozenth time.

Dillon handed over the offending footwear as Sophie sat down on a log.

"I think, if I take off my socks, I might not have so much trouble," she told Dillon, who just nodded with big puppy eyes. "The shoes will stick to my feet."

"Um, that might not be the best idea—," Nick started.

"It's brilliant!" Dillon interrupted. "Who needs socks?"

Chelsea snapped a photo of Dillon making a goofy face while Sophie wriggled her bare toes, free from sweaty socks, and then they set off down the trail again, following Nick and Charlotte.

"Come look what I found!" Charlotte called them all over to a dark, damp hollow between two giant boulders.

"Cool! A cave!" Dillon ducked inside, and Chelsea took more pictures.

"Watch out!" Sophie yelped and grabbed Charlotte's arm as something mouse-sized flew out over Dillon's head. "What was that?!"

"A bat, probably." Charlotte shrugged.

"Don't you have bats in France?" Nick asked.

"Bats?" Sophie thought hard. "But of course. I just don't hang out with them!"

The kids all laughed. *Sophie is being a good sport,* Charlotte thought, *even though she is out of her element.* Sophie even climbed inside the cave with Dillon, after he checked the rock walls thoroughly for more bats.

The trail climbed up and around the boulders, then along a ridge lined with birch trees. They'd been walking quietly for a few minutes when Sophie complained that her feet were sore.

Charlotte diagnosed the little red bump of Sophie's left heel. "It looks like a blister."

Nick opened up his first-aid kit. "I have a blister kit." He handed a special Band-aid to Sophie, and Charlotte helped her put it on. "I tried to tell you it's not a good idea to hike without socks." He shot a told-you-so look at Dillon.

"Okay, I will wear the socks." Sophie looked around in her pack, but could only find one!

"Mon dieu!" Sophie exclaimed. "I've lost a sock!"

"Just wear one sock, on the foot with the blister," Chelsea suggested.

"That will look crazy!" Sophie immediately rejected the notion. "I will just go back to look for my sock."

Charlotte shook her head. "Not when we've already come this far!"

"Just wear the one," Nick agreed with Chelsea. "At least the blister will be protected."

"You can have one of my socks," Dillon offered, but when he untied his shoes, stinky-foot smell wafted up.

Nick plugged his nose and protested. "Ewww! Put them back on! That's *gross*, dude!"

Sophie laughed musically. "It is not as bad as my school after the science disaster. Thank you, Dillon, for your chivalry, but I will just wear the one sock."

This is a bold move for Sophie, Charlotte had to admit. *I bet she's never worn just one sock before! Wouldn't it be funny if that became the new fashion craze at AAJH?*

As they got moving again, Dillon stepped ahead of Sophie, kicking stones out of her way and holding tree branches back.

"*Merci.*" Sophie smiled each time he helped her out.

Chelsea walked behind Dillon and Sophie, with Nick and Charlotte bringing up the rear. From where Charlotte stood at the back of the pack, all she could hear was the chirping of birds and Sophie going "*merci.*" "*Oh, merci.*" And then "*merci.*" Again.

"It sounds like she's calling for mercy," Nick commented back to Charlotte.

"That's not a good thing when we still have almost six miles to go!" Charlotte said with a grimace. "Maybe I should switch places with Dillon." Charlotte tried to dodge around Nick and scoot up closer to Sophie.

"I think Dillon has this one covered," Nick replied, jokingly blocking Charlotte's path, trapping her in place at the end of the line. "He *wants* to help her."

"*Merci*, Dillon." It went on as the birches made way for majestic pines.

"*Merci*." As Dillon helped Sophie cross a log placed over a wide brook.

So it went for another mile, until it ended with "*Merciiiii*. Oof."

Charlotte rushed past Nick and up the trail to find Sophie sprawled out on the trail. She'd tripped over a tree root that even the hyper-gentlemanly Dillon couldn't protect her from. Her scarf was snagged on a thornbush, and her sockless foot had lost its shoe.

"Help!" Sophie cried out in distress, discovering that she was tangled.

Dillon helped Sophie sit up, retrieved her shoe, then struggled with the thornbush until his hands were all scratched up. But the scarf wouldn't come loose!

"I think it's even more tangled than before," Chelsea commented as Sophie tried untying the scarf from her neck . . . but both ends were trapped tight.

"Let me try." Charlotte tugged with all her might, until the bush was bending over backward, but Sophie was still stuck.

Nick cut in with his pocket knife and snipped at twigs and strings until Sophie was free.

"Looks like you're taking the bush with you." Chelsea pointed to several sawed-off twigs still dangling from the end of the scarf.

"And some of the scarf is staying here." Dillon nodded at the frayed silvery fabric tangled in the bush. "Couldn't you be more careful?" he chided Nick.

"Sorry," Nick apologized.

"It's all right." Sophie kept her head high, and Charlotte felt so proud of her. If she'd been the one tangled in the bush, she'd be mortified right now!

"When we get back to Boston, I'll buy you another one," Dillon offered. "An American scarf to remind you of your hiking trip."

"*Merci, non.* I think I will remember this hike no matter what!" Sophie exclaimed. The others laughed in agreement.

Dirt, Roots, and Bugs

Finally it was time for a rest. As they chowed down on sandwiches, carrot sticks, and granola bars on top of a flat rock overlooking the woods, Charlotte realized that Sophie looked a little less than her usual bubbly self.

Apparently she wasn't the only one who noticed. "What's up?" Dillon asked Sophie. "Do you wanna stop soon or something?"

"No, no, please. I think I am slowing you all down and ruining the hike."

Dillon shook his head. "You could never ruin anything." His smile was warm and sincere.

"We don't have to go all the way around," Nick said. "We're only about ten minutes from the halfway mark."

"We are not even halfway?" Sophie sounded stunned.

"But we *must* have come almost eight kilometers already, *non*?"

"Umm, the whole hike is eight *miles*," Charlotte explained. "That's about thirteen kilometers."

The color drained from Sophie's face. *"Mon dieu!"* she exclaimed, collapsing backward into a clump of moss and grass, dropping the granola bar she'd been eating.

Sophie looked over at it with sorrow. Then her expression turned to horror as a zillion happy ants swarmed the granola bar.

"I can't do this." She groaned with a sigh. "I won't make it. I shall just lie here and let the ants carry me away."

"No, you won't! And yes, you can make it," Charlotte insisted, overhearing Sophie's lament. "It seems like we found out something important today. I like hiking. You don't. That's okay. It's nice when friends have differences." Charlotte gave Sophie a hand up. "But I won't let you quit, just like you don't give up on me when I have my clumsy moments at school. Let's go."

Chelsea poked Sophie's arm and held up her camera. "Group shot?"

When they got going again after Chelsea took their picture, Sophie hung behind the group, taking each step slowly.

"Come on, Sophie, you can do it!" Dillon cheered her on.

"Put a little power to it," Nick continued the cheer.

"Gooooo, Sophie!" Chelsea finished.

"You're doing great, Soph. Hang in there!" Charlotte hung back next to her friend.

It's strange to see her so dejected, Charlotte thought. *My put-together friend has met her match. Who would have guessed she'd be bested by Mother Nature? I should be the one getting tangled in a bush or tripping over rocks.* Charlotte chuckled to herself. *Of course, there's still time for that!*

The path wound up and down another steep hill. Sophie walked very quietly between Dillon and Charlotte.

Something rustled in the trees.

"Aughhh! Help!!!" Sophie screamed, running behind Dillon for cover!

"A bug! There's a bug. A huge, deadly bug!" Directly in front of Sophie, a furry brown-and-black striped animal was standing on the path, washing its face with its tiny little paws. Chelsea grabbed her camera and took a few shots of the furry fellow, who didn't seem to be afraid of people at all.

"Get away!" Sophie shouted at it, trying to scare the little guy away. "I hate bugs!"

"Umm, I think you've got the wrong word." Charlotte squeezed her friend's hand. "Chipmunks are definitely not bugs."

"I think they're related to mice," Nick offered.

That didn't help. "I hate mice and bugs and bats and woods," Sophie cried. "He's going to bite me. I will get the plague!"

"He's more afraid of you than you are of him." Dillon tried to soothe Sophie, but she ignored him and backed up until she was only one step away from a huge patch of poison ivy!

"Stop!" Charlotte cautioned her, but it looked like Sophie would rather tangle herself up in a thornbush again than face the gnashing teeth of that terribly vicious chipmunk.

It was up to Dillon to play the rescuing hero. "Ay ya!" He leaped into a ninja warrior stance, hands raised to challenge the furry critter to a fight to the death. "Ya. Ya." Dillon moved in one of his practiced karate sequences, his hands chopping in perfect arcs.

The chipmunk merely blinked at the unmasked avenger. It was one brave little guy!

"Yeeeeeaaa!!!" Dillon exclaimed, and whipped around with a spinning, jumping back kick that finally sent the chipmunk scampering away.

Nick dropped to the ground in thanksgiving. "All praise, Master Dillon. I was nearly eaten alive!" he said, arms raised dramatically skyward in a mocking pose.

"The Chipmunk Ninja has rescued us all!" Chelsea added, putting the back of her hand across her forehead, like she was about to faint. "The best part? I got the whole battle on camera!"

Charlotte rolled her eyes and drew Sophie away from the poison ivy. "Are you okay?" she asked, but Sophie was staring straight at Dillon.

"You are my hero!" Sophie put a hand on Dillon's shoulder and kissed him lightly on the cheek. "A real live kung-fu master! Thank you!"

Dillon blushed, one hand floating up to his cheek. "You're welcome," he mumbled, all his bravado completely dissolved.

"Come, my Ninja Chipmunk Warrior, lead the way!" Sophie cheered, ready to finish the hike.

And they did. They made it all the way up to the overlook point, where they rested and watched cars traveling along the highway into the city. Charlotte called her dad to say they were going to finish the whole hike. Then they climbed back down, telling jokes to keep themselves going and to keep Sophie's mind off her sore, blistered feet.

"What do you call a monkey that eats chips and dresses in black?" Dillon asked as they started back on the path. "A ninja chipmonkey!"

"Lame," Nick said, snickering.

"I have one." Charlotte went next. "How many Chipmunk Ninjas does it take to screw in a lightbulb?"

Chelsea stepped adroitly over a rock. "No one knows. When the light comes on, they all scatter!" The group burst into giggles.

The rest of the way down the trail, they took turns frightening birds and squirrels away with bold karate moves and making up Chipmunk Ninja jokes.

Finally, they made it back to the parking lot, where Mr. Ramsey was leaning against the hood of his car, waiting for the gang. "Hey!" he called, waving to them.

Sophie practically flung herself into Mr. Ramsey's car.

"Thank you for the hike," she told her friends when they all settled in for the ride home. "But now I think I need a hot bath and perhaps, a paraffin pedicure and a hot meal, then everything will be back to *magnifique!*"

CHAPTER

18

French Romance and American Secrets

"How'd you do on the math test?" Isabel asked Maeve as they waited for the rest of the BSG outside school on a warm and sunny Tuesday afternoon.

"I got a B plus!" Maeve grinned. "Working with Austin is like a miracle cure for both of us. It makes me think about how I learn, and for the first time *ever* I'm not completely dreading homework."

"That's fantabulawesome!" Katani came up behind Maeve, cheering her math success with Maeve's new favorite word.

"Totally," Isabel agreed.

"Hey, guys!" Avery came running over, already changed into her soccer uniform for her usual afternoon pickup game. "I only counted *ten* girls wearing scarves today. The Scarfless Wonders are totally taking over!"

Isabel whipped a scarf out of her book bag and looped it around Avery's neck before she could get away. "Gotcha!" She giggled.

Katani touched the simple choker she was wearing. She hadn't worn a scarf since Sophie walked into school on Monday in jeans and a Red Sox T-shirt! After the hike on Sunday, Sophie had explained, she decided she needed some casual wear. So she bought herself a few T-shirts and a good pair of sneakers, too.

"Everyone is back to dressing like normal, boring, sloppy Americans," Maeve commented. "I can't believe I'm saying this, but . . . it's refreshing."

"Everyone except you two!" Isabel shoved Katani and Maeve playfully. They may not have been wearing scarves, but they were both wearing sundresses, for no particular reason except that it was a nice day.

"And Dillon," Avery said with a grin. "He's still wearing those dumb pointy shoes."

"I'm no fashionista," Isabel piped up, "but someone" — she coughed out Katani's name—"has to tell him that you can't wear pointy shoes with a sports jersey and shorts!"

"I'm not telling him. Let the QOM tell him," Katani suggested. "They like French fashion."

"I actually heard"—Maeve leaned forward like she was revealing a big secret—"that after Sophie bailed on everyone Saturday, the QOM were so mad they cancelled the French fashion club."

"It's true," Charlotte said as she and Sophie joined the group. "No more fashion club. But the French language club is still going strong."

"Who needs designer scarves when you have comfy T-shirts?" Sophie preened a little, showing off her pink and white Red Sox shirt. "I am no longer French. I am oh-so-American, duuudes!"

Charlotte laughed and plopped down on the grass next to Maeve. "What's up with you, girl?" she asked. "You've been MIA a lot lately."

"Bat Mitzvah on the horizon—four days and counting." Maeve grimaced. "My family starts coming in tomorrow! My great-grandma Gigi is arriving in the morning from New York. Uncle Marty and my cousin Stacy are getting here on Thursday."

"Yikes," Avery whimpered on Maeve's behalf. "Can we do anything to help?"

"We already are—," Charlotte started, but then quickly stopped herself.

"Are what?" Maeve asked.

"Are . . . available!" Katani finished Charlotte's half sentence. "We are available for anything you need. And of course we're coming to the service Saturday morning. We can't wait!"

"Great!" Maeve said. "It would be awesome if you guys came to my rehearsal at the temple tomorrow. You could hang out with Grandma and Grandpa Taylor while I run through the service with the rabbi. I think it would help calm my nerves if I had my friends there."

"I'm totally in. What time?" Avery asked. "I'm free after—"

"No!" Isabel interrupted. "You can't go. You have that *thing* with me and Katani." She gave Avery a strong stare. "We have to go to *that* place. It was *your* idea after all."

"Oh, yeah," Avery said, realizing what Isabel meant. She turned to Maeve. "Oops. Sorry. Can't be there."

Maeve found the looks passing among her friends quite odd, but Avery had always been kind of hyper. It wasn't worth delving into the details, especially with Austin to tutor, a dress to save up for, and Hebrew to practice!

"Maybe Sophie and Charlotte can come?" Maeve pleaded.

"We, uh . . ." Charlotte searched for an excuse.

"We'd love to," Sophie said, putting her arm firmly around Charlotte and dragging her close. "If we all ditch out, Maeve will know something's up. We must go to the rehearsal," she whispered.

Charlotte nodded, realizing Sophie was right. "We'll be there!" she told Maeve enthusiastically.

Triple Date

The next afternoon, Charlotte and Sophie followed Maeve and her grandparents out of the temple.

"You did a great job!" Grandma Taylor cheered. "Didn't she do well?" the tiny old woman asked Charlotte, then leaned in and gave Maeve a big, sloppy kiss on the cheek.

"Thanks, Grandma and Grandpa, for coming today. I'm glad you're here." Maeve was speaking from her heart.

"We're so proud of you! This will be the finest Bat Mitzvah I've ever attended!" Grandpa Taylor told her, hugging Maeve tight.

Maeve smiled, realizing that this was actually the *only* Bat Mitzvah they'd ever attend—her father's parents weren't Jewish, and this was the first time they'd been inside a temple since her mom and dad got married! Thankfully, none of the family had said anything about the separation, and both sets of grandparents *and* great-grandma seemed to be having a blast.

"Will you drop us off at Montoya's Bakery?" Maeve asked. "I'm gonna hang with my friends awhile. Mom knows. I'll be home later, in time for dinner."

The girls climbed into Maeve's grandparents' rental car.

"I messed up the Hebrew a little on the third part of my reading," Maeve told Charlotte and Sophie on the way to the café. "I'll have to review it one more time before the big day."

"Sounded just right to me," Charlotte told her.

"Yeah, because you don't speak Hebrew!" Maeve laughed. "Botching the Hebrew is like when an actress forgets a line. Only the director, I mean, the rabbi, knows, but it's still a mess up."

Charlotte and Sophie hugged Maeve, who was in the middle.

"You'll do *fantabulous*," Sophie added with a wink and a grin.

The girls were still chitchatting about the service when they got to Montoya's.

"OMG! Do you think Riley's here yet?" Maeve peered into the car's rearview mirror and fluffed her hair. "I'm totally not ready. . . ." They had set up a triple date after the rehearsal. Maeve and Riley. Charlotte and Nick. Sophie and Dillon.

"You look beautiful, Maeve, as always!" Charlotte dragged her dramatic friend away from the car and into the bakery. Riley and Dillon were waiting at the BSG's usual table.

"Hey, dudes!" Dillon waved. A pair of scruffy sneakers poked out from the bottoms of his jeans.

"What happened to your pointy shoes?" Maeve teased.

"Avery gave me a talk about being myself." Dillon shrugged. "And she backed it up with threats of bodily harm." He widened his eyes like this was the worst thing ever.

"Say no more." Sophie waved his words away. "I absolutely agree! Fashion is about so much more than designers and popularity. It is about expressing your true self." She paused before adding, "And, being *confortable, non*?"

"A good lesson for next time we go hiking," Nick agreed, joining the group with a tray of freshly baked chocolate-chip cookies.

"I don't think there will be a next time for me," Sophie said gently. "My new sneakers are just right for walking in a mall or on a sidewalk, but not the forest. I'm full with roots, dirt, and bugs." She paused, then added with a grin, "And Ninja Chipmunks."

They all laughed, and the girls went to sit down.

Nick jumped in front of Maeve and pulled out a chair facing the window out onto the street. "Why don't you sit here?"

Maeve looked confused for a second, but when Riley scooched over so he could sit next to her, she relented. Charlotte and Nick took their seats facing the back of the restaurant.

"What was that all about?" Charlotte whispered. Then she saw a door in the back of the restaurant open, and Katani, Avery, and Isabel snuck out! Their secret meeting had run long and they were just now leaving Montoya's.

"Maeve! Did you tell Riley about the dress you're saving up for?" Charlotte distracted her friend.

By the time Maeve was done describing every sequin of her dream dress in intimate detail, the other BSG were safely out of the building. Charlotte let out a sigh of relief.

Mrs. Montoya brought them iced hot chocolate to go with their cookies. Dillon offered Sophie a cookie, and she nibbled off one end, laughing as the crumbs landed in her iced hot chocolate. Charlotte smiled shyly at Nick when he handed her a straw and pushed his iced hot chocolate her way. "I think my mom put an extra shot of chocolate sauce in mine. Want to try?"

It was the best iced hot chocolate Charlotte had ever had. If she had eyes for anyone other than Nick, she would have noticed that Riley and Maeve were lost in their own little world as well!

When they finally got up to leave, Maeve saw Fabiana,

Nick's older sister, coming out of a door she'd never noticed before.

"Do you have another room back there?" Maeve asked Nick, squinting her eyes toward the open door.

"No!" Nick said, too quickly. "I mean, it's just storage."

"So what was Fabiana doing back there?" Maeve asked, intrigued. "Inquiring minds want to know."

Charlotte held her breath, but Nick replied smoothly, "She has a secret life. I try not to pay attention."

"I read this book where everyone had a secret life," Charlotte said, helping Nick with his cover-up.

"I don't have one," Riley remarked. "Where can I get a mysterious, intriguing, rock star secret life?"

Maeve laughed. "When I'm famous, the tabloids will report on all my friends' lives. If you don't have any secrets, they'll make some up for you!"

"Sophie Morel wrestles rabid chipmunks in her secret life." Dillon spread his hands, as if this were a newspaper cover story.

Sophie and Charlotte started laughing and couldn't stop until they got home.

Counting Pennies

I can't believe it! I have $191! Just in time to buy the amazing dress that has MY name on it in the window of Think Pink! Maeve thought as she skipped home from tutoring Austin. It had been her third session that week, and each day she'd checked on the dress. Just to make sure.

"Wait up!" Sam whined, dragging a backpack full of plastic army men.

Since her mom was busy ushering more family from the airport to hotels, Maeve had arranged with Mrs. Franklin to bring Sam with her to Austin's. It had gone well, even though Sam insisted on turning every story they read into some sort of battle for his army men. When Maeve got the envelope from Mrs. Franklin with her payment, she instantly added it to the wad of cash growing in a secret pouch inside her babysitting bag. Finally it was enough!

Think Pink will be closed now, but I'm just going to stop by to say hello to the amazing, soon-to-be-mine, red-carpet-worthy number! Maeve thought as she picked up the pace. *By tomorrow everyone will be here. Tomorrow night I go to the Friday night service at temple. We'll have a nice dinner and then go to sleep. The next morning it's pink-sequined-gown grown-up Bat Mitzvah Maeve showtime! Wow,* Maeve thought. *All these months and months of preparation. It feels like years! I can't believe it's actually almost here.*

"Are you listening to me, Maeve? 'Cause I don't think you're listening." Sam had finally caught up to his older sister and poked her in the side.

"Sorry, Sam." Maeve took his hand as they crossed the street. "I zoned out."

"You've been doing that a lot lately," Sam remarked. "Is it your dyslexia?" The large word rolled easily off her little brother's tongue. They stepped up on the curb and started down the sidewalk.

Maeve laughed, then started in seriously, "I hate to tell

you, Sam, but I am almost positive I have a very serious disease. Worse than dyslexia. It's making my brain turn to mush. It's called . . . drumroll, please!" She drummed her feet on the sidewalk. "Bat Mitzvah-itis."

Sam poked Maeve again and said, "You're verrry funny."

Maeve poked her little brother back, saying, "No, you are."

"Know what?" Sam asked, suddenly all serious. "Austin told a bunch of kids today how much he *loves* his new tutor." Sam smiled mischievously, "So, I said, 'If you love her so much, why don't you marry her!' How cool would that be, Maeve-y? Too cool for words!"

"Austin's kind of young for me, don't you think?" Maeve asked with a giggle.

"He'll grow up someday," Sam said. "We could be related!"

"Ha-ha." Maeve rolled her eyes.

"And now all these other kids want a tutor. I said if they paid me, I'd ask you." Sam opened his hands and showed Maeve two quarters, a dime, and three pennies. "I made sixty-three cents!"

"Sam, you're brilliant!" Maeve stopped in her tracks so suddenly Sam bumped into her.

"I know I'm brilliant," he said. "I know what a square root is."

But Maeve wasn't listening. "I could make my tutoring work with Austin my Bat Mitzvah project!" she exclaimed. "And maybe tutor other kids with learning differences, too! There could be a whole program matching up older kids and younger kids with things like dyslexia, so they can teach one another. They'd, like, help one another with more than just school."

Sam nodded. "Uh-huh. A square root is when there are two of the same number that multiply together—"

"You weren't even listening!" Maeve threw her hands up in the air, too excited about her new idea to get really angry at her brother. *I'll make a difference in the world after all! That's what becoming a Bat Mitzvah is all about,* Maeve told herself as she turned down the street that would take them past Think Pink on the way home.

As they got closer, Maeve's fingers gripped her savings and her heartbeat started racing. *One-hundred and ninety-one dollars. Enough to pay for the dress, plus one bag full of Swedish Fish!* After all the drama, all the trouble and disappointment, Maeve had finally set herself a goal and achieved it. *What could be more fantabulawesome than that?*

Finally, Maeve reached the fancy pink awning and stopped to gaze in the window. But something was wrong. . . . Her smile vanished, and she started to tremble. Mostly the display case looked just as she expected: There was a stack of pink hats, a stuffed flamingo, a wicker chair, and a mannequin. But the mannequin, *her* mannequin, was wearing a pink plaid jacket.

Her dress was gone. Gone!

Life as she knew it was over.

Maeve clenched her fingers around her money so tightly, the bills crumpled. It was the most she'd ever saved up in her whole life, and suddenly it was all for nothing. Her eyes frantically searched the window display. *This is all a bad dream! It can't be real!* She grasped out to hold onto something, and Sam took her hand.

"No. No. No," Maeve wailed. "Where is my dress???!!!"

Sam just looked at her, then looked away. "It's okay, Maeve-y. It's only a dress."

"It's *not* okay! This is the least okay I've ever been in my entire life!" Maeve pronounced dramatically, and stared in the store window again, studying the ghastly jacket now on display.

The dress was still gone. *Someone else must have bought it. How dare she!* Maeve moaned inside. *Some other girl will be wearing the most glamorous gown on the face of the Earth, MY gown, to her party. I hope she's happy.*

Somehow, this had gone from the best day to the worst day of Maeve's life. Head down and shoulders slumped, Maeve walked with Sam the rest of the way home, tears streaming down her face.

CHAPTER
19
Changing the World

"*N*otain Ha-Torrahhh*," Maeve chanted the last bit of Hebrew after her Torah reading. She had been so nervous all week that she would stumble over her part in the service, but once she got up in front of everyone, the actress inside Maeve kicked into gear. She threw back her shoulders, stood up tall, and spoke the Hebrew words she'd practiced a million times before. *Whew. I survived. I did it!* Maeve smiled, looking out into the sanctuary. Her mom and dad were smiling. Even Sam was blowing Maeve kisses from his place in the front row. She saw the BSG and Sophie staring up at her, beaming with pride. *It's okay that I don't have that dress*, Maeve told herself for the hundredth time, finally starting to believe it. *They're all here because of me and the meaning of the ceremony. I didn't need a fancy gown for this day to be special.*

Maeve took a minute and scanned the crowd; friends from school and the neighborhood, a few teachers, her pals from Hebrew school, aunts, uncles, cousins, grandparents—they'd all come to hear her read her special portion and watch her become a Bat Mitzvah. Now it was almost over.

There was only one last thing she needed to do: give her speech. During their meetings over the last few months, Maeve had worked closely with Rabbi Millstein to write something about the ancient words she'd read in Hebrew and their relevance to her today.

"Uh hum." Maeve cleared her throat, stepping into position in front of a microphone. "Shabbat Shalom." *I wish you a day of peace.* That was the traditional greeting before the speech.

Maeve opened her mouth to continue, but at that moment she caught her cousin Stacy's snide smirk. Maeve suddenly felt nauseated.

Stacy had confronted her before the service, looking up and down at Maeve's Valentine's Day dress. "I hear you're having a tiny family-only luncheon after your service." Stacy had spoken in a tone reminiscent of the QOM. "My Bat Mitzvah is next month, and afterward my party is going to be on a yacht. I'll have music and dancing and fruity drinks with little umbrellas that are to *die* for and party favors like nothing you've ever seen."

"So?" Maeve had retaliated. "I'm going to have a sleepover with my best friends next week that will be waaay more fun than your lame boat ride." It was the first time she'd thought about having a sleepover to celebrate, but once the idea took form, Maeve was instantly excited about it.

But Stacy made the idea seem pathetic. "Sleepovers are sooo sixth grade. Ugh. I still can't believe my dad dragged me all the way up here, and there's not even a party! Don't you think that's a little rude?"

Maeve had wanted to snap back at her spoiled cousin, or at least stick out her tongue and tell her she hoped she'd get seasick at her party, but something stopped her. Out loud, Maeve said simply, and with so much maturity that Katani would be proud, "Thanks for coming today." Then she turned on her heel and walked away.

Now, at the podium, she let that same feeling wash over her again, chasing away the nausea. *I'm a Bat Mitzvah now, and I understand what today is really all about. It's not about parties or even a fancy dress with lots of sequins. It's about growing up and becoming a responsible adult. A member of the community. Someone who can make a difference.* Maeve gripped her speech notes.

"Today I became a Bat Mitzvah," she started. Then stopped. Her mom and dad and Sam were all focusing their complete attention on her, glowing with pride. She glanced over at her BFFs; Avery gave her a quick thumbs-up and Sophie blew a kiss. In the back row Maeve caught Austin's eye. She'd chosen to invite his family at the last minute and wasn't sure they'd come. And yet there they were. Little Austin was staring up at Maeve with awe, like she had accomplished something absolutely amazing simply by turning thirteen.

But it's not just my age that's different, Maeve realized, and lowered her eyes back down to her speech. The words she was supposed to say were there, but there was something else she wanted to add. Something that she had just come to understand and *needed* to share.

"Today I became a Bat Mitzvah," Maeve repeated. She needed the time to gather her thoughts as she forged ahead without a script. "Over the last few weeks I've realized something really, mega-important. Even though I feel a little sad that I am not having a big blowout bash tonight, I really, truly, absolut-ively *know* that becoming a Bat Mitzvah is about *way* more than having some fancy *fête*. Um, that means 'party' in French. Anyway, I know now that a party won't make me a better person."

Maeve was on a roll. She rested her hands on the sides of the podium and let her gaze sweep the sanctuary. "Becoming a Bat Mitzvah is about being responsible and sharing an extraordinary moment with your family and friends. It took me a while to figure it out, but now I know that it's also about listening, even when no one is talking. This was a pretty hard lesson for me to learn. Sure, I like to help when there's something obvious I can do, like when we did Project Thread at Jeri's Place, but sometimes there are things about yourself that you don't know you have to give."

Maeve told everyone about how she'd spent her whole life working with different tutors, and she thanked every single one of them. "You all helped me become who I am today, and I'm sorry about the times I was totally uncooperative." A few people laughed, Maeve's Hebrew tutor and her math tutor, Matt, among them. "You see, I recently became a tutor myself. I never thought I was smart enough to teach someone else. But now I know that I really do have something to offer."

Maeve stood up straight and took a deep breath. "I know how hard some kids have to work to learn something that everyone else just gets right away, because I'm one of those kids. I have dyslexia, and normal things like reading are a lot harder for me." Maeve was aware that she had just admitted her difficulties at school, something she'd spent her whole life trying to hide, to a giant room full of people. But somehow it didn't bother her.

"So this is what I realized. I can totally help other kids with learning problems, because I'm just like them! I've decided to embark on a *new* Bat Mitzvah project. It'll be like a tutoring program, but all the tutors and tutees will be kids with learning differences. Kids like me. We'il share our experiences and figure things out together. This is the small way that I, Maeve Kaplan-Taylor, can help change the world."

The sanctuary fell silent, in awe. Maeve was stunned. Somehow this felt like the most spiritual moment of the whole morning.

Maeve flashed her special Academy Awards smile and then looked down at her printed speech. "Thank you all for coming today and celebrating with me," Maeve began the real speech, just like she'd written it with the rabbi. At the end, Maeve gave special thanks to her friends and family, then said "Shabbat Shalom" again.

A few more prayers and the service was over.

"You were stupendous!" Katani gushed when Maeve came out of the sanctuary into the social hall.

Avery held up her hands for a double high-five. "Way to go!"

"Brilliant," added Charlotte.

Isabel and Sophie spoke at the exact same time, "Fantabulous!" Then everyone wrapped Maeve in a big group hug. When they pulled back, Maeve realized, for the first time that day, what her BFFs were wearing.

Since Maeve was wearing her dress from the Valentine's Day dance, all the BSG had decided to wear their Valentine's Day dresses too! Maeve hadn't even gotten a chance to tell them about the pink gown disaster, but somehow, they'd known that she'd need some solidarity.

Before Maeve could thank her friends, her cousin Stacy passed by. "Are these your *sleepover* friends?" she jibed.

Maeve smiled and put her arms around Katani's and Isabel's shoulders. "They are, in fact. Shall we walk you to your car? I wouldn't want you to waste even one more second of your precious time."

"No thanks." Stacy sneered. "Will I see you at *my* Bat Mitzvah boat party next month?"

"Hmmm." Maeve pretended to think about it.

Isabel squeezed Maeve tighter. "I think we might have a sleepover planned for that evening already."

"Sorry!" Avery added.

The girls managed to keep it together until Stacy was just out of earshot, then collapsed with laughter. Maeve's eyes started to tear. "You are the greatest BFFs a girl could ever have," she said, choking on the words.

"You have no idea how great we really are!" Avery blurted out.

"Huh? What?" Maeve looked at her suspiciously.

"She's just saying." Charlotte covered Avery's tracks. "We're better friends than anyone could ever realize."

"Oh." Maeve grinned. "Of course!"

"Gotta run." Katani grabbed Avery's hand and yanked her toward the door.

"*Hasta luego!*" Isabel followed them, with Charlotte and Sophie close behind. "Have fun at your lunch!"

"Aren't you guys going to hang out awhile?" Maeve dashed after her friends. "We might not be having an official party, but there is a small reception in the social hall. I was hoping you'd stay at least a few minutes."

"I'm sorry," Charlotte told Maeve. "But my dad is driving us all . . . home. And he just drove up!"

Maeve looked to Katani for confirmation.

Katani nodded. "We'll catch up later. Okay?"

"Wait!" Maeve protested. "It's Sophie's last day in town. We should at least have a good-bye party that's better than the welcome one when she first came. How about we meet in the Tower later, okay?"

"But of course." Sophie nodded vaguely.

Then Isabel checked her watch in a way that was so dramatic, Maeve wondered if she was vying for a Best Supporting Actress Academy Award. "Mr. Ramsey is probably sitting out in the car right now," Isabel proclaimed, overenunciating and tapping her foot.

"Maeve! Congratulations!" Grandma Taylor engulfed Maeve in a hug that smelled like lavender, and then a whole swarm of cousins from Atlanta rushed in, shouting, "Mazel Tov!"

When Maeve finally managed to come up for air, her friends were gone. But Austin was waiting to give her a card he'd drawn himself, the rabbi wanted to congratulate Maeve on her new project idea, Great-grandma Gigi had to see the photo of Maeve in her horrible lavender dress, and her parents both needed to tell her how grown-up and responsible she had sounded.

"You never cease to surprise me, Maeve," her mom confessed, tears leaking out of her eyes. "My little girl. All grown up!"

"You made us all so proud, Maeve," her father added, misty-eyed.

After what seemed an eternity of well-wishing, the cousins and the rest of the extended family headed over to the luncheon, and the temple was finally quiet. Maeve gathered her preparation binder, her speech, and the lip gloss she'd stashed in a corner, and met her parents in the parking lot.

The luncheon was quiet and ordinary, but still lovely. Maeve was happy, honestly happy, for the time with her extended family. Of course, it helped that Stacy's family wasn't there. They had to leave early to catch their flight back to New York. *I kinda feel bad,* Maeve realized, *that Stacy doesn't know what it's like to have such awesome friends as I have.* Maeve couldn't wait to see them in the Tower later!

Some things would never change.

Coffee Break

"We need to make a quick stop on the way home," Maeve's mother said as they turned down Beacon Street from the restaurant.

"A stop?" Maeve asked.

"Oh, Maeve," Ms. Kaplan gushed. "You know how much I love Montoya's coffee! I need a hot cup."

"But, Mom," Maeve said, "you had coffee at the restaurant. Can't we just go straight home? I was going to change and then head over to the Tower to see my friends."

"I want a hot chocolate," Sam added from the backseat. "Can I get one?"

"Sure, sweetie." Their mom smiled. "We're almost there now."

"Yippee," Sam cheered. "Thanks, Mom."

"Well, hurry up!" Maeve ordered.

As they turned into a parking space outside the BSG's favorite hangout, Maeve noticed a lot of familiar cars lined up. Apparently the entire Kaplan and Taylor families had all been possessed by sudden caffeine and sugar cravings! Maeve's cousins, aunts, uncles, grandparents, and father were all getting out of their cars here, too.

"A cup of coffee sure would hit the spot," her father remarked.

"I want a slice of chocolate cream pie," Grandma Taylor explained.

"I am craving donuts," Great-grandma Gigi chimed in.

Maeve went inside with her mom and Sam, her

family close behind. The restaurant buzzed with the normal hustle and bustle of a Saturday afternoon.

"Come with me, Maeve-y." Sam grabbed her hand. "I need to show you something." He was tugging her toward a door in the back.

She pointed. "It says 'Employees Only.'"

"I know," Sam said, dragging her along. Maeve tried to tug her hand free from Sam's, but he held on with the grip of death, pulling her closer and closer to that door. "Fine. Whatever. Just show me, then let's get going so I can get together with the BSG and debrief," Maeve proclaimed with a dramatic, Hollywood air.

Sam opened the door.

Surprise!

"SURPRISE!" shouted about a hundred voices.

The room behind the door was filled to the brim with all the people Maeve knew and loved, and decked out from floor to ceiling with streamers, balloons, shiny stars, and flashing strings of holiday lights spelling out "Maeve Kaplan-Taylor!"

"It's . . ." Maeve was too stunned to speak for a moment. "It's my party," she murmured, gazing around the room at all the cheering faces. Absolutely *everyone* was there! The BSG, Sophie, *all* the kids from school, including the QOM, Mr. Ramsey, Mrs. Martinez . . . In fact, all the BSG's parents were there! Mrs. Weiss, Yuri, Mrs. Fields, and even shy Miss Pierce had shown up. And of course Marty was there too, yipping and dancing around the room!

"*Félicitations*," Sophie congratulated.

"What do you think?" Katani waved a hand at the room.

"Sorry we had to leave you hanging at the temple," Charlotte added. "But we had things to do!"

As a response, Maeve gave each of her friends a kiss on each cheek, European style. "I don't know what to say!!!" she gushed.

"You don't have to say anything!" Isabel said with a laugh. "Just have fun!"

As Maeve wandered across the room, hugging and thanking every person she passed, she didn't notice the low ceiling, odd corners, or the one cracked window. All she saw were the decorations her friends must have spent hours putting up, and the love and friendship it all stood for.

A red carpet stretched from the door to the back wall, where more red velvet was draped, like a grand theater curtain, gathered at the sides with ornate, gold tassels. Gold and silver stars hung from the ceiling, and there was a line of stars around the edge of a little dancing area with Maeve's favorite actors' names inside—Isabel had made the walk of fame she'd promised! Old movie posters that her father must have gathered were plastered on the walls, there was a stage for a band, and the dance floor was just the right size for Maeve and her friends to cut loose and boogie!

"You guys did all this?!" Maeve returned to the corner where the BSG had staked out a table just for themselves. "This is beyond nice!"

"Well . . . we had help," Isabel admitted.

"This used to be just a storage room," Charlotte explained. "But Nick's family always wanted to fix it up for hosting parties. They just never got around to it."

"They said if we could clean it out, we could have your party here, no charge!" Katani declared. "And all these decorations—the curtain, stars, centerpieces, everything— we made from things we found in our basements and closets."

The tables were draped in red velvet, like the curtain, and each table seemed to have a different theme, like doves, butterflies, and movie stars—all the things Maeve had said she wanted when she was planning her mega-bash. There was even a big picture of a limousine on the side wall!

"Isabel made all those drawings," Charlotte pointed out.

On the walls, between the movie posters, Isabel had hung sketches of Maeve's favorite actors and actresses. And there, in the very middle of the party room, Isabel had mounted a beautiful, life-size cutout of Maeve herself, holding an Academy Award.

It was just a drawing, but seeing her dream for her future standing in the middle of the room made her heart melt. *I am so lucky!* Maeve thought, gazing around the room once again. *I have amazing friends, an amazing family, and life just couldn't be any better than this!*

20

A Bat Mitzvah to Remember

"Sorry I'm late!" Ms. Razzberry Pink stepped into the room and held out a big, flat pink box with an enormous matching bow on top. "I think this belongs to you." She handed the box to Maeve.

"For me?" Maeve stared at the gift.

"Go ahead. Open it," Ms. Pink insisted. The BSG gathered around, and so did the rest of the crowd, murmuring questions about what could possibly be inside the beautiful box.

Maeve set the present on one of the beautifully decorated tables and carefully removed the bow. With each passing second she could feel her pulse accelerating. Finally the lid slipped off, and Maeve reached between the folds of soft, rose-colored tissue paper.

"OMG!!!" she exclaimed. "The dress! *My* dress!" Maeve held the dress tightly to her chest and swung around, giddy with joy. "My dress! I can't believe it!" She hugged

Ms. Pink hard. "Oh, thank you. Thank you so much!"

"My pleasure," Ms. Pink said gladly. "But you should thank your friends and your little brother, not me!"

"Sam?!" Maeve turned over the gift tag tucked under the bow and saw her brother's name.

Sam crept out of the crowd and just stood there smiling, so Ms. Pink explained. "Your friends called, begging me to reserve the dress. I told them I couldn't do that, but I'd take it down from the window. The very next morning, in comes Sam with a wad of crumpled cash, asking if anyone bought it yet!"

Maeve knelt down next to her brother. "Where did you get enough money?" she whispered.

"Welllll . . . ," Sam admitted. "Most of it was yours. From your babysitting stash. I'll pay you back! Here, I have sixty-three cents so far."

"Oh, Sam!" Maeve laughed and hugged her little brother. "How did you know? You're the best little brother ever!"

"Go and put it on!" Katani urged.

"Yeah! We wanna see it!" Avery cheered.

"Be right back!" Maeve exclaimed, rushing out toward the restroom.

"Wait! Maeve!" Sophie called after her. "You need the shoes."

"Shoes?!" Maeve was very near tears as she turned back to take the small gift bag that Sophie was holding. She peeked inside. The shoes were the same color as the dress, with matching sequins across the top of the toes.

"I brought them with me from Paris," Sophie told

Maeve. "But I think you must have them. They fit your lovely Hollywood style!"

"Oh, wow!" Maeve fanned her face to keep herself from crying. "*Merci*, Sophie. *Merci beaucoup!*"

"Come on, Isabel," Katani said as she took Maeve's arm and led her toward the bathroom. "We've got work to do."

With a nod, Isabel followed closely behind.

Shining Moment

When Isabel, Katani, and Maeve returned to the party room, Maeve looked like the superstar triple threat her friends knew she'd one day become. It was her shining moment.

Katani had helped her change into the dress and then swept Maeve's hair up into a stunning arrangement, with little crystal beads twisted into the top knot.

Isabel had brought her makeup bag and worked her artist's magic, painting Maeve's eyelids and glossing her lips.

"Wow! What did you do with my sister Maeve-y?" Even Sam couldn't hold back, seeing how pretty his sister was in her new gown.

"You guys really are the best, most fantabulawesome friends ever!" Maeve said as she hugged each of her BFFs.

"We know," Avery said, grinning. "I told you that earlier." She winked, "It was my idea to ask the Montoya's if they had a room we could use. And finally *they* listened to me!" Avery added with a lopsided grin, catching sheepish glances from Katani, Isabel, and Charlotte.

"Very sneaky," Maeve remarked. "I didn't have a clue what you guys were up to."

"That's only because you were so busy!" Charlotte laughed. "We weren't always very subtle . . . like during our triple date when Fabiana was back here getting stuff ready." Then Charlotte told Maeve how she manned the communications for the party, making sure everyone knew their job and got it all done in time. "I was IM central."

"Most of the plates and silverware are from my house," Avery said. "I lugged it all in here myself."

"Katani was in charge of decorating and scheduling," Isabel put in. "Betsy arranged transportation. Sophie came up with the table themes and made centerpieces—"

"And wait until you see the photo slideshow Chelsea made!" Katani interrupted.

"Slide show?" Maeve was thrilled. "There's a slide show?!"

"After the cake!" Avery said. "Elena Maria and Scott baked a triple-decker, chocolate-strawberry masterpiece. With no help from dogs or parrots this time!"

Marty jumped up on Avery and yelped. "No chocolate for dogs!" she reminded him.

"What about me?" a little voice next to Avery piped up. She looked down at Sam and remembered her pinkie promise.

"Of course, you most excellent secret keeper! You kept your side of the bargain so you get the biggest slice!"

Maeve walked up to the gorgeous cake—decorated

with sliced strawberries and delicate curls of chocolate. It seemed such a shame to cut into it!

"Who's got a camera?" Maeve asked, then laughed because dozens of flashes were already going off. Her mom and dad both had cameras practically glued in front of their noses, capturing every moment of their daughter's special party.

Dance Party

Maeve got a chance to eat only one bite of the delicious cake. Every aunt, uncle, cousin, friend, and grandparent needed a picture with the special girl in her fabulous new dress. As she spun from one group to the next, Maeve kept her eyes peeled for Riley. She'd seen Dillon talking to Sophie, and Nick and Charlotte were sitting together sharing their cake. . . . But where was the oh-so-cute Mustard Monkey band leader?

"Looking for someone?" The Queens of Mean snuck up behind Maeve after she had just finished posing for a photo beside Isabel's life-size Maeve drawing for the gazillionth time.

"This is sooo not like the party you promised," Anna taunted.

"What are you talking about?" Maeve demanded. Avery had just told her how hard Dillon, Nick, and Fabiana had worked, putting in multihours, cleaning out this old storage room.

"You said your party would be radder than Henry's," Joline reminded her.

Maeve looked around. Henry Yurt's family had donated a photo booth, just like the one from his Bar Mitzvah. Katani's father had helped build the stage, and someone had brought a sound system that was pumping out dance tunes. Every single family had donated food and beverages, and her own brother had not only kept the party a secret, but made sure Maeve got the dress of her dreams. And then there were the BSG who had somehow pulled all this together in only one week!

If this isn't radder than the Yurtmeister's party, what is? Maeve realized.

"This party," Maeve announced, waving her hand

around the room, "has everything I said it would have. Including a limo." She pointed to the picture on the wall. Maeve felt so happy that nothing the QOM might say would bring her down!

Isabel danced over and handed Maeve a cookie. "Try this! Mrs. Weiss made them," she said, then noticed Anna and Joline. "I see you've already enjoyed some of that delicious cake," Isabel commented, pointing at the chocolate crumbs both on Anna's mouth and the front of Joline's light blue dress.

"We aren't enjoying anything," Joline said snottily, dusting off the crumbles.

"Yeah." Anna drew a hand across her mouth. "We only came because we thought it would be a big bash with some, like, famous band. Instead"—she looked at the stage where a band was setting up—"Mustard Monkey is playing."

"Mustard Monkey!" Maeve squealed, spinning around to see Riley and his buddies take the stage. "Go have more cake," she told the Queens, then, turning her back on them, Maeve bounded out across the dance floor.

"Hey," Riley greeted, his face turning the same shade as the strawberry decorating his slice of cake. He'd set it on top of the speakers while he plugged in his guitar.

Maeve practically lunged at him, knocking Riley back a bit as she flung herself around his neck. "Thank you for playing. And for helping. And for EVERYTHING!" She was holding on so tightly, Riley had to struggle to get her to loosen up.

"Can't breathe," he choked out.

"Ooops, sorry." Maeve giggled, loosening but not removing her arms from his neck. "Let's try that again. Thanks, Riley." This time, instead of grabbing him in a stranglehold, Maeve kissed Riley softly on his cheek. "Will you play that song . . . you know?"

Riley was speechless. He just nodded, and his cake sat on top of the speaker, forgotten, for the rest of the night.

BFFs+e

The opening bars of Mustard Monkey's seventh-grade hit, "You, You, You" rang out across the room. It was the same song Maeve and Riley had sung together at the end of the Valentine's Day dance, except Sophie had helped translate one of the verses into French just for the occasion!

"I love this song!" Maeve exclaimed, twirling around to the beat. The sequins on her dress sparkled, casting little rainbows all over the party room.

Avery laughed. "You love *every* song Riley plays."

"Of course I do!" Maeve gushed. "Isn't he amazing?"

"I think"—Sophie leaned over and whispered in Charlotte's ear—"someone has a, how do you say, crush?"

"Yeah," Charlotte answered, noticing Dillon standing off to one side. "And I think someone else, how do you say, wants to dance with you!"

"*Bonjour, mademoiselle,*" Dillon greeted Sophie with a little bow before he swept her into a spin around the floor. "*Comment ça va aujourd'hui?*"

"Awesome, dude," Sophie replied. "Your French accent

is totally coolio!" Then, spontaneously: "Will you come visit me in Paris?"

Dillon looked down at his shoes. He'd worn the fancy, pointy ones just for this occasion. "Uhhh . . . sure."

"You already have a scarf and fashionable shoes. You'll fit right in!" Sophie winked.

As Nick spun her around, Charlotte stole a glance at Dillon and Sophie dancing together. She'd overheard Sophie invite him to France and had no idea if that could ever really happen. . . . But it was nice to dream. And maybe Sophie would come back to visit Boston again some time. *I would really love that,* Charlotte said to herself, swallowing a lump of sorrow about this being Sophie's last day. Her plane was leaving early the next morning. *I'm really going to miss her,* Charlotte realized.

". . . and life will be brighter, bigger, kinder, crazier, now that I have youuuuu!" Riley finished the last song in the set with a flourish of guitar picking. It was a new tune, one Maeve had never heard before. She jumped up and down and clapped as loud as she could, until she felt a hand on her shoulder.

"Maeve," her mom began, "your father and I are so impressed with the maturity you and your friends have shown. This party truly upholds our feelings about what becoming a Bat Mitzvah means. I love you so much, my grown-up daughter."

"You were wonderful today," her dad added. "I am so proud of you. Your friends really came through with this party, once they explained what they were up to—how this was a true community effort—we were happy to pitch in and help." He swept Maeve into a bear hug and added, "I love you, darling."

Maeve hugged her parents, one in each arm.

"I love you both, too. Mom and Dad," she said, stepping back and breaking free. "And now, there is something I need to do." Her parents watched her walk to the stage.

"Uh hum," Maeve said, taking the microphone off the stand. As long as the stage was empty, Maeve figured she should be on it. "Testing one, two, three." Her voice reverberated around the room.

All eyes turned to her.

I love this feeling, Maeve thought. *I was born to be right here, center stage, mic in hand.* She smiled, enjoying the moment, trying to capture the feeling and bottle it forever. *I bet this is exactly what it feels like when you go up to accept your Academy Award,* she decided.

"I want to thank you, Mom, Dad, the BSG, and everyone yet again," Maeve began. "I just want you to know how much I appreciate all the love and work you put into this party. I don't think I can tell you all enough times how happy I am!!!"

The whole room broke into applause and cheers, thanking the party organizers. When it died down, Maeve continued, "You should know that this party isn't just for me. It's for Sophie too. The sixth Beacon Street Girl is headed back to France—today's her last day here." She looked directly at Sophie. *"Bon voyage, mon amie."* Maeve came down off the stage and gave Sophie two *bisous*, one on each cheek, and wished her a safe trip home.

"Now," Maeve said, "in honor of Sophie's last night and my Bat Mitzvah celebration, there is only one other thing we need to do. As the character named Julian Marsh says in the 1933 classic movie, *42nd Street*, 'You're gonna dance until your feet fall off—and you're not able to stand up any longer!' So, let's boogie!"

Mustard Monkey came back onstage.

Maeve declared, "Hit it!"

Epilogue
Bon Voyage, Mon Amie

At the airport Sunday morning, Charlotte was all mixed-up. As she handed Sophie a small, wrapped gift, she felt nervous, excited, and sad. Sad to say good-bye, but also sad that Sophie was leaving *just* when they'd started to really feel like BFFs again.

"What is this?" Sophie asked, her eyes wide.

"A farewell present," Charlotte said, not wanting to give away the secret.

Sophie shook the box. "Is it another cap like the one Dillon gave me?" She was wearing that hat right now, for the flight. Charlotte wondered briefly if Sophie's parents would recognize their new, American daughter!

"Nah. You have plenty of sports gear now." Charlotte poked at Sophie's matching Red Sox T-shirt.

Sophie peeled back the wrapping paper. "Perhaps it is a new scarf to replace the one I got all tangled up during our long, dangerous hike?"

Charlotte looked at the scarf Sophie was wearing. It was bright pink; a gift from Maeve. "Nope," she said. "You have too many scarves already, anyway!"

Sophie shook the box. "Is it a—"

"Just open it already!" Charlotte groaned. The anticipation was killing her. *I can't wait to see her face when she opens the lid*, Charlotte thought.

"A book?" Sophie asked, pulling the gift out of the box and looking at the cover. Her eyebrows drew together as she read the title out loud: "'Orangina's Travels.'"

Charlotte watched the shift in Sophie's face as she realized what she was holding in her hands. Her features softened and her eyes widened. Sophie's mouth curled up into a huge smile.

"You finished it!" Sophie cheered. "When? How?"

Charlotte couldn't contain her joy at seeing Sophie's excited reaction and began jumping up and down, just like when Sophie had first arrived at the airport. "I finished it a few days ago. When you took Marty to the park. My dad printed it out on nice paper, then Isabel drew the cover. Katani sewed the book together. Maeve wrapped it and Avery glued on the bow. This book is a gift from the entire BSG."

"I can't wait to read the ending," Sophie marveled, cradling the book to her chest as if it were the most priceless treasure she'd ever held. "I'll read it on the plane."

Charlotte hugged Sophie tight and gave her two *bisous*, one on each cheek. "I will miss you terribly, my dear friend."

Sophie kissed Charlotte back in the same Parisian fashion and repeated Charlotte's sentiment, only this time, in French, *"Tu va me manquer terriblement, toi, mon cher amie."*

"Write to me," Charlotte called out, her voice breaking with emotion as Sophie walked up to join the line waiting to go through security.

Sophie turned back toward Charlotte and promised, *"Chaque jour*, Charlotte. I will write to you every day. You are my best friend, for always."

The End

Sweet Thirteen

BOOK EXTRAS

 Young Authors Contest Winner

 New Tower Rules

 Sweet Thirteen Trivialicious Trivia

 Book Club Buzz

 Charlotte's Word Nerd Dictionary

Young Authors
Contest Winner

Caitlyn Dwyer, New York
Age 14

Orangina's Travels
Part 7
The Three Companions

A feline figure stepped out from the shadows in the mossy pumpkin forest—it was the black cat from the storybook.

She trotted up to Orangina and Big Bruce. "Ah, Bruce," she said. "We meet again. After that last incident, I didn't think you'd have the nerve to show your face in this forest." The cat chuckled.

"Who are you?" Orangina asked.

"I am Serena. I come down to Earth from the heavens every October by means of a shooting star. I'm the black cat you should watch out for, if you're superstitious."

Serena rolled her green eyes. "Ever since he"—she gestured toward Bruce—"messed up the pumpkin forest by creating butterbees, I haven't been able to get back up to the sky!"

Orangina saw real sadness in the black cat's eyes. "Maybe I can help you," he told Serena. "What could I do?"

"There is this old riddle that says:

If autumn squash should grow on trees,
Companions three pick the magic leaves,
Watch out for the new crossbreed,
They disappear if you do succeed.

"But I couldn't perform the task by myself. The butterbees would attack me right away! And besides, there need to be three companions. But now I seem to have found someone the color of a pumpkin. . . ." Serena gazed at Orangina hopefully.

"But what exactly are these 'magic leaves'?" Orangina asked.

"I know this one!" said Big Bruce. "The three magic leaves are scattered among the trees."

"They are golden, and sparkle like the sun," added Serena. "Please help us!"

Orangina didn't need persuading. He set off in search of the first leaf, followed by Big Bruce and Serena.

"So how exactly did you mess up the forest?" Orangina asked Bruce as he scanned the trees for a golden leaf.

"I'm an adventurer, see. So I was adventuring," Bruce explained. "I found a gold leaf, and I was running back to the tunnels . . . but then I knocked a beehive out of a tree onto three butterflies. Long story short: butterbees. Serena was pretty mad at me when she found out about my accident. . . ."

"So I shrunk him," Serena finished.

Just then, Orangina spotted the first leaf. He gracefully climbed up the tree and started to rip the leaf off the branch—but a sudden swarm of butterbees caught him off guard!

"Look out!" Serena shouted, but it was too late. Orangina fell out of the tree.

Of course, cats *always* land on their feet, and Orangina held the golden leaf safely in his mouth. *Charlotte would be so proud of me*, Orangina thought. *I'm helping a friend in need!*

"Run!" Serena shouted as the butterbees dove and stung.

The trio ran as far as they could before Bruce shouted, "Mate, there's the next leaf!" Serena was quick to claw the leaf off the tree, and they kept running.

There were several hundred vicious insects trailing the group, but all of a sudden Big Bruce stopped and reached into a small hole at the base of a tree. Orangina soon realized why: The last leaf was tucked away inside! The three companions held up their leaves triumphantly, and the butterbees disappeared.

"Now you just need to put the leaves into a beehive-shaped pumpkin, and I'm back in the sky!" Serena told them.

"And I'm back to my normal height!" Big Bruce added.

Orangina saw the perfect pumpkin hanging from a

nearby tree at the edge of a meadow. And he was *just* tall enough to reach up and pick it.

When he placed the golden leaves inside the pumpkin, Serena rose up in the air, and Big Bruce grew from tiny to medium to gigantic!

"Thank you, thank you both!" Serena called out, rising higher and higher until she was just a silvery dot in the sky.

Big Bruce looked around, then down at Orangina from his new, giant height. "Big Bruce is back! Thanks, Orry. Now I can send you home. . . ."

Orangina's vision blurred, and he squeezed his eyes shut as the ground seemed to fall away. When he opened his eyes, he was on a familiar boat, floating down the Seine river. *Home sweet home!* he thought.

The New Tower Rules
Created by the Newest Order
of the Ruby and the Sapphire

Be it resolved that *all* girls are created equal!

1. We will speak our minds, but we won't be, like, obnoxious or anything.
2. We won't put ourselves down, even if we aren't supersmart, super-coordinated, or a supermodel.
3. We'll be loyal to our friends and won't lie to them, even if they make a mistake or do something totally embarrassing.
4. We will go for it—how will we know what we can do if we don't try?
5. We will try to eat healthy and stay active. How can you chase your dream if you can't keep up?
6. We won't just take from people and the planet. We'll try to give back good things too.

··

Amendments:

1. We can add as many amendments as we like.

2. We will dare to be fashion individualistas—like, we're all different so why should we dress the same?

3. Sometimes we'll veg out—just because we feel like it!

4. We should have as much fun as we can.

5. We should try to save money so if we ever want to, we can start a business or something someday.

6. We will try to keep an open mind about new people.

7. When in doubt . . . phone home!

8. We won't let people take advantage of us. . . . We deserve respect!

9. We won't let competition ruin the BSG—friendship is way more important than winning.

10. We won't judge people by their looks.

··

Note from Maeve
Proposed new amendment:

Maeve: Family and friends are way more
important than glitz and glamour—so don't
forget it!

What's the Vote?

Katani—family before fashion!
Charlotte—so true.
Avery—sweet new rule!
Isabel—I love it.
Sophie—*Bien sûr!*

Sweet Thirteen trivialicious trivia

1. Where was Henry Yurt's Bar Mitzvah?
    A. At his house
    B. At a fancy hotel
    C. At a science museum
    D. On a cruise ship

2. What is the fruit that makes Isabel's parrot, Franco, fly around like crazy and ruin the BSG's baking?
    A. Oranges
    B. Mango
    C. Strawberries
    D. Pineapple

3. What is the name of the little man in Charlotte's story?
    A. Terrible Tunneling Tommy
    B. Big Bruce Barley
    C. Gruff Gus
    D. Lucky Larry

4. What does Dillon teach after school?
    A. Karate
    B. Basketball
    C. French Club
    D. Soccer

5. What DOESN'T Austin do during Maeve's first babysitting job?
    A. Throw LEGOs
    B. Stomp all over his carrot sticks
    C. Rip up his homework
    D. Lock himself in the bathroom

6. Which American slang word does Sophie have a lot of trouble pronouncing?
    A. "Dude"
    B. "Rad"
    C. "Fabulous"
    D. "Totally"

7. In the lunchroom, Ms. O'Reilly tells Charlotte a story to help her deal with Sophie's popularity. What is it about?
   A. Rock stars
   B. Scarves
   C. Tulips
   D. Skype

8. What kind of animal does Dillon fight off for Sophie while they're hiking?
   A. A skunk
   B. A chipmunk
   C. A bug
   D. A pigeon

9. What is Maeve's final mitzvah project?
   A. Collecting movies for sick kids
   B. A tutoring program for kids with learning differences
   C. Volunteering at a soup kitchen
   D. Fixing up the park at Jeri's Place

10. How did Maeve end up getting her dream dress?
   A. Miss Pink donated it
   B. The BSG had a fund-raiser to buy it
   C. Sam bought it (with Maeve's money)
   D. Ms. Kaplan gave it to her

Book Club Buzz

1. Maeve wants her Bat Mitzvah party to be glamorous, with a red carpet theme, while Henry Yurt's is all about science. What would be the theme of your ideal party?

2. Everyone at AAJH wants to be BFFs with Sophie! How does this make Charlotte feel? Have you or one of your friends ever been superpopular or felt left out by someone who was? What do you think it's like to constantly be in the spotlight?

3. Events from real life inspire Charlotte's writing. Have you ever written a story based on something from your life? Name two things that happened to Charlotte in this book that turned into ideas for Orangina's story.

4. Franco and Marty wreak havoc in Isabel's kitchen. Describe the grossest or messiest cooking disaster you've ever had!

5. Maeve's Bat Mitzvah is an important rite of passage for her. Have you ever had a meaningful personal experience like this one? What kind of effect did it have on you?

6. When Dillon wants to impress Sophie, he totally changes his look and even how he acts. Would you change yourself for a crush? Why or why not?

7. Sophie's fashionable scarves create a major fad at AAJH. Has there ever been a fashion craze at your school? Did you participate or stick with your own sense of style?

8. Maeve realizes that she can use her own experience with dyslexia to help Austin with school. Have you ever helped someone else like this? How do you deal with a super-difficult homework assignment?

9. Sophie says yes to too many activities and ends up overbooked! Have you ever been in a situation where you had to choose between two - or more! - activities and

risk disappointing one set of your friends?
How did you choose?

10. Everyone works together to pull off Maeve's
surprise Bat Mitzvah party. Have you ever
planned a surprise party before? How did it
go? Did people keep it a secret?

Charlotte Ramsey

Charlotte's
Word Nerd Dictionary

French Words

Meilleures amies: (p. 32)—*best friends*
Petit ami: (p. 32)—*sweetheart*
Je t'adore: (p. 32)—*I love you*
Entre: (p. 33)—*enter*
Merci: (p. 34)—*thank you*
Ça va bien: (p. 34)—*It's going well*
Bateau: (p. 35)—*boat*
Je t'aime: (p. 54)—*I love you*
Bienvenue: (p. 59)—*welcome*
Ma chérie: (p. 60)—*my dear*
Ma petite: (p. 60)—*my little one*
Adieu: (p. 60)—*good-bye*
Bon anniversaire: (p. 60)—*happy birthday*
Non: (p. 62)—*no*
S'il vous plaît: (p. 63)—*if you please*
Au revoir: (p. 63)—*good-bye*
Bien sûr: (p. 63)—*absolutely, of course*

Fête: (p. 64)—*party*

Incroyable: (p. 65)—*incredible*

Triste: (p. 68)—*sad*

Premier séjour a Boston: (p. 71)—*first stay in Boston*

Quelle bonne surprise!: (p. 71)—*What a great surprise!*

J'ai une idée: (p. 72)—*I have an idea*

Marveilleux: (p. 72)—*marvelous*

Il est très mignon!: (p. 76)—*He's very cute!*

Tu as le bon goût!: (p. 76)—*You have good taste!*

Allons-y!: (p. 76)—*Let's go!*

T'es folle?!: (p. 76)—*You're crazy?!*

Bisous: (p. 80)—*kisses, like XOXO*

Bonne nuit: (p. 80)—*good night*

Mode: (p. 88)—*fashion*

Garçons: (p. 89)—*boys*

Un par un: (p. 90)—*one by one*

Oui: (p. 90)—*yes*

Il est un joli chien: (p. 103)—*He's a cute dog*

Qu'est-ce qui se passe?: (p. 106)—*What's going on?*

Canard: (p. 106)—*duck*

Grandpère: (p. 109)—*grandfather*

Amusant: (p. 110)—*fun*

Qu-est que c'est?: (p. 123)—*What is it?*

Merci beaucoup: (p. 128)—*thanks so much*

Parfait: (p. 130)—*perfect*

L'amour: (p. 142)—*love*

Très françai: (p. 167)—*very French*

C'est la vie!: (p. 174)—*that's life*

Délicieux: (p. 175)—*delicious*

Parler français: (p. 179)—*speak French*

Paix: (p. 181)—*peace*

Quoi de neuf?: (p. 192)—*What's new?*

Combien?: (p. 207)—*How much?*

C'est une catastrophe: (p. 208)—*It's a catastrophe*

Aide-moi: (p. 208)—*Help me*
Dangereux: (p. 213)—*dangerous*
Comme un oiseau: (p. 213)—*like a bird*
Chacun voit midi à sa porte: (p. 217)—*Be true to yourself*
Félicitations: (p. 258)—*congratulations*
Comment ça va aujourd'hui?: (p. 267)—*How are you doing today?*
Tu va me manquer terriblement: (p. 273)—*I'm going to miss you terribly*
Chaque jour: (p. 273)—*every day*

Hebrew Words

Bar/Bat Mitzvah: (p. 1)—*coming-of-age ceremony for a Jewish boy/girl*
Mitzvah: (p. 42)—*a good deed*
Yafe m'ode: (p. 84)—*very cool*
Shabbat Shalom: (p. 249)—*wishing you a day of peace*
Mazel Tov: (p. 255)—*congratulations*

BSG Words

Humongo-gigantic: (p. 5) adjective—*humongous and gigantic*
Supermarvtastic: (p. 11) adjective—*super, marvelous, and fantastic*
Mega-awesomicity: (p. 15) noun—*super awesomeness*
Wowmazing: (p. 34) adjective—*amazing*
Stupend-delicious: (p. 39) adjective—*stupendous and delicious*
Perfectomundo: (p. 44) adjective—*perfect*
Ginormous: (p. 102) adjective—*gigantic and enormous*
Unvitations: (p. 126) noun—*the opposite of invitations*
Defreakify: (p. 140) verb—*to make less freaky*
Fantabulawesome: (p. 177) adjective—*fantastic and fabulous and awesome*
Absolut-ively: (p. 251) adjective—*absolutely positively*

Other Words

Taffeta: (p. 10) noun—*type of fabric*

Etiquette: (p. 21) noun—*manners*

Bloke: (p. 36) noun—*guy*

Surmised: (p. 54) verb—*figured out*

Martyr: (p. 92) noun—*someone who sacrifices something for the good of others*

Vehemently: (p. 98) adverb—*with energy and passion*

Amphibious: (p. 114) adjective—*able to go on land or in water*

Emphatically: (p. 117) adverb—*strongly*

Forlorn: (p. 142) adjective—*sad*

Charismatic: (p. 143) adjective—*charming, fun*

Unintelligible: (p. 167) adjective—*not understandable*

Linguistics: (p. 180) noun—*rules of language*

Palpable: (p. 181) adjective—*obvious, real*

Inevitable: (p. 183) adjective—*unavoidable*

Blithely: (p. 201) adverb—*casually*

Spontaneously: (p. 204) adverb—*impulsively*

Cacophony: (p. 207) noun—*loud mix of sounds*

Maelstrom: (p. 223) noun—*an unstable and disorderly situation*

Chivalry: (p. 229) noun—*gentlemanly behavior*

Lament: (p. 232) noun—*cry of sadness*

Bravado: (p. 234) noun—*bravery, daring*

Adroitly: (p. 235) adverb—*skillfully*

Sanctuary: (p. 248) noun—*safe, peaceful place*

Reminiscent: (p. 249) adjective—*recalling, suggesting*

Reverberated: (p. 269) verb—*echoed*

Collect all the BSG books today!

#1 Worst Enemies/Best Friends   ☐ **READ IT!**
Yikes! As if being the new girl isn't bad enough . . . Charlotte just made the
biggest cafeteria blunder in the history of Abigail Adams Junior High.

#2 Bad News/Good News   ☐ **READ IT!**
Charlotte can't believe it. Her father wants to move away again, and the
timing couldn't be worse for the Beacon Street Girls.

#3 Letters from the Heart   ☐ **READ IT!**
Life seems perfect for Maeve and Avery . . . until they find out that in
seventh grade, the world can turn upside down just like that.

#4 Out of Bounds   ☐ **READ IT!**
Can the Beacon Street Girls bring the house down at Abigail Adams Junior
High's Talent Show? Or will the Queens of Mean steal the show?

#5 Promises, Promises   ☐ **READ IT!**
Tensions rise when two BSG find themselves in a tight race for seventh-
grade president at Abigail Adams Junior High.

#6 Lake Rescue   ☐ **READ IT!**
The seventh grade outdoor trip promises lots o' fun for the BSG—but will the
adventure prove too much for one sensitive classmate?

#7 Freaked Out   ☐ **READ IT!**
The party of the year is just around the corner. What happens when the
party invitations are given out . . . but not to everyone?

#8 Lucky Charm   ☐ **READ IT!**
Marty is missing! The BSG's frantic search for their beloved pup leads them to
a very famous person and the game of a lifetime.

#9 Fashion Frenzy   ☐ **READ IT!**
Katani and Maeve are off to the Big Apple for a supercool teen fashion
show. Will tempers fray in close quarters?

#10 Just Kidding   ☐ **READ IT!**
The BSG are looking forward to Spirit Week at Abigail Adams Junior High, until
some mean—and untrue—gossip about Isabel dampens everyone's spirits.

Also . . . Our Special Adventure Series: